# Tripp

## A Walker Brothers Novel

### Seven Sons Ranch in Three Rivers Romance™
#### Book 2

## Liz Isaacson

ISBN-13: 978-1-63876-363-5

# 1

Tripp Walker rolled his shoulder, the ache there bothering him and it wasn't even lunchtime yet. He needed to get up from this computer, take a walk, and breathe in some of the summer air, even if it did have the consistency of soup.

Right after he finished this last animated sequence. Then he'd be done with this project for at least a week while the on-site animators in Seattle went through his work and pieced it together. They'd send him notes, and he'd fix whatever they wanted him to fix.

But not today.

Right now, he wanted to spend a few minutes with Penny, Rhett's dog, and then he wanted lunch.

His chair scraped the wood floor as he stood, and he exhaled heavily as he stretched.

"Done?" Liam asked from his desk.

"Yes," Tripp said. "I'm heading outside for a few minutes. Then we should get lunch."

"I'm in," Liam said. "I have maybe twenty minutes of work left before I can go."

"Take your time," Tripp said, but his stomach wasn't happy with the words. "I'm going to go teach Penny how to roll over."

His twin laughed, and Tripp knew enough to laugh at himself too. Penny was a great dog, but she did not want to roll over, especially in the dirt. Tripp wasn't going to give up on her though. He was simply going to take advantage of Penny living at Seven Sons for the next few weeks while Rhett and Evelyn were on their honeymoon.

He missed his older brother, though Rhett had been living in the house he'd bought on Quail Creek Road for a few months now.

After stopping at the fridge for a piece of cheese, Tripp stepped onto the back deck and let the summer sunshine beat down on his shoulders. He whistled, hoping Penny would hear him and come running. He heard a bark, and he whistled again.

The dog came running, and when she reached him, he laughed at her and bent down to give her a healthy scratch. "You ready to roll over?"

Penny barked as if saying, *No thank you, Tripp. Where's the treats?*

He took the cheese out of his pocket, and Penny sat down,

her front paws twitching as she kept her eyes right on that treat in his hand. "Good sit," he said, smiling at the dog. "Shake." He put his hand out for Penny, and she put her paw in his fingers.

He gave her a bit of cheese. "Lay down."

She did. Treat. He worked through all of the things she could do really well, and then he said, "Roll over."

Penny went onto her side, but she would not roll all the way over. She whined, and Tripp tilted his head at her. "Just roll over, girl," he said. "You've done it before. Go on. Roll over." With a little more coaxing, Penny did what he wanted.

He cheered and gave her the rest of the cheese, scrubbed her ears and said, "Good girl. Rhett is going to be so proud of you."

He straightened, realizing what his life had become. The best part of his day was getting a cattle dog to roll over. Standing in the brutal June sun was enjoyable.

Tripp really needed to get out more. And not to lunch with his twin. But with a woman.

A specific woman who hadn't answered his last text. "Ivory Osburn," he whispered. He'd been out with her a dozen times over the last nine months, but she was hot and cold with him. She'd go out with him three or four times and then say she needed some space.

He'd given it to her when he really wanted to keep seeing her. Meet her son. Ivory hadn't allowed him to meet Oliver, and Tripp didn't want to push her on that. A mother should get to decide when to bring people into her child's life.

The thought to text her and ask her to dinner crossed his mind, but he crossed it off his list just as quickly. She'd just ignore him again, driving the pin further into his heart.

He wished he could let her go, but for some reason, he couldn't. Hadn't, at least. Maybe with some effort, he could.

"Ready?" Liam asked, and Tripp spun toward him. His mind cleared, and he'd made it a personal rule not to eat out twice in one day. Besides, Jeremiah would make dinner, and Tripp loved his brother's food.

"Yes," he said, following Liam back into the house. "I'll drive."

"You and that fancy truck." Liam chuckled, but Tripp just took his keys off the hook in the kitchen and went into the garage.

He'd bought a new truck a couple of months ago, true. It was dark blue and full of all the bells and whistles. The truck made the twenty-minute drive to the town of Three Rivers almost fun, and Tripp adjusted the radio and the air conditioning when he got behind the wheel.

"Okay, where are we going?" he asked once they got off the lane where the ranch sat, the truck's wheels rolling well over the asphalt.

"I'm feeling like Chinese," he said.

"The one by the post office?" Tripp asked. "That's the one I like."

"China Isle," Liam confirmed. "That's the one. I'm feeling like the chicken noodle bowl."

"You and your love of noodles." Tripp shook his head as he smiled.

A mile or two passed before Liam asked, "Do you think we should've invited Wyatt?"

"Oh," Tripp said, surprise moving through him. "I mean, maybe. He wasn't in the house, though." He glanced at Liam. "And we didn't invite Jeremiah."

"I'm just saying I forget about Wyatt sometimes," Liam said. "He's so quiet."

Tripp laughed then, and that definitely wasn't quiet. His mother had always told him he had the best laugh out of any of the boys, and Tripp liked his laugh.

"Yeah, well, compared to us, anyone would be quiet." Tripp caught sight of the outskirts of town, and his stomach grumbled as if he needed a reminder that he was hungry. "Wyatt seems happy enough, though."

"Yeah, he has a way with the horses," Liam said. "And he doesn't want to train them for the rodeo, which I don't get."

"Well, he's working at Bowman Breeds, and that's what they do. Maybe he feels like this town is too small for two rodeo training operations."

The truth was, Tripp didn't really know how Wyatt felt. His brother had said he needed some time to figure out his life without the rodeo in it, and everyone had left him alone to do that.

"It's fun having him here," Tripp said as he turned to go down the right street.

"Yeah, totally," Liam said. "I just don't want him to feel like we've left him out."

"Fair point," Tripp said. "We should be more careful of that." Sometimes the two of them got in their twin space and didn't realize that the other brothers might feel like they weren't welcome.

He turned into the parking lot and started looking for a spot. "Wow, this place is popular during lunchtime." He swiveled his head left and right, searching. "Anything over there?"

"No, and I had no idea this many people liked Chinese —watch out!"

Tripp slammed on the brake pedal, having just saw the woman bent over in the middle of the parking lot. She'd dropped a bunch of packages, and a very keen sense of déjà vu hit him right in the chest.

So hard that he unbuckled his seatbelt and slid from the truck. "Ivory?" he asked. The first time they'd met, she'd dropped an armful of packages right in front of him at the post office.

She sniffled and snatched the last package before he could help her. His pulse sang and skipped through his veins. At the same time, he realized that there was something wrong with Ivory.

"Are you okay?" He actually glanced at the front bumper of his truck just to make sure he hadn't touched her.

"Tripp." She balanced the packages in one arm and used her free hand to swipe that dirty blonde hair out of her face. "I'm fine."

But she wasn't fine. She'd been crying, and while Tripp wasn't well-versed with crying women, he sensed an opportunity here.

"Let me help you," he said, taking some of the packages before she could protest. With three or four in his hands, she only had a couple left to carry. "You're taking these to the post office?"

"Yes," she said, walking now. He met his brother's eyes through the windshield, and even without their freaky twin communications, Liam would've gotten the message to slide over and get the truck parked.

*This is Ivory Osburn,* Tripp thought, suddenly so glad he'd waited for Liam to finish his work before coming to lunch.

"Why'd you park over here?" he asked.

Ivory just glared at him, then she picked her way across the decorative rocks that separated the restaurant parking lot from the post office one. "No reason."

"Ivory, wait," he said, frustrated she was already pushing him away again. "There's something wrong. A blind man could see it. Let me help you."

"You want to help me?"

"Yes," he said, though her voice bordered on dangerous.

She stepped onto the sidewalk and faced him, her face filled with irritation and anger. Her eyes brimmed with

7

tears. "I don't need help. They're just necklaces." She started taking the packages from him and ended up bobbling all of them, dropping them to the ground again.

A frustrated moan came from her mouth, and she bent to collect the packages again.

"Ivory," he said, feeling helpless with a hint of humiliation.

"I'm fine, Tripp," she said. "I mean, if you can get more people to buy my jewelry, I might be better. Or if you could get my addled mind to remember where to turn to park at this blasted post office, that might be good too. Or you know what?" She straightened, all of the packages securely in her arms again.

"Maybe you could get my ex to drop the custody challenge he started. Can you do that?" She cocked her eyebrows at him, and Tripp had no idea what to say.

"I didn't think so." She turned and marched away from him. "Don't offer to help if you can't actually do it," she said over her shoulder.

Tripp turned to look behind him, sure some help would be standing there. No one stood there, and Tripp watched Ivory walk into the post office and right out of his life.

Again.

# 2

Ivory leaned against the counter, her breaths coming in huge gulps. She was seconds away from having a panic attack in the Three Rivers post office, where everyone would see her.

She could not believe Daniel was suing her for full custody. And the worst part? His claims were true. She had no money. She could barely afford to feed herself and Oliver. The cable had been turned off. Their Internet. Anything Ivory didn't have to have to survive, she'd gotten rid of. They needed air conditioning and heat. Electricity. And her phone, which she used for Internet service too.

But she was months behind on the mortgage, and it was only a matter of time before she didn't have a house either.

And that meant Oliver wouldn't have a place to sleep.

So Daniel's claims that she couldn't adequately provide for their son were one-hundred percent right.

"I can't lose him," she murmured to herself only a moment before a fresh flood of tears arrived.

And running into Tripp in the wrong parking lot was just icing on a really ugly cake. The man called to her very soul, and it had been very hard for her to push him away. Every time he got a little too close, she'd put the brakes on their relationship. She didn't need another man walking out on her. Another man proving to her how unlovable she was. Another man trying to tell her how to live her life, what to wear, how to be.

She opened the pre-stamped mail chute and put her pathetic packages in. Only six this week, and that meant she'd only earned a hundred and twenty dollars. She couldn't afford much with that, because half went to buying the supplies she needed to make the necklaces.

"Look," a man said, and she turned to find Tripp Walker standing there. He was dark, stormy, and beautiful. She wanted to run to him and let him hold her upright. Whisper in her ear that everything would be all right. Kiss those lips she'd kissed before.

"I don't know how to do any of that stuff you just said," he said, taking a step closer, those sexy cowboy boots making a clunking sound on the hard floor. "But I'm not going to just let you walk away when you're so upset."

"I'm fine," she said, though she was anything but fine. In fact, fine and Ivory weren't even on the same continent at the moment.

"Let me take you to lunch," he said.

"Liam was in the truck."

"Liam knows how to order his own food."

Ivory's stomach cramped with hunger. She wanted—no, needed—to eat. And if she were being completely honest with herself, she wanted to be with Tripp.

"I don't think so," she said.

"Why not?"

"Because I don't want you getting the wrong idea," she said, going for snappy truths again. "I'm fine. I just needed to mail my packages." And now she needed to go home, make a pancake out of the giant, ten-pound bag of mix she had, and figure out how to get more people buying jewelry from her online store. What new pieces could she make with the supplies she already owned?

*What do people want?* she begged. She'd been asking God the same question for months, but so far, He hadn't struck her with any inspiration.

"Let's go to lunch with Liam, then," Tripp said. "I can't get the wrong idea then, right?"

Ivory considered him, thinking of the gossip mill in town. The Walker brothers were a little removed from it, but Ivory wasn't. She'd heard plenty of talk at the salon, while she got her nails done, and at the boutiques where she liked to shop. Well, when she had money to do all of those things.

Nails, hair, and shopping had all been cut from her life, the same way the cable had been.

"Come on, Ivory," he said, clearly exasperated. "I stood

over there and watched you have an anxiety attack. One meal. I won't text you afterward."

Ivory wished she could tell him why she'd gotten so scared and cut him out of her life a few times. But she hadn't dared then, and she didn't dare now either.

"Fine," she said. "One meal. With Liam."

"I'm texting him now," Tripp said. He looked up a moment later. "Ready when you are."

Ivory gestured for him to go first, and instead of walking out, Tripp reached over and took her hand.

"Tripp," she said, but he didn't let go. Outside, the sun had heated the air beyond tolerable, and Ivory felt the sweat start to slide down her back with the first step.

He released her hand when he was obviously satisfied that she wasn't going to run away. They walked over those decorative rocks again, and the silence between them made Ivory's nerves strain.

"How have you been?" she asked.

"Not fair," he said, not even glancing at her.

"What's not fair?"

"You asking me how I've been," he said. "That's not fair."

"*You* asked me to lunch."

"You don't seem fit to drive right now," he said. "I want to make sure you're okay."

"I told you I was fine."

"And I've heard you say that before, when you weren't fine." He looked at her then, and Ivory's steps slowed. "I don't know why you've pushed me away on three separate occasions. I really don't. When we've been together, I've had a great time. I like you." He drew in a deep breath, his frustration like a third person between them.

He looked at her, clearly expecting her to say something. "I'm sorry," she said. "I just...needed a break."

"Must be nice," he said, striding forward again. "To take a break from your life whenever you want one."

Fury moved through her, and she stared after him. "You have no idea what you're talking about. I never get a break."

"That's because you refuse to ask for help." He tossed the words over his shoulder, the length of his strides broadcasting his anger. "Have a good day, Ivory." He touched the brim of that sexy cowboy hat and continued toward the entrance of the restaurant.

"I guess I'm uninvited," she said to his retreating back, nowhere near loud enough for him to hear. She watched until he disappeared inside the surely air conditioned restaurant, and then she sighed, running her hand through her hair.

It felt tangled and messy, and she hated that he'd seen her like that. She hurried to her car and turned on the air conditioning. "I took a break from *you*, Tripp, when you were getting too close to me. When things got too real. When I was afraid I'd fall in love with you, only to have you break up with me."

Ivory hung her head, everything in her wrung out. An

alarm went off on her phone, and she sucked in a breath. Pulled everything back inside. Laced it tight.

After all, it was time for her to pick Oliver up from school, and he deserved a mother that wasn't one tick away from a breakdown.

———

"OLLIE," she called from the sliding glass door. "Come on, baby. Dinner's ready."

Her son left his toys in the sandbox and skipped toward her. "Look, Mama. I can skip." He grinned so wide, his whole face shone with joy. He had no idea she'd spent too much at the grocery store that afternoon so they could have sausage with their pancakes that night.

"Good job," she said, stroking her hand over his silky hair. "Are you ready for summer?"

"Yeah," he said. "Dad said he'd take me horseback riding."

"Yep," Ivory said as cheerfully as she could. Daniel had moved to Amarillo after their divorce, but he came to Three Rivers twice a month for his son. And he'd take Oliver the day after school got out for half of the summer.

"Pancakes again?" Oliver asked, and Ivory flinched.

"That's right," she said brightly. "With your favorite— sausage links." She put the plate in front of him as he climbed up on the barstool. She'd added water to the syrup and heated in the microwave, stirring it all together. It was a little thin, but Oliver didn't say anything about that.

She flipped the pancakes on the griddle and served two to her son a minute later. She kept her smile on her face as she ate, but she could barely gag down another bite of pancake. She'd bought hot dogs as well, and she'd definitely have to switch up their diet tomorrow.

Helplessness filled her, but she held back the tears until Ollie finished dinner. "Bath time, bud," she said, her patience for this day almost gone. And she'd have to see Daniel on Saturday, look him in the face, and pretend like he hadn't turned her world upside down with a few pieces of paper.

Oliver didn't get up and skip down the hall to the bathroom. He never did. She didn't have the energy to fight with him tonight, so when he got down and went into the backyard instead of to take a bath, she said nothing.

She sat at the kitchen counter and stared at the watery syrup. The empty plate which had held the sausage links. The pancakes she hadn't been able to swallow.

"What am I going to do?" She tilted her head toward the ceiling. Her parents lived in Tennessee, and she had absolutely no desire to call them. She'd left for college and never gone back, as her father had a drinking problem and turned mean when he drank.

Daniel's parents lived in the Texas Hill Country, and she hadn't spoken to them since the divorce, three years ago.

They'd never offered to help her, but they may have made arrangements with Daniel.

He paid his child support, and without that, Ivory would've been in much worse condition than she was now.

She exhaled, determined not to sit here and cry. Her jewelry-making wasn't working out. So she'd get a job.

With an ache in her bones, she got up and went to the back door again. "Ollie, come on," she said. "Bath time."

"Mom," he whined, and Ivory gestured to him. He argued a little bit, but he eventually came in and stomped down the hall to the bathroom. Ivory cleaned up the kitchen, glancing at the small cowboy figurine on the windowsill above the sink.

Ollie had made it for her in school, and for some reason, Tripp's handsome face appeared in her mind.

If he was her husband, she'd have plenty of money....

The thought waltzed through her mind so slowly. She really had time to think hard about it, ultimately dismissing the idea.

"You're not even talking to him," she muttered to herself as Ollie started singing down the hall. And marrying him?

Wasn't going to happen, even if he did say he wanted to help her.

# 3

Tripp spent the rest of the week on the ranch, working on moving the first harvest of hay into the right barn. He wasn't a born and bred cowboy like his brother Jeremiah, but he did love being out on the ranch, under the hot sun, the scent of dust, horses, and hay in the air.

He rubbed his nose as he tossed another bale onto the belt, sneezing a moment later. His altercation with Ivory was a few days old, but he couldn't get her out of his mind. He'd wanted her to follow him into the restaurant and tell him off for judging her.

He hadn't meant to do that, and he'd spent a couple of nights on his knees, trying to repent of saying she'd taken a break from her life whenever she wanted one.

She was a single mother, for crying out loud. Tripp didn't have any kids, but he knew enough to know Ivory didn't truly get a break from all she had to do, ever. He'd seen her jewelry, and she was really talented. She had an eye for colors and textures that his mind would never come up with.

They'd spent afternoons riding horses, and she loved Texas though she wasn't from the state.

He knew she liked iced coffee and that her favorite pie was banana cream. They'd been together for Thanksgiving and Christmas, but she'd ended things sometime in January. Then he'd seen her again for a few weeks at the end of March and the beginning of April, and then she'd retreated again.

She never gave much of an explanation for her exits from his life, and that alone drove frustration through him whenever he thought about it.

"Gotta stop thinking about it," he told himself, grabbing a hay bale in each hand. When Ivory was talking to him, he spent a lot of his spare time with her. When she wasn't, he hit the weights at the gym, so he was really ripped right now.

He thought about the woman at the front desk at the gym. Tammy wore leggings and a tight T-shirt every day, and she'd asked Tripp for his number that morning.

And he'd given it to her. With a smile.

"Gotta move on," he said, though he had very little conviction behind the words.

"Talking to yourself again?" Jeremiah came up beside him and tossed a bale onto the belt.

"Hey," Wyatt said from up above. "I can't get them off that fast."

"Sorry," Jeremiah called up to him.

Tripp glanced at him and let a few more seconds go by before putting another bale on. He wasn't going to deny talking to himself. He was the brother who did that, and he often muttered to himself in front of his computer as he animated the characters others had drawn.

"So what's goin' on?" Jeremiah asked.

"Nothing," Tripp said, because this particular brother was still very much anti-female. But it had been two years now since the Walker brothers had left Austin and come to Three Rivers. Well, four of them, at least.

"So Ivory," Jeremiah said, adjusting his cowboy hat.

"Liam told you."

"He may have mentioned that you ran into her the other day when you guys went to lunch."

"Why would he mention that?" Tripp hefted another bale onto the belt.

Jeremiah picked up the next one, and Tripp took a moment to stretch his back. "Because he's realized he doesn't like Kiley."

"That's because he's still hung up on Callie. I don't know why he doesn't just ask her out."

"He's working on a strategy for that." Jeremiah put his bale on the belt.

Tripp threw on the last one, and Wyatt took it off at the top. Then he switched the direction of the belt and rode it back to the ground.

"Lunch?" he asked.

"Simone is making lunch at Shining Star," Jeremiah said. "That's why I came out. She called and invited us." He cocked his eyebrows at Tripp. "Sure is nice to be invited."

"Hey, we said we were sorry," Tripp said, frowning at his older brother. "Everyone is invited to lunch." He and Liam hadn't meant to leave anyone out.

"I know." Jeremiah smiled, and he truly wasn't upset. Thankfully. An angry Jeremiah was something to behold, and Tripp didn't need to see it anytime soon. "But let's go clean up. She said we can come anytime."

"I'm starving," Wyatt said.

"That's because you eat five million calories a day," Tripp said. He'd literally never seen a human being consume as much as Wyatt did. Or wear a belt buckle so large, even to just load hay into a loft.

"Hey, I'm not the one at the gym seven days a week," he shot back.

"Me either," Tripp said. "I'm not going tomorrow."

"And he's only been going this week because of Ivory," Jeremiah said.

"Ivory...." Wyatt said thoughtfully. "She's the blonde you like, right?"

"Been out with her a *ton*," Jeremiah said. "She can't make up her mind."

"I don't know what she can or can't do," Tripp said, disliking Jeremiah's assessment of her. "And we haven't been out a ton."

"Enough to kiss her," Jeremiah said, peering at him. "Right?"

"That was last year," Tripp said, like it was old news. He whistled for Penny to come, and she trotted out of the shadows and followed them back to the homestead. He wasn't going to admit he'd been dreaming of kissing Ivory again. Or that he'd tapped out a dozen texts to her this week, only to erase them and then turn off his phone to remove the temptation.

Jeremiah looked like he was going to argue with Tripp again, but Liam burst out of the house and said, "I got the job!"

"No way," Tripp said, bounding up the steps. "The Marvel contract?"

Liam's whole being glowed, and he tipped his head back and laughed. "The entire universe. It's going to be *amazing*."

His brother was one of the best computer-generated imagery artists in the country, and landing a contract from one of the biggest names in the entertainment industry proved it. "You've been working on that for *so* long." Tripp threw his arms around his brother and hugged him. "Congratulations."

"It's a four-year project," he said, accepting congratulations from Jeremiah and Wyatt too. "I can't wait to get started. I have to go to California in a few weeks." They went into the house, shutting out the heat while they washed up for lunch.

Over at the Shining Star, Callie and Simone waited in the kitchen, chatting about something.

"Ladies," Liam said, always the charmer in a crowd. Tripp used to follow his younger brother of eight minutes around both his high school and college campuses. That way, they'd both walk away with a date.

But here in Three Rivers, it seemed like those tables had turned. Of course, Tripp wasn't doing well in the dating pool since wading in. But if there was someone doing worse, it was Liam.

He slung his arm around Simone's shoulders. "What's cookin' today."

She rolled her eyes as she giggled and pushed him away. "Burger bites," she said. "We know how you Walker boys like red meat."

"I know I do," he said, sidling over to Callie. "Heya, Callie."

"Afternoon, Liam." She smiled at him with pure joy on her face, but something pinched around her eyes.

"What's wrong?" he asked, his voice dropping. Amidst all the other hellos, their conversation got lost, but Liam hugged Callie and held her at arm's length, saying something to her.

Wyatt didn't say a whole lot, but Jeremiah could talk about food until the cows came home, and he complimented Simone on the burger bites.

"Okay," she finally called. "Let's eat."

Tripp was glad he was surrounded by so many people,

because it meant he couldn't disappear inside his head. Couldn't obsess about Ivory Osburn, the woman who'd made it very clear she didn't want anything to do with him.

———

FOLLOWING morning found him at the gym, despite his denial that he went every day. He couldn't help how early he got up, and he couldn't stand to putz around the house. Might as well get on the treadmill and build muscle before the rest of the world rose.

He sweated through his leg workout, and he decided he'd earned a baked omelet from the pancake house. He stopped there and got a table for himself. He didn't have to feel guilty for eating breakfast alone and not inviting his brothers. He'd asked them to go to the gym with him, and they'd all declined.

Wyatt and Jeremiah had plenty to do around the ranch, and Wyatt had taken over some of the chores at the Shining Star while Rhett was on his honeymoon. And Liam was a sleep diva, and heaven help the man that woke him before nine.

He'd ordered and sugared up his coffee when a woman sat down across from him. Surprised laced through him when he met her eyes.

"Hi," she said with a smile.

Tripp was a nice guy, so he smiled back. "Hello."

"My name is Billie."

Oh-kay. "Hello, Billie," he said, thinking she was way too young for him. She glanced out into the restaurant, and he followed her gaze. Sure enough, a table of three women stared at them, and Tripp lifted his hand in a wave.

"Oh, honey," Sandy said. "Don't encourage them." She pierced Billie with a glare. "Leave the man alone."

Billie just grinned at Sandy, who didn't leave. "Tripp."

"Yeah?" He looked up at her, unsure of what to do in this situation.

"Did you ask her to sit with you?"

"No," he said, spying his waitress coming with his food. He just wanted to be left alone.

"Come on, Billie. Back to your own table." Sandy snapped her fingers at the woman, and she heaved a sigh as she slid out of the booth. "He's too old for you anyway," Sandy added, and Tripp ducked his head as a smile touched his lips.

"Be right back," she said, and she escorted Billie back to her own table, leaned into it, and started lecturing the women there. Tripp was far enough away that he couldn't hear what they were talking about, and his puffy, delicious omelet arrived, so he was a little distracted.

Sandy returned to top off his coffee. "Sorry about that," she said.

"It's fine," he said.

"Your brother used to draw quite a crowd of female fans too," she said with a smile. "I'm not complaining. You come in everyday if you want." She patted him on the shoulder and returned to work.

Tripp kept his head down as he ate and sipped his coffee, wondering if this was what his life was going to be. Forty years old, eating breakfast alone, pining after a woman who wanted nothing to do with him.

When he'd wasted a couple of hours at the pancake house, he finally slid out of his booth, tossing some money on the table. "Thanks, Val," he said to his waitress, who smiled at him as he turned to leave.

His phone rang, and he expected it to be one of his brothers, asking him where he was.

Ivory's name sat on the screen.

"Ivory," he whispered to himself. As if he was doing something wrong, he glanced around the pancake house to see if anyone had heard him. He hurried outside, where the hot air almost punched the oxygen out of his lungs.

He swiped on the call. "Ivory?"

Sniffling came through the line, but she didn't say anything. Maybe she'd pocket dialed him. "Hello?" he tried again.

"Are you busy right now?" she asked, her voice an octave higher than normal. She was obviously crying.

"Not even a little bit," he said.

"Can you come over?"

*Absolutely*, he thought, almost breaking into a jog to get back to his truck. He forced himself to walk and to say, "I think I can make that work."

"I'll text you my address if that's okay. Do you need a few minutes?"

"I'm actually in town," he said, feeling like a hopeless fool. Was he really going to go running back to this woman the moment she called? "I just finished breakfast at the pancake house."

She didn't answer immediately, because she was very obviously upset about something. Probably her ex-husband.

He'd thought about buying every piece of jewelry available in her online store, but she'd know it was him. Trying to give the woman charity had never ended well for him.

"Okay," she finally said. "I'll see you really soon then."

"Okay," he said, and she said she'd text him and ended the call.

He positioned himself behind the wheel and turned on the truck so the air conditioning would start blowing. His phone chimed, and there was Ivory's address.

He'd never been to her house before. She'd always insisted on meeting him somewhere when they'd gone out before. She'd wanted to keep some distance between him and her son, whom he hadn't met yet.

His pulse thrummed in his neck as he put the truck in reverse. "Help me help her," he prayed aloud as he backed out. He'd been praying to get the woman back in his life, and if he could only be her friend, well, that might have to be enough.

"But let it be more," he whispered to himself and maybe God too.

# 4

I vory paced in her house, her face so, so hot. She clutched the paperwork in her fist, thinking of all kinds of things she should've said to Daniel while he was there.

Instead, she'd just taken everything he'd said and done, kissed Ollie goodbye, and then she'd broken down.

Completely. Huge, chest-wracking sobs that left her breathless and her heart hollow.

She was going to lose her son.

Pure desperation filled her again, but she shoved the feelings away. She'd pulled herself together enough to call Tripp, and he was coming.

Somehow, he'd help her figure out what to do.

A knock sounded on the door, and it had Tripp's name written all over it. She drew in a deep breath and squared her shoulders. After crossing the room, she opened the door and looked at him through the screen.

"Hey," he said, pure concern in his voice and his expression.

She released the latch on the screen door and pushed it open. "Come in."

Tripp did, his broad shoulders and tall frame filling her doorway in the most comforting way. "Can I hug you?"

She practically fell into his arms and held on tight, refusing to cry. She'd done enough of that. It was time to do something useful.

"Tell me what's going on," he said, clearing his throat and stepping back.

"Daniel is trying to take Oliver from me," she said. "Daniel's my ex. Oliver is my son."

"Right, right," he said. "Why would he think he could do that? Don't you guys already have shared custody?"

"Yes," she said, pacing away from him. Her heartbeat sprinted in her chest, and she hadn't anticipated having to tell him so much. But he'd need to know everything.

"I tried to find a job this week," she said. "It's not going well, because every teenager in the world wants to work too." She didn't mean to sound so bitter. But she needed money, and at this point, she was willing to do anything.

She shot a glance at Tripp. Calling him had been very difficult, but she didn't have many options at this point.

*Dear Lord,* she prayed. *I need help here.*

She wasn't sure why she kept praying. God never seemed to hear her at all. And if He did, He obviously didn't care what she wanted or needed, because things with her business had only gotten worse over the last six months, not better.

Tripp put his hand on her shoulder. "Hey," he said.

A thrill moved down her arm from his touch.

"Take a deep breath," he said. "You're looking for a job?"

She collapsed onto the couch and ran her hands over her face. "I'm broke. Completely. I'm four months behind on my mortgage. We've been eating pancakes for every meal for a couple of weeks now." She shook her head, tears brimming in her eyes. "I'm selling very few things from my jewelry shop, and Daniel's filed for full custody, citing that I can't provide the necessities of life for Ollie."

By the time she finished talking, her voice was barely a whisper.

Tripp sat next to her on the couch and took both of her hands in his. "Ivory," he said, his voice low and kind and dripping with emotion. "Are you asking for my help?"

She looked at him—right into those deep, dark eyes that she'd fallen for in the past. He wore a nicely trimmed beard, which was a new development since Monday, when she'd seen him in the post office. He was handsome, and his spirit called to her, the same way it always had.

She nodded, the moment between them charged and serene at the same time.

"I know you won't just accept charity," he said, his brow furrowing. "The Foster sisters need help on their ranch." He shook his head. "They can't really pay you, though...." His voice trailed off, and he looked like he was thinking really hard.

"I don't want you to give me a job," she said, feeling like everything inside her was about to splinter.

"Oh, okay." He watched her, clearly waiting for her to tell him what she wanted from him.

"I need to prove to Daniel—and a judge—that I can take care of my son."

"Okay."

Ivory was going to have to say exactly what she wanted. "I think...." She swallowed, finding her throat so dry. "I think maybe if I was married—" She choked, because her last marriage had not gone well at all. And she had absolutely no desire to walk down the aisle again. Ever.

"Married," Tripp repeated.

"I would pay you back," she said.

Tripp shot to his feet and walked over to the window, turning as he took his cowboy hat off. "Okay, let me get this straight. You want me to...get you caught up on all of your bills, marry you, and convince a judge that *we* can take care of Oliver." He gestured between the two of them, his eyes sparking with heat.

Ivory's heart fell to the ground. "When you put it like that...." But that was what she wanted. And she hated herself for wanting it. For calling him and asking him to do this for her.

"I'm sorry," she said, standing up. "Really. I'm sure I'll get a job next week, and I'm sure things will start to look up." Her voice broke on the last word, because she wasn't sure how working the graveyard shift at the convenience store on the road leaving town would work. Who would stay with Oliver?

She had a friend down the street that took him when Ivory needed help, but she couldn't have her son sleep over there every night.

*He's gone for the next seven weeks*, she thought. She could take that job at the convenience store. She could. She would.

"Forget I said anything, okay?" She begged Tripp to agree, but he stood there, saying nothing. "I'm so sorry, Tripp. I was just desperate there for a minute. I shouldn't have called you."

He blinked, his shoulders drawing back. "Did you really just call a man you can barely tolerate and ask him to marry you?"

Ivory wanted the floor to open up and swallow her whole. "I'm so sorry." She shook her head. "And you're wrong. I can tolerate you." And a lot more than that, she really liked him.

"Is that so?"

"Yes," she said, lifting her chin.

He took one step toward her. "Why'd you break up with me three times in the past nine months?"

"Fear," she said bravely, the word sticking in her throat. So she wasn't the bravest woman on the planet.

"Fear of what?" he asked, still closing the distance

between them.

"Being intimate with you," she said. "Telling you about my past. Introducing you to my son." She held up a finger for each thing she said. "Three break-ups."

"You didn't like kissing me?" he asked.

"I liked it," she said, swallowing. Her eyes dropped to his mouth right now. "And I got scared, because I liked it. I *like* you. Not past tense."

He touched his fingers to hers, and the spark between them flared to life. "I want to know about your past. Your present. What you want in the future," he said, ducking his head. "And I'd love to meet your son. I told you that."

"I know," Ivory said. "I'm just...protective of Oliver."

"Understandable." He glanced around. "Where is he now?"

"Daniel has him for the next seven weeks."

A new light entered Tripp's eyes. "Seven weeks. So if you liked kissing me, and you're okay sharing your life with me, we can spend the next couple of months doing that. And then when Oliver gets home, I'd love to meet him—if you're ready for that then."

"Seven weeks." Ivory couldn't believe what was happening right here.

"And if you think we need to get married...I'm willing to consider it."

"Really?"

"Ivory," he said, taking off his cowboy hat and pressing his cheek against hers. "I've tried to get you out of my head.

I've tried to move on. I haven't been able to figure out how." He swayed with her, and Ivory closed her eyes, this feeling of safety so foreign and so welcome.

"Let's start with dinner," he said. "Tonight?"

"Okay," Ivory said.

"Great," he said. "I'll pick you up at seven." He brushed his lips against her cheek and fell back, putting all kinds of proper space between them. Their eyes met and hooked, and a rush of gratitude moved through her.

"Thank you, Tripp," she said.

"I've always said I'm willing to help you," he said. "And I meant it."

She nodded, and he moved over to the front door. He stepped out onto the porch and turned back to her. "Seven."

"Seven." She gripped the door as he repositioned his cowboy hat on his head, went down her steps, and climbed into his truck.

Then he was gone.

She closed the door and sagged against it. "What a disaster," she said, but for the first time in four months, hope existed in her heart.

"All right." She straightened away from the door and wiped her hair out of her face. "Up next: Calling back the manager of that convenience store." All she could do was hope that she didn't have to start work that night.

———

"I GOT A JOB," she said when she opened the door to Tripp's handsome face that evening.

"You did?" He grinned at her, and he looked good enough to dream about in that pair of dark jeans, his peach-colored shirt, open at the throat, those cowboy boots that got her heart racing, and that cowboy hat.

Oh, that cowboy hat.

She'd always had a soft spot for a man in a cowboy hat, and she had the strangest desire to reach up and take it off. Put it on her own head. Or just kiss him without that brim in the way.

But she didn't move. She knew cowboys didn't like it when someone touched their hat. And wearing it? She'd had one boyfriend in Tennessee who'd accused her of "misshaping" his hat when she'd worn it for ten seconds.

"Where are you going to work?" Tripp asked.

Ivory grabbed her purse and stepped out onto the porch with him. "The convenience store on the west side of town," she said. "Graveyard shift." She beamed at him, so proud of herself. "I mean, I might have to change things up when Ollie comes back." She shrugged and linked her arm through his.

"Graveyard shift?" he asked. "At Gus's? Isn't that the place where they've had those robberies?"

"What?" she asked, her stomach swooping and not because she'd caught a whiff of his sexy cologne. "I haven't heard of any robberies."

"Yeah, I'm sure they were at Gus's." He paused at the

end of her sidewalk and pulled his phone from his back pocket. He tapped and typed, swiping and then showing his screen to her. "Yeah, look. This says, 'Third robbery at gas station has owner hiring security guard.'"

Ivory took his phone and read the article. "Three robberies in six months," she said, the familiar fear and helplessness threatening to join her on this date. "No wonder Wade was so glad I'd called him back." Disgust flowed through her. "I can't put myself in danger like that," she said, looking at Tripp. "What would you do?"

# 5

What would he do?

Tripp didn't know how to answer. Couldn't answer. He had no idea what Ivory's life was like, what it had been like. He didn't even think about money, ever. And the weight of not having any crushed Ivory, so he couldn't understand. Couldn't answer.

"I don't know, Ivory," he said. "Honestly, marrying me is less dangerous." He couldn't believe he'd just said that. But he was right.

She sighed and turned away from him, running both hands through her gorgeous hair. Tripp wanted to do that. He wanted to hold her close and tell her everything would be okay. He wanted to meet her son when Oliver came home.

He stood there, wondering what he needed to do or say. "Ivory," he tried, wondering how Rhett and Evelyn had gotten to the point where they'd gone to City Hall and gotten married when it wasn't real.

Was he about to do the same thing?

He wished he could call his brother and get more details. Get some advice.

The blonde he'd liked for so long turned back to him, her eyes filled with emotion. "I don't know, Tripp."

"Well, I do," he said, quickly closing the distance between them. He slipped his arm around her waist, and she didn't jump away from him. Push him away. Protest. She just gazed up at him, and Tripp really wanted to kiss her.

He'd kissed her before, and he didn't want the next time they kissed to be at their wedding—which was totally happening.

He cupped her face in one hand, a sure sign of what he was about to do. She said nothing, and Tripp lowered his mouth to hers, barely touching her, giving her the opportunity to stop him.

She didn't. In fact, she tipped up onto her toes and *kissed* him.

Tripp's pulse blipped through his body faster and faster as the kiss lengthened. "Okay," he whispered, pulling away. His cowboy hat had fallen off at some point, but he didn't care. "So let's go to dinner and talk about this wedding."

"I don't know, Tripp," she said, fiddling with the collar on his shirt.

"You need help," he said. "And I can help you." He

touched his cheek to hers. "I like you, Ivory. I don't think that's a secret."

"I feel...stupid," she said, the word bursting from her mouth. "And helpless. I'm not helpless. I can do this."

"Of course you can," he said. "You got a job already. You're a good mother."

"You don't even know that," she said, stepping out of his arms.

Tripp felt her slipping away from him, physically and emotionally. "Ivory," he said. "I have so much money, I don't even know how much."

She turned and pierced him with a glare. "Not helping."

"I'm not saying that to be arrogant," he said. "I'm just saying that I have what you need, and *I'm willing to give* it to you. You don't have to pay me back."

She looked torn, and Tripp felt like backing off a little bit. "And I know you're a good mom, because you'd do anything to keep your son. And I'm *willing* to do it."

"Do what?"

"What you suggested."

"Marry me and pay my bills."

"Yes," he said. He'd say yes over and over again for her.

"What do you get out of this?" she asked.

Tripp drew in a deep breath, about to lay everything on the line. As if he hadn't already. "You," he said. "Ivory, I get *you*."

She shook her head, clearly exasperated. "Tripp, this isn't some sort of sex trade thing."

He flinched and fell back a step. "Wow, that kind of hurts." And it did. Who did she think he was?

"Sorry," she murmured. "I just...it wouldn't be real."

"Okay," he said, his hopes crazily bouncing around his head anyway. The pinch of pain in his chest dissipated, because of course Ivory didn't think he was just looking for sex.

"We'll stay married just long enough for you to get your ex off your back." He reached out and touched her fingers with his. "Just long enough for you to get back on your feet. And who knows? Maybe then we can try a for-real relationship."

Ivory considered him for a moment, and then she ran her hands up his chest. "Tripp, you're too good for me."

"That's not true," he said.

"I do like you," she said, and he saw the fear she'd spoken of right there in her face. So maybe she just needed more time to come to the same conclusion he had: that they were meant for each other.

"Let's go to dinner," he said, threading his fingers through hers and tugging her toward the front door. "And I don't think you should take that job at the convenience store."

"If we're really getting married, I won't."

"I already said yes," he said. "I'm waiting for you to agree to the idea."

"Let's see how dinner goes," she said, a giggle accompanying the words.

Tripp was willing to see how everything went. He couldn't believe how happy he was to have Ivory back in his life, but he was. He'd always liked the woman, from the very first moment she'd dropped a couple of dozen packages at his booted feet in the post office.

Now, he held her door while she scampered up into his truck, glad he hadn't turned it off to go to the door. Because, wow, summer had arrived, and the temperature in the air stole his breath. Or maybe all of that heat was because of Ivory's rose-scented perfume and the gentle curl in her hair. The way she glanced at him as if *he* made *her* nervous.

"Okay, listen," she said before he'd even backed out of her driveway. "I'm still going to get a job. I mean, I can't just sit around and do nothing, especially while Ollie is gone."

"You make jewelry, don't you?" he asked.

"A little," she said, her voice taking on an evasive quality. "My business...hasn't been going so well."

The Foster sisters flashed through his mind. He didn't know all the details of their ranch, but he knew it floundered a little bit. They worked hard, just as he was sure Ivory did, but sometimes success wasn't in the cards.

"I understand that," he said.

"You do?" she asked.

"A little," he said with a shrug. "My father was a computer engineer and entrepreneur. He had a job with a company when I was young, but about age seven, he quit and started his own thing." He glanced at Ivory to find her watching him fully now. "There were lean times. We ate

47

pancakes for every meal for a while too." He gave her a smile, hoping to get her to do the same.

He also wanted her to know she wasn't alone.

"And there are a lot of you Walkers," she said.

He chuckled. "Sometimes it felt like a zoo," he said. "At least that's what my mother says." Tripp had loved growing up with six brothers. They'd had a big house out in the middle of the countryside outside of Austin, and he'd spent more time outside than in any day it wasn't raining.

"How's Destiny?" he asked, hoping he could ask her about her family and not get shut down. His other relationships with Ivory had been slow, not that Tripp had minded. But every time he got too close, she pulled back.

Tonight, though, she said, "She's good. She just got a new job."

"Oh yeah?"

"Yeah, she moved into recruiting for her company. She seems happy." Ivory turned and looked out her window, and Tripp wanted to know what she was thinking.

So he asked, and that brought her attention back to him.

"I'm thinking we might be crazy," she said. "My sister can barely make her marriage work, and it's real."

Tripp reached over and took her hand in his. Even her fingers were full of tension, and he wanted to erase it for her. "I think it would be amazing."

"Well, you've always seen things with rose-colored glasses," she teased.

Tripp shrugged one shoulder, but he couldn't deny it. "Things usually work out, Ivory."

"Except when they don't," she said quietly.

"I haven't been married," he said just as softly. "So I don't really know, but I think if we work at it, we'll be fine." He pulled up to a stop sign and looked at her. "Besides, it's not real, right? You need your son back. You just need some time to get back on your feet. I can help by doing this, so let's just go down to City Hall and get it done."

Of course he had ulterior motives—he couldn't help hoping that Ivory could somehow fall in love with him during their fake marriage—but he did want to help her.

"We can't get married at City Hall," Ivory said.

"What?" Tripp didn't care that another pair of headlights had come up behind him. He hit the hazard button to turn on his flashers, and they went around. "Why not?"

"Daniel is a lawyer," she said. "He won't buy that for a second. He'll know we didn't really tie the knot." She shook her head. "No, we'll have to have a small ceremony. Maybe out on the ranch?"

Tripp felt like she'd tossed a bucket of ice water in his face. He opened his mouth to speak, but nothing came out. A wedding at the ranch. No. A *fake* wedding at the ranch.

Jeremiah would go ballistic. Absolutely bonkers.

"I'll talk to my brothers," he said. "I'm not sure we're equipped for a wedding."

"It will be very small," she said. "But a few friends. A

real dress. Maybe a bouquet. Then it will look real, even if it's not."

*Even if it's not.*

*Dear Lord*, he prayed as he took off his cowboy hat and ran his fingers through his hair. *Is this the right thing to do?*

No answer came, because Tripp couldn't detangle his own feelings from the situation. What he wanted and what God wanted and what Ivory wanted was just a giant ball of emotion, and he couldn't tell what was right and what wasn't.

"I know I'm asking a lot of you," Ivory said, squeezing his fingers and bringing him out of his mind.

"It's just...I think maybe we should think about this for a day or two," he said quietly. "I'll see how I feel at church tomorrow."

"Fair enough," she said. She sucked in a deep breath, and Tripp felt like he needed to do the same. "All right. Enough wedding talk. Let's go eat, because I'm starving."

Tripp met her eyes, the moment still sober. Then he said, "All right. How do you feel about steak?"

She swatted his arm, because he already knew steak was one of her favorite things. He was willing to bet a sizable sum that she hadn't eaten anything of that caliber in a while. He eased around the corner, glad that she'd been able to take a heavy topic and make it lighter.

She'd always been able to do that, and Tripp reminded himself just how much he liked this woman.

*Enough to marry her and not really have her?* he

wondered. But he pushed the thought away, because he wanted to enjoy his dinner with her. It might be the only one they had, and he didn't want to waste the time he got with her.

———

THE NEXT MORNING, Tripp joined his brother in the kitchen. "Where's Jeremiah?" he asked, noting the pan of hash on the stovetop.

Liam looked up from his phone, where he read the news each morning. "He and Wyatt went out to get the ranch chores done, same as always." Something glinted in his twin's eye, and Tripp looked away. "You were out late last night."

Tripp reached into the cupboard and got down a mug. "I told you I had a date with Ivory."

"Yeah, but sometimes those only last an hour."

True, but Tripp wouldn't give Liam the satisfaction of being right.

"So things must have gone well," Liam pressed.

Tripp sighed as he turned around to stir sugar into his coffee. "I guess."

"You guess?" Liam wore his cowboy hat inside, which Tripp normally did too. He just hadn't showered yet, so he hadn't gotten dressed.

"It's kind of like with you and Callie," Tripp said, and the softness went out of his brother's face.

"There's nothing with me and Callie," Liam said.

Tripp glanced out the sliding glass doors behind his brother. "Look, it's just me and you. I know you like that woman, and if you'd just ask her out—"

"I did," he said.

Surprise moved through Tripp. "Oh."

"She said she didn't want to ruin our friendship with 'feelings'." He made air quotes around the last word, and he looked and sounded disgusted. "So please, just stop trying to tell me if I'd just ask her out, she'd go with me." He got up and practically stomped over to the sink, where he dumped the last couple of swallows of his coffee.

"Liam," Tripp said, desperate now to make things better for his brother and Ivory. "I'm sorry. I didn't know."

"It's okay." Liam stood very still at the sink, his head bowed. "I just...I really like her, and I just can't figure out what's wrong with me."

"I'm sure it's not you. Callie doesn't go out with anyone."

"I know." He straightened and looked at Tripp. "I'm done talking about this. What's with you and Ivory? Is she going to let you see her again?"

"Yeah," Tripp said slowly, his mind moving quickly. "And she's in a bit of a hard place, and I just keep thinking about what Rhett and Evelyn did, and well, we're thinking about getting married."

Liam's whole face rounded. His eyes. His mouth. "Wow. For real? Or like what Rhett and Evelyn did the first time?"

52

Tripp glanced back to the windows and doors that showed the backyard and on to the ranch. "Probably more of the first time," he said miserably, lifting his coffee to his lips. "But no one would know that. She wants it to look real, because her ex is suing her for custody of her son."

Liam said nothing as he moved to stand beside Tripp. They watched the sun bake the world outside, both of them lost in their own thoughts. Finally, when he caught movement out on the ranch, Tripp breathed in deeply.

"Please don't say anything to anyone," he said. "I'm— *we're*—still thinking about it. I'm going to see how I feel at church today." He picked up the spoon and put some hash on his plate.

"You know we'll support you," Liam said. "At least I will. And Jeremiah—"

"Is coming in right now," Tripp said under his breath. "This looks great, Jeremiah," he said in a normal voice. "I swear, when do you sleep?"

# 6

I vory looked at herself in the mirror, wondering when the lines around her eyes had appeared. Or that one between her eyes, the perpetual frown she couldn't make go away. She'd really enjoyed dinner with Tripp last night, and thoughts of the man had kept her awake too.

He was kind, and strong, and smart, and faithful. He was everything she'd wished Daniel was.

She wasn't sure what reservations had come over him while they'd been talking in his truck on the way to the restaurant, but she didn't have any about marrying him. And she *would* pay him back.

She absolutely would.

Turning away from the fierceness in her eyes in the reflection, she went down the hall and got her keys. Without Oliver, she didn't have anyone to sit by at church. That

Liz Isaacson

didn't matter. She'd find a friend or an elderly woman who needed someone to sit by, and she'd be fine.

After a short drive, she entered the church, a sense of pure peace coming over her. It was as if there was something attached to the doorframe that lifted away troubles and problems, and Ivory couldn't feel the burdens she'd been carrying during the week.

She caught sight of her friend, Kate, only a couple of steps away from the door. She didn't have her husband with her either. Only her two kids. Dexter was the same age as Ollie, and Ivory and Kate had helped each other a lot over the past few years with their kids.

"Hey," she said as she approached Kate. "Can I sit with you guys today? Ollie's with his dad."

"Of course." Kate grabbed onto her and hugged her. "How are you?" She looked at Ivory with her dark hazel eyes that knew so much. She was really asking how everything was going. And if Ivory was okay with her son's absence, especially since it was going to be so long.

"Good," she said, her voice maybe a little too bright and a little too false. "Good."

But things weren't good. She wasn't good. And she knew it.

Oliver was only going to be in Amarillo for seven weeks, and she was already lost without him. What would she do if Daniel won full custody?

Panic paraded through her, but Jenny, Kate's five-year-

56

old, put her hand in Ivory's. "I want to sit by you," she said in her angelic, childlike voice.

"Sure," Ivory said, even more brightly. "Let's go." They entered the chapel, and Kate chose a bench on the side, about halfway toward the front. Perfect. Not too close. Not too far away. Out of the way.

That was exactly what Ivory wanted. Out of the way. No spotlights. No attention. No need for anyone to look too closely at her, see what she was doing.

And marrying Tripp Walker would bring her right into the spotlight.

As if summoned by her thoughts, the Walker brothers sat down on the bench in the middle, one in front of where she sat. Her breath waltzed in her lungs, which was quite painful. Those four men had no idea what they were doing to the women in this town, and it was as if a hush had fallen over the congregation and the pastor hadn't even gotten up to start yet.

Tripp had gone into the row first, and she could barely see him past all those other broad cowboy shoulders. His twin, Liam, leaned over and whispered something to him, and she caught half of Tripp's smile as he shook his head.

Jeremiah sat next to Liam, with Wyatt on the end. Ivory had never met Wyatt in person, though Tripp had talked about him plenty during their last try at a relationship. Well, *his* last try. If Ivory were being honest with herself, she'd never tried with Tripp at all.

Desperation moved through her now, but she couldn't help feeling broken. Like she was completely unlovable, and that no one would ever want her. After all, Daniel had left at the first sign of trouble.

So Ivory had learned to run from hard things. Hard conversations. Hard feelings. Difficult situations. Why put herself through those things?

She stole another glance at Tripp. *He's not Daniel,* she thought. *So what's the right thing to do?* She closed her eyes and leaned her head slightly back, as if light from heaven would bathe her face.

It didn't, but she still felt the same as she had last night.

If Tripp agreed, she'd marry him. Win the lawsuit for full custody. Keep Daniel where he'd fled to—in Amarillo and out of her life.

Tripp turned and looked at her, and Ivory's face heated. Her pulse bounced in her veins. But she couldn't look away. He smiled again, and then the pastor said something, drawing his attention to the pulpit.

Ivory looked up there too, but she knew she wouldn't hear a word. No, she was going to spend the next hour praying that God would let Tripp know that it was okay to marry her.

*I won't hurt him, she told the Lord. I'll pay him back. It'll just be a few months. I won't hurt him....*

---

Tripp didn't call after church, which put Ivory on edge. Without her son, she didn't have much to occupy her time. She made a new necklace and posted it on her online shop. She searched for jobs in Three Rivers, and found a new listing for a clerk at Verona's, the oldest dry cleaner in the county.

She jotted down the number and decided to take a chance and call, even though it was the Sabbath.

An older gentleman said, "Hello?" in a shaky voice.

"Hello," Ivory said in a bright voice. She wondered if she'd somehow swallowed light bulb filaments for how much she'd spoken so brightly today. "I just saw your listing for a clerk at your dry cleaner. I'm interested to know more about the job."

"We need someone over the age of twenty-five," he said.

"Oh, I meet that requirement, sir," she said with a laugh.

"And someone who can work the day shift," he said. "Even when school starts again."

"Double-check," she said. "This is Ivory Osburn. I'm looking for something I can do while my son is at school to bring in some extra money. I'm willing to learn whatever I need to. I have a degree in business management, and I run my own online jewelry-making company."

A long pause came through the line, and then the man said, "Can you come in tomorrow morning for an interview?"

"Absolutely," she said, hoping she wouldn't have to

detail how she'd used her business management degree. Because she never had. She'd only finished the degree so her father wouldn't make her pay back all the tuition, and she'd promptly enrolled in art and jewelry-making classes upon her college graduation.

She'd been making jewelry full-time for a decade now, and things had only started going downhill in the past year or so. Maybe only nine months.

"Eight o'clock?" the man asked. "You can ask for me, Harmon, or my wife, Verona."

"Eight is great," she said. "At the shop?"

"Yes, we'll be here."

"See you then." Ivory hung up and pressed the phone to her heartbeat and her eyes closed. "Please, Lord, let me get this job," she prayed. It wasn't graveyards, and she could work while Oliver was at school.

And penny by penny, she'd pay back Tripp Walker. That was, if the cowboy billionaire ever called her and let her know what and how he felt about everything she'd proposed.

---

THE NEXT MORNING, Ivory made sure every piece of her appearance was in the perfect place. Her jewelry was all homemade and original. Wearing it made her feel powerful and feminine at the same time.

She'd put on her nicest black skirt, with a pale blue blouse, and heels. Heels. She literally never wore heels. Heck, most of the time, she barely upgraded to jeans and closed-toed shoes. After all, she could wear yoga pants to drive Oliver to school and drop him off. No one had to know.

She'd slept little as she toyed with the idea of texting Tripp. But she didn't want to rush him, and she felt foolish enough as it was. The man had taken three beatings from her, and he'd come back for more. She wasn't sure what that said about her—or him.

But she couldn't let go of the hope that seemed to keep zipping through her at the most inopportune times. Like now, when she should be eating something to quell the nerves in her stomach.

In the end, she skipped breakfast so she wouldn't be late to her interview. Her phone rang the moment she pulled up to the dry cleaning building. Tripp's name sat on the screen, and she had ten minutes before she had to be inside, ready to dazzle Harmon and Verona.

"Hey," she said. "Before you say anything, I'm just letting you know that I'm ten minutes away from a job interview."

"Oh, hey," he said. "Okay. What job?"

"Something new came up yesterday. Day shift at the dry cleaner." She hated that she was thirty-seven years old and desperate for a job at a dry cleaner. She wasn't sure what her life had become, and another wave of negative emotions hit her right in the throat. She couldn't seem to speak at all, and she hoped this would pass so she could complete the interview.

"I was just calling to see if you had time for lunch," he said.

She nodded, tears pressing behind her eyes.

"Ivory?"

"Yes," she said, her voice choked. Surely he'd know she was crying, not that it mattered. The man had seen her in complete turmoil at the post office.

"Are you okay?" he asked.

Her first instinct was to snap at him. Didn't he know he held her entire future in his hands? If he said he didn't feel good about marrying her, she'd lose Oliver. She'd lose her house. Her business.

Everything.

She'd lose *everything* she'd been clinging to so desperately these last few months.

*How did I get here?* she asked herself. Or maybe God. She wasn't sure. *Is this my life now?*

"I'm going to be late," she said, unbuckling her seat belt and getting out of her sedan. For some reason, she couldn't stand being constrained inside the car.

"Okay, I'll pick you up around noon?"

"That's fine," she said, watching a woman walk into the dry cleaner. They were open already, and she wondered how early she'd have to come in. She wasn't what anyone would call a morning person, but she could do it.

*You will do it*, she told herself.

"Great, see you then." Tripp ended the call, and Ivory absently slid her phone in her purse. Then she put her plastic, professional smile on her face, and followed the other woman into the dry cleaner.

# 7

Tripp pulled up to Ivory's house a few minutes late, his hands slick against the steering wheel. He wasn't sure why he was so nervous. He'd kissed this woman on Saturday, and as far as their tumultuous relationship had been, that was amazing progress.

"It's fine," he coached himself. He'd had to say the same thing ten times just to get himself out of the house. Into the truck. Driving down the road.

And now he was here.

He glanced at the front door, thinking maybe he should just back out of the driveway, text Ivory that he wasn't feeling well—because he wasn't—and put off this conversation until another day.

Or never.

After all, she'd been extremely good at doing that. Pushing him away. Avoiding difficult conversations.

"It's okay," he told himself. The conversation wasn't even going to be hard. But he wanted...something. The fantasy romance, maybe, where he swept Ivory off her feet with a proposal, they got married, and then sailed away into the sunset to start their new lives together.

And that so wasn't going to happen.

Before he could get out of the truck, her front door opened, and she came bounding down the steps. She wore a pair of white shorts with a bright blue top—and a big smile.

Tripp's heart rate doubled, and he opened his door.

Ivory laughed as she jogged the last few steps to him. "I got the job at the dry cleaner." She threw herself into his arms, and everything inside of Tripp aligned.

"That's so great," he said, chuckling as he held onto her. "So this lunch is a celebration." That was so much easier for him to think about than an engagement meal.

"Yeah," she said, stepping back. "I start tomorrow morning." She wiped her hands down her shorts and looked at him, the moment between them soft and beautiful. "Where do you want to eat?"

"I was thinking Sevano's," he said, the words tripping in his tight throat.

Her eyes widened. "Wow. Are they even open for lunch?"

"They are today," he said evasively. Maybe he'd made a couple of phone calls to see if they'd open just for him. He'd heard rumors of the posh, upscale restaurant doing that—for the right price.

A warning sounded in the back of his mind, but he ignored it. Ivory didn't typically like a lot of attention lavished on her, but Tripp didn't want everything about this engagement to be fake.

*Probably would be easier if it was, though, he thought.*

"Should we go?" he asked.

"Sure. Let me just grab my purse."

She didn't need it, but Tripp waited for her to walk back into the house and get it. Once she was in the passenger seat, and he was behind the wheel again, Tripp started to relax. "So what will you do at the dry cleaner?" he asked.

"I'll be the front desk clerk," she said. "I have to deal with all of the customers. Learn their filing system. Work with the money."

Tripp had never worked in retail, so he wasn't sure what all of that entailed. "You'll be great at that. You love the details."

She gave a short laugh. "I really do." She seemed so happy today, and Tripp wanted that for her every day.

He drove down Main Street, with its old buildings, big, beautiful park, and rows of shops. He did love this small town in the Texas Panhandle, though he'd been dubious about coming here. "As long as there's great Internet," he'd told Rhett. And his brother had delivered.

He'd been in town for a couple of years now, but Ivory had been here for five. "Have you ever been to Sevano's?" he asked.

"Nope," she said. "It's a little out of my price range."

The sarcastic quality of her voice wasn't lost on Tripp. He didn't say anything, because what was there to say?

He pulled into the restaurant, and there wasn't another car in sight. But they'd be open. He'd asked John to be there at noon, and his friend had agreed.

"They don't look open," Ivory said, peering through the windshield.

Tripp pulled into the front parking spot. "They're open." Why was he so nervous? They'd already talked about getting married.

"Are you okay?" Ivory asked, and Tripp released the death grip he had on the steering wheel.

"Yes," he said at the same time she said, "Are you going to tell me no? Because if you are, you can save your money. I don't need a fancy meal." She folded her arms and looked away. "I don't need to be let down easy."

"It's not that," he said. He reached into the compartment on the door and grabbed the black ring box. "And I do need a fancy meal. So let's go." He got out of the truck before he sprung the ring on her right then. He did not want to propose to her in his truck. How unromantic.

Ivory joined him at the front of the truck, and he laced his fingers through hers. "I really don't think they're—" She cut off as John opened the door and stepped outside, a bright smile on his face.

"Tripp," he said, and Tripp grinned at his friend. He released Ivory's hand to shake John's, and said, "This is Ivory Osburn, my girlfriend."

He honestly had no idea if the label fit, but he very well couldn't say she was just a friend. The bulky box in his pocket testified of that.

"Welcome," John said, gesturing for them to enter the restaurant. Ivory went first, and John touched Tripp's arm. "You owe me big time, cowboy."

"Whatever you need," he said. "Signage, animation, whatever. I mean it." He clapped his hand on John's shoulder. "Thank you. Really. Thanks." He followed Ivory into the restaurant—somewhere he'd actually never been. His brothers were simple, like him, and Jeremiah's cooking was sufficient for them.

"Wow," he said, gazing around at the rich woodwork, the clear glass finishes, the candlelight. John had done everything right, just as he said he would.

"Right this way," John said, leading them past several tables to an intimate booth that practically wrapped around itself.

Ivory cast a doubtful look at Tripp, but she sat down and accepted the menu from John. As soon as he'd walked away, though, she set it down and said, "Tripp, this place isn't open. What's going on?"

Swallowing hard, Tripp removed the ring box from his pocket and snapped it open. Ivory sucked in a breath, which made him pause. But he plowed forward, his heart tapping out staccato beats in his chest.

"Ivory," he said. "I've thought a lot about it. I've prayed about it. And I think the right thing to do is to marry you.

Help you however I can." He cleared his throat, because this was a stupid speech. "Will you marry me?"

She looked from him to the diamond in the box. "Where did you get this?"

"I bought it," he said.

"When?"

"This morning." He nudged it closer to her, and lowered his voice when he said, "I know you wanted this to be as real as possible from the outside. Now you have the engagement story."

His chest caved in a little bit with the words, but her face shone with such light that it was worth it.

She shook her head, her eyes glassy. "Tripp, you're too good for me."

"I am not," he said. "Stop saying that." His words had a little bit too much bite, but he really did want her to stop saying that. He took a deep breath to find his center, a place of calm and peace. "I think we can agree on a seven-week engagement. We'll get married as soon as Oliver gets home." He lifted his eyebrows at her, but she still hadn't looked away from the ring. "Right?"

Ivory did focus on him them, and something hot and crackly moved through the air, striking him right in the back of his throat. And he knew in that moment that this relationship wasn't one-sided. He wasn't the only one with feelings at this table.

This woman liked him.

"Yes," she said. "Yes, I'll marry you."

Relief like Tripp had never known filled him, and he plucked the ring from the box and slid it on the appropriate finger. "Great," he said with a smile, leaning forward to kiss her.

He'd kissed her before, but with the diamond and that lightning still cracking through him, this kiss with his fiancée was different.

Tripp really hoped he and Ivory could make whatever was fake between them into something real. If not in the next seven weeks, then after that. He did not want this relationship to be trivial—and for the first time in a long time, he thought he had a chance of it becoming big, and beautiful, and absolutely real.

———

"Family meeting," Tripp said later that night, the same nerves prancing through him that had been aggravating him in the morning.

Liam already sat on the couch, but Wyatt lingered at the kitchen table, his dinner dishes still in front of him as he texted someone. Jeremiah worked in the kitchen, as usual, and Tripp actually felt guilty for all his brother did around the homestead and the ranch.

But he left the rest of the dishes and came over to the couch. Tripp exchanged a look with Liam, who nodded slightly, as Wyatt joined them. He looked around at everyone and said, "I feel like I'm missing something."

"That's why we have the family meeting," Liam said. "So no one misses anything."

Tripp felt like he'd be missing his head in a minute, and he glanced at Jeremiah and away again quickly. *It's fine*, he told himself, really tired of the self-reassurances.

"I'm going to need help with the horses tomorrow," Jeremiah said. "We need to move them out of the pasture they're in."

"No problem," Tripp said. "I still don't have notes back from Pixelate."

"I have a conference call in the morning," Liam said. "But I can help after that."

"I'm free in the morning," Wyatt said. "I'm headed out to Brynn's in the afternoon. She's got a couple of new horses, and she's asked me to come see if I'd be interested in working for her permanently."

Surprise flowed through Tripp as he looked at Wyatt. "Really? That's great. I mean, if you want to do that." His brother had recently retired from the professional rodeo circuit, and he had tons of experience with the livestock required for the events. And Brynn Greene ran Bowman's Breeds out at Three Rivers Ranch. She and her husband, Ethan, were both former rodeo stars, like Wyatt.

"I do want to do it," Wyatt said with a smile. "I mean, the last six months without anything to do has been nice, but—"

"You do stuff," Jeremiah said. "Tons of stuff around the ranch."

"More than me," Liam said.

"You have a job," Tripp said, realizing the conversation had devolved from where he'd wanted it to go.

"I know," Liam said. "I sometimes feel bad, though. You've made the ranch so awesome."

Tripp echoed his brother's sentiments, but Jeremiah just shook his head. "We all do things around here," he said. "Some are just more visible than others." He folded his arms, and a flash of affection for his brother moved through Tripp.

He cleared his throat and said, "Okay, I have some news. I asked Ivory Osburn to marry me, and she said yes."

No one moved. No one spoke. Tripp enjoyed the quiet, the calm, because he knew it was only a precursor to a complete explosion.

"Wow," Liam said, surprise in the three letters.

Wyatt just blinked and said, "Is she that woman who broke up with you a few months ago?"

And Jeremiah just got up from the couch, glared, and stomped down the hall to his bedroom, the slamming door a very final punctuation mark that expressed exactly how he felt about Tripp's news.

Tripp sighed and sat down on the coffee table. "Well, there was no yelling like when Rhett announced he was getting married."

Liam chuckled, but it wasn't an entirely happy sound. "No, Rhett didn't announce he was *getting* married. He announced he *was* married. Big difference."

"True." Tripp looked back and forth between Liam and Wyatt. "The wedding isn't until mid-July. She wants to have it here at the ranch."

"Wow," Liam said again. "You might want to really talk to Jeremiah about that." He groaned as he got up. "Because the ranch is his baby, and...yeah."

"I just thought he might be more receptive this time."

Liam smiled at Tripp and extended his hand to him to help him stand. "Yeah, no you didn't."

Wyatt burst out laughing, and that got Tripp and Liam going too. Tripp was glad the mood had lightened, but as he glanced down the hall where Jeremiah had gone, he knew he'd definitely need to have a better conversation with his brother. Soon.

# 8

Ivory walked down the street early the next morning, her running shoes laced on her feet. She couldn't sleep because of the anticipation of starting her new job, so she figured she might as well get up and get moving.

She wasn't known for loving exercise, but if she was going to get married in seven weeks, she could definitely lose a few pounds. Several groups of women were out walking already, because early morning in Texas really was the best time for such things.

A pang of sadness hit her. She wished she had a walking group in the morning, especially when she caught sight of Kate's dark ponytail swishing from side to side as she power walked with another woman.

She felt left out of a group she didn't even know she'd wanted to belong to. And in reality, if Oliver were here, she would never leave him to go walking, even at five o'clock in the morning.

"Ivory," Kate said as she and her friend turned to come back down the street where Ivory was. A smile spread across Kate's whole face. "Hey, do you want to join us?"

"There is no way I can walk as fast as you," Ivory said. "I'm not even close to in shape."

"We're winding down," the other woman said, and Ivory blanked on her name. She should know her, but she didn't.

"This is Jennika," Kate said, indicating the tall brunette. She could probably take one step for every two of Ivory's. "Her son goes to the same story time as Jenny."

"That's great," Ivory said, and her words sounded too chipper, even to her own ears. If she was home on Tuesdays and Fridays for the story time hour Kate took her son to, she must be married, probably with a nice, new house on the north side of town.

"I'm Ivory Osburn," she said, trying out the last name of Walker in her mind.

*Ivory Walker.*

The name had a nice ring to it.

The three of them continued down the street, and Ivory didn't quite know what to say to keep the conversation going.

"How many kids do you have?" she asked Jennika, reaching up to brush her hair out of her face.

Kate sucked in a breath. "Ivory Osburn." She grabbed Ivory's hand and yanked it toward her.

Her left hand.

"What in the world is this?" She practically shouted the question, and a couple across the street looked their way.

Ivory smiled at the diamond ring, which boasted a large, round diamond in the middle of the setting, with concentric circles of gems surrounding it. Around and around they went, and Ivory had stared at the ring last night for a long, long time.

She couldn't believe it was hers, number one.

"Oh, um, I got engaged yesterday?" Why she'd phrased it as a question, she didn't know.

Kate lifted her eyes to Ivory's. "To who?"

"Tripp Walker."

"Dear Lord in Heaven," Kate said, pressing her palm to her heartbeat, her eyes wide and glittering. "You got a Walker brother."

"They're elusive," Jennika agreed. "I can't help looking at them, and I'm married."

"Right?" Kate said with a giggle. She looked back down at the ring. "This is *incredible*. You have to let me do the flowers." She met Ivory's eyes with hope in hers now.

"Oh, no, I couldn't," Ivory said, sliding her hand out of her friend's. "I can't afford much. I just want a bouquet."

"Aren't those Walkers billionaires?" Jennika asked. "I bet he'd buy you every flower in the state if you wanted him to."

Yes, Tripp probably would. But Ivory wasn't going to ask

him for more than she already had. She couldn't tell either of them the true reason behind the engagement. So she just smiled and shook her head. "I'm sure he could, but I don't want a big, fancy wedding. Been there. Done that. Ended badly." She shrugged like her divorce and single parenthood didn't matter that much. In reality, her insides felt shredded from the past three years, and that raggedness inside her had contributed greatly to her ability to push Tripp away at the drop of a hat.

A cowboy hat.

"I can do the bouquet," Kate said. "Please?"

"Just the bouquet," Ivory said. "I can't afford more than...fifty dollars." And even then, she shouldn't use it for perishable flowers she'd only hold for twenty minutes. If that. Guilt moved through her. That fifty dollars could go right into Tripp's pocket, getting her closer to being out of his debt.

"I don't even need to be paid," Kate said, picking up speed again as they reached the corner and turned back the way they'd come. "Tell me what kind of flowers you want. When are you getting married?"

"Right after Oliver comes home from his father's," she said. "About seven weeks. Mid-July." She and Tripp hadn't even really set a date yet. They hadn't set up another time to see one another, and Ivory's memories of when she and Daniel had been engaged came forward in her mind.

At that point in their relationship, they didn't *need* to set up a time to see each other. It was implied that they'd spend their afternoons and evenings together after work. Maybe they'd arrange a spot to meet for dinner, or he'd text and say he was coming over to her place. But it wasn't like he *asked*.

And she felt like Tripp would probably still ask.

"You definitely need bluebonnets," Kate said. "And roses. The red and purple are *so* pretty together."

Ivory smiled at her friend, her calves burning and her breathing coming so quickly that she couldn't respond.

Foolishness filled her. How could she ask her friend to spend her time and money on a bouquet for a fake wedding?

*She offered,* Ivory thought, but the guilt still twined through her.

"I can put in some white roses too," Kate said. "Red, white, and blue." She looked absolutely delighted at the opportunity, and Ivory didn't have the heart—or the guts—to tell her the truth.

"How did you get engaged?" Kate asked next, her excitement over this wedding infectious. Ivory was excited, of course, but she hadn't really let herself get too deep into the thought process of it. "Tell me everything. Don't leave a single thing out."

"Oh, boy," Jennika said with a smile. "I forgot how much you love weddings."

"I *love* them," Kate said with a laugh. "Now come on, Ivory. I want to know exactly how this Tripp Walker got you to say yes."

Ivory grinned at her and Jennika, but she couldn't talk. She reached the end of the sidewalk and bent over, her hands braced against her knees.

"First," she said, panting. "I need to get in shape for the wedding. Then maybe I can tell you." She sucked at the air, feeling a little light-headed.

"What does that mean—how he got her to say yes?" Jennika asked.

"Oh, Ivory doesn't date," Kate said so matter-of-factly. "She actually told me once that she'd never get married again."

Ivory straightened and met her friend's eye. She had said that, because that was exactly how she felt.

Kate's whole soul seemed lit up from the inside. "Something *huge* must've happened." She nudged Ivory with her hip, her smile playful but her eyes a bit predatory. "So start talking, girl. What did he do that got you to agree to tie the knot?"

Ivory swallowed the part about Tripp catching up with her mortgage and providing the means she needed to fight Daniel's custody challenge. "He's a great guy," she said. Not a lie. In fact, absolutely, one-hundred percent true. "And I don't know, I just fell for him."

"She's caught her breath," Jennika said. "So how did he propose?"

"He took me to Sevano's yesterday," Ivory said, a sigh already slipping between her lips. "For lunch."

"Sevano's isn't open for lunch," Kate said, her eyebrows drawing down.

"I know," Ivory said. "He called the chef, who he's apparently friends with, and they opened *just for us.*"

"Wow," Jennika said at the same time Kate sighed.

"How romantic," her friend said, linking her arm through Ivory's. "I'm so happy for you."

And the funny thing was, some of that joy seeped into Ivory. She hadn't felt anything but desperate and tired for so long now.

*Thank you, she prayed, giggling with her two new walking friends. Thank you so much, Lord. I promise I won't hurt him.*

———

IVORY HAD four dry cleaning shifts under her belt now, and she almost had the computer system memorized. Almost. She worked from eight to five each day, and she went home at night, utterly exhausted. Except for her lunch hour, she spent all of her time on her feet, running here and there to fetch garments, take payments, hang up new items that needed to be cleaned, wiping the countertops after sticky toddler fingers had been on them, and dozens of other tasks.

With each day that passed, her happiness grew. She hadn't even realized how stifled she'd become, sitting in front of her laptop, trying to find a new way to advertise her jewelry.

She hadn't even been in her jewelry studio since last week, when she'd finished her pieces and gone to the post office, only to be served with custody papers on her way out the door.

She'd been making lists and checking them twice, just the way Santa Claus did. Most weddings had plenty of moving parts, but Ivory had spoken true when she'd said she didn't want a big wedding.

She couldn't afford one, that was for sure.

So she'd put the venue on her list, and Tripp had said he'd talk to his brother about having their nuptials at the ranch. That was free.

She was getting the bouquet from Kate. She'd need a cake, but Tripp had said one of the Foster sisters could do it. Their ranch butted up against Seven Sons, and Tripp said the two families were close.

Since Ivory had never actually been out to the ranch, she wouldn't know.

He'd also said he'd cater for their dinner, and she'd argued with him. In the end, though, they did need food, even for a small wedding, and she'd simply added it to her private list of things she'd pay him back for.

She wasn't doing anything huge for décor. Just tables and chairs for the ceremony and dinner.

*Flowers.*

*Cake.*

*Venue.*

*Dinner.*

*Décor.*

*Music.*

She couldn't afford a band, and she'd told Tripp they'd be dancing to recorded music, on a speaker system. He'd said he and Liam would figure out all the technical logistics of that. Since he was a computer engineer, Ivory felt confident leaving that task in his capable hands.

Everything was coming together, and it had only been four days. The only thing she needed was a wedding dress. She had some serious research skills when it came to the Internet, but she hadn't been able to find a dress she could afford that didn't look like it was made in 1922.

The back door slammed, jolting her out of her mind. There were a few lulls at the dry cleaner, but Harmon wanted her to be busy all the time. So she reached down below the counter where she checked people out and picked up the duster.

"Afternoon," the older man said as he joined her up front. "Can you see if you can find this for Verona?" He handed her a ticket, and Ivory smiled at him.

"Sure thing." She traded him by passing over the duster, and then she went into the depths of the building. Verona's didn't have all the fancy equipment the bigger places did in bigger cities, and Ivory had to physically walk through the racks of clothes to find the garments she needed.

And this ticket was old, and as she went further and further into the racks, she started to feel a little claustrophobic. She finally located the blouse in question and had just pulled it down from the rack when her eyes caught on the white satin of a wedding dress.

"Oh," she whispered, her pulse going from zero to sixty in a single breath. She pushed the clothes around the dress out of the way and looked at it. Yes, it was an older style, but not last-century old.

She took it down from the rack too and examined the slip of paper stapled to the plastic sheeting. No name. Just a number.

Feeling brave and like perhaps God had put this wedding dress here for her to find, she took it with her up to the front counter, where Harmon waited. The duster lay on the counter next to the cash register, and the old man was asleep with his arms folded, sitting upright on the barstool.

"Harmon," she said, and the gentleman snorted as he woke. "Whose dress is this?"

"I have no idea," he said in a crotchety voice. "Did you find the blouse?"

"Right here," she said, passing it to him.

He took it with a "Thank you, Ivory," and started for the back exit. Ivory wanted to call him back and ask him more questions about the wedding dress, but she didn't.

She'd look it up herself first.

After typing in the number on the ticket attached to the dress, she got the name of the woman who'd dropped the dress off-thirteen months ago. With that same recklessness flowing through her, she dialed Millie Montgomery.

"Hello?" she said when someone answered the line.

"Yes?" a woman said.

"Hello," she said, putting in her professional voice box. "My name is Ivory Osburn, and I work for Verona's dry cleaning in Three Rivers, Texas." She paused, hoping for some sort of recognition, but none came.

"Anyway," she said, some of her earlier bravery fading away under the silence. "We have a wedding dress here that's ready for pick up." Way past ready, but Ivory wasn't going to say that. In fact, she wanted this woman to say she didn't want the dress and Ivory could keep it.

"Oh, yes," the woman said. "That was my daughter's."

"Okay," Ivory said, expecting more. No further explanation was provided. "Is she going to come pick it up?"

"I don't see how," the woman said. "She lives in Key West now."

"Can you come pick it up?"

"Heavens, no," Millie said. "She didn't need it to actually get married in, and I don't want it. If she hasn't picked it up by now, I doubt she wants it."

"Oh, okay," Ivory said. "So what should we do with it?"

"I don't really care," Millie said. "Is that all?"

"Yes," Ivory said, hanging up more confused than she'd been going into the phone call. But her mind worked quickly, and she pulled out her phone to call Harmon.

"Hello, Ivory," he said.

"Hey, Mister Wheelwright. So I called on that wedding dress, and the woman says they don't want it. What should I do with it?"

"Put it back on the shelf, I suppose," he said.

Ivory bit her lip. "I was actually wondering if I could… borrow it."

"Borrow it?"

"Yeah, I'd pay to have it cleaned afterward. I'm kind of getting married in a few weeks, and I need a dress."

A pregnant beat of silence came through the line. Then Harmon asked, "You called the owner?"

"Yes, sir."

"And they're not going to come pick it up?"

"She said it was her daughter's dress, and she lived in Key West now."

Another long silence, as if Harmon was wrestling with his thoughts to get them to line up the way he wanted. "Then it's yours," he said. "You can have it."

"Have it?" Ivory asked, her surprise matching her excitement.

"That's right," he said. "We don't need to store something no one is ever going to come pick up."

A squeal built in the back of Ivory's throat, but the chime on the front door sang, and she turned toward the customer, not truly seeing him. "Someone just came in, Mister Wheelwright. I have to go. Thank you *so* much."

"Ivory, wait," he said. "Maybe you should go through all the clothes that are more than a couple of months old and contact the owners."

"Sure thing, Mister Wheelwright," she said, feeling happier than she had in a long time. She hung up with a massive smile on her face. She'd just gotten herself a free wedding dress. "Hello," she said, blinking out of her euphoria. "How can I help—Daniel?"

Her ex-husband stood at the counter, his eyes very, very angry as they bored into hers. "You're engaged?" he clipped out between his perfect teeth she knew he paid to whiten. He was just that vain.

"Yes," she said, her pulse bouncing around in her chest for an entirely different reason now.

He shook his head, a cruel laugh coming from his mouth. "This isn't going to work, Ivory."

"Where's Oliver?" she asked, looking past him.

"At a friend's," he said.

Oliver had not mentioned any friends when he went to his father's, but Ivory didn't argue with Daniel. She knew that was a fruitless activity she didn't want to deal with.

He leaned into the counter, a deep growl in his throat. "When's the big day?"

"July fourteenth," she said, because she and Tripp had discussed things that far ahead since her walk a few days ago. "And I'm going to fight you on your custody challenge." She lifted her chin. "I have a job, and I *can* provide Oliver with everything he needs."

Daniel just shook his head, his exasperation coming off him in waves. "You're four months behind on your mortgage."

"That's not true," she said. "Those bills were caught up this morning."

Daniel blinked, clearly not expecting that. "Did your sugar daddy pay out?"

"No," she said, because technically, Tripp was only three years older than her. He was wealthier and more successful, but she wasn't his sugar baby, because they were close to the same age. "My fiancé helped me get back on my feet."

"This isn't going to work," Daniel said again. "I'm a lawyer, Ivory. I can smell a fake marriage from a hundred yards away."

She didn't say anything, because she'd rather not lie to anyone. And she definitely didn't want to fight with her ex where she worked.

"That's it?" he challenged.

"I'll see you in court," she said quietly. "And we'll let the judge decide." Every cell in her body trembled, and she prayed that Daniel would just leave her alone. Someone on high still liked Ivory, because Daniel scoffed, turned, and strode out of the dry cleaner as quickly as he'd come in.

Ivory sagged against the counter, beyond glad he was gone. She glanced at the wedding dress, some of her earlier excitement returning. Daniel had never wanted Oliver, and she wasn't sure why he was fighting for him now.

The chime sounded again, and Ivory warily looked up. Only this time, the cowboy walking toward her was a welcome sight. "Tripp," she said, surprised.

"I brought lunch," he said, holding up two brown paper bags from Triple Roast Beef Deli.

"Bless you," she said, rounding the counter and slipping herself easily into his embrace. She tipped up onto her toes and kissed him, because she had the very real feeling that Daniel was watching.

He wanted a show?

He'd get one.

# 9

Tripp wasn't sure why Ivory had kissed him, but he wasn't complaining. He'd told her he'd bring her lunch today, and he hadn't even gone anywhere nice. He cradled her face in both of his hands, kissing her back as enthusiastically as she'd started this little game.

"Wow," he said when she finally pulled away. "You must be starving."

She trilled out a little giggle that didn't sound entirely like it belonged to her. "You'll never guess what I found just now." Her blue eyes lit up, and Tripp chuckled.

"No, I don't suppose I will." He bent down and picked up his cowboy hat. He put it back on and busied himself with pulling out the sandwiches he'd bought for lunch. When Ivory didn't say anything, he looked up.

She stood behind the counter, a wedding dress in a bag

held up against her body. Tripp blinked. "Isn't it bad luck to see the bride in her dress before the wedding?"

Ivory just laughed. "You're not my real groom," she said, clearly not understanding the punch those words carried.

Tripp ducked his head again, this time taking the potato chips out of the bag. "Right," he said, mostly to himself. Because Ivory was beaming as she admired the dress.

"I found it right here," she said. "In the back. The woman who dropped it off isn't going to come get it, and Harmon said I could have it."

"Great," he said, but he didn't really mean it. "I told you I'd buy you a dress."

"And then I'd just have to pay you back for it," she said, her smile losing some of its shine. "This way, I can bedazzle it with some of my beads or something, and we're good to go."

"Good to go," Tripp repeated, forcing himself to put a smile on his face. He knew this wedding was fake. He knew Ivory didn't have any money. She'd given him the username and password for her mortgage company, and he'd logged on that morning to get caught up on her mortgage. It had literally taken him five minutes, and he wouldn't miss the money.

Heck, he could buy her the most expensive wedding dress in the world and not miss the money.

He smothered his sigh and looked around for somewhere to sit. "Is there another stool back there?" he asked.

"Let me get the chair from the office," she said, hanging

the wedding dress on the hook where she usually put customer's garments. She scampered away from him, and Tripp let her go. She returned, and with his chair behind the wall so customers wouldn't see him, they sat down to eat.

"How's everything else coming?" he asked.

"Great," she said. "With the dress, I have everything we need for a wedding."

"What about pictures?" he asked.

"Pictures?"

"Yeah." Tripp looked at her. "Callie Foster asked me if we were going to send announcements. Honestly, I wasn't sure what she was talking about, and she knew it." Tripp shook his head, the humiliation of that conversation filling him again now. "She said most couples get engagement pictures, have someone at the wedding taking professional pictures, all of that."

"Wedding photographers are very expensive," she said. "We don't need to do that."

"What are you doing?" he asked, wondering if any of his wants would make it into the wedding. Because he'd love a professional picture of him and Ivory. Foolish, he knew. Pathetic, even. But he couldn't help wanting the pictures all the same.

"Well, my friend Kate is making my bouquet," she said. "We're having the wedding at your ranch, and you said you'd take care of all the tables, chairs, décor, and food for that."

"Right," he said, because he didn't want to tell her he'd

done none of those things. He hadn't even talked to Jeremiah again since Monday night. His brother got up early and he ignored Tripp in the evenings.

"And you said one of the Foster sisters would make my cake."

"Callie," he said. "I did talk to her about that. She said she'd love to." He didn't mention that the Fosters were about as bad off as Ivory was, and that he'd be paying for whatever Callie needed to make the wedding cake.

"Your brother is dealing with the sound system. I found a dress." She ticked off her last finger. "That's everything."

Tripp nodded and stuffed another bite of sandwich in his mouth, buying himself some time to figure out how to insist on pictures. He hadn't discovered a way to start a hard conversation with his brother, and Ivory was twice as hard to argue with.

Finally, he just looked up and said, "I'd really like to have someone take our pictures. Callie gave me the name of someone who's great, and you don't have to pay me back."

"Tripp—"

"The groom pays for some things, doesn't he?" he challenged.

Ivory searched his face, and Tripp didn't know what to hold back from her so she couldn't find it. He didn't want to hide anything from her, but the ground they were on felt fragile.

"You've already done so much," she said.

"Yeah, and yet I have time to waste, eating lunch with

you." He grinned at her, the edits he'd gotten in his inbox that morning suddenly at the forefront of his mind.

Ivory scoffed, but she didn't laugh. The moment didn't lighten. The chime on the door rang, and she got up to attend to her job. Tripp stayed in the chair, out of the way, tapping and swiping on his phone.

Whitney Wilde had a beautiful website, full of gorgeous brides. Maybe if Ivory saw these pictures....

She finished up with the customer, and Tripp stood up. "I did get edits on my project this morning, so I have to go." He swept a kiss across her cheek. "But just look at these for a minute, would you?"

He handed her his phone, and she sucked in a breath. Her eyes darted to his and back to the device as she started to scroll. Several seconds later, she said, "I can't afford her."

"*We* can, though." Tripp gently took his phone from her. "I'd like the photos, Ivory. Think about it." He held his back straight as he walked toward the exit. "Text me later, okay?"

"Okay," she said, her voice quiet and far away. Tripp left the dry cleaner and drove back to the ranch, one thing on his mind—talking to Jeremiah.

Yes, he had work to do on the three screens in his office. But the animation could wait.

He changed into a long-sleeved shirt, because work on the ranch often caused injuries without some sort of protection, and headed outside. "Where are you going?" Liam called after him. "Your computer's been blowing up for an hour."

"Mute it," he called back. "I have to talk to Jeremiah."

"Whoa." Heavy scraping followed Liam's words, and his brother came jogging down the hall and into the kitchen. "You're going to talk to Jeremiah now?"

"Yes," Tripp said, watching his brother. "Why? Did something happen?"

"Oh, something happened," Liam said.

"What?"

"Simone asked him to be part of the Fall Festival."

Tripp wasn't following. "Okay. We went to that last year. Simone had an awesome booth with all that furniture she restored."

"Yeah, and there's a bachelor auction." Liam cocked his eyebrows.

"Oh." Tripp sighed and removed his cowboy hat. He felt drenched with sweat, and he'd been in the air conditioning this whole time. "Well—"

"I told Simone I'd do it," Liam said. "And Jeremiah went muttering outside. He was not happy."

"He's got to get over Laura Ann," Tripp said.

"He *is* over Laura Ann. He just doesn't want a repeat of Laura Ann, and you setting up an altar where he has to see it every day? Not going to help."

Tripp turned and looked out the wall of windows. "What am I supposed to do?"

"Find somewhere else to marry her," he said. "There's got to be a billion places."

"Maybe you could ask Callie if we can use the Shining Star."

"I'm not talking to Callie at the moment," Liam said stiffly. "Ask her yourself." He turned and started back down the hallway.

Tripp twisted to watch his brother go. "Is this how we are now?" he called. "We don't have crucial conversations?"

"I guess," Liam said, disappearing. His footsteps continued until he made it to his desk, and then his chair squealed as he sat down.

Tripp sighed. Maybe having the wedding here would be too triggering for Jeremiah, who'd been standing at the altar for his own wedding when he'd learned his bride-to-be wouldn't be coming. Tripp couldn't go back in time and fix that for his brother, though he wanted to. Just like he wanted Callie and Liam to open their dang eyes and see how perfect they were for each other.

"You're already dressed," he muttered to himself, and he pulled open the back door. Penny panted in the shade, and he said, "Hey, girl. Where's Jeremiah, huh?"

The cattle dog just closed her eyes and kept sucking at the hot air. "All right," he said. "I'll find him myself."

Down the steps and down the stone path through the grass, and Tripp stepped onto the ranch. He'd been helping his brother with the horses, the pastures, the clean-up of troughs. Whatever Jeremiah needed. With Wyatt splitting his time between Seven Sons and Shining Star *and*

Liz Isaacson

Bowman's Breeds, Tripp had been happy to pick up some of the slack.

He found Dicky with the goats, holding a nursing bottle for one of the new babies. "Hey, Dicky," he said. "You seen Jeremiah?"

"He's with Orion in the south corn field," he said. "Something about pests."

"Great," Tripp said, though it was anything but. If there were pests in their corn, Jeremiah wouldn't be in a good mood. He went that way, though, the sun beating down on him. Sure enough, he saw Orion and Jeremiah standing on the edge of the field, pulling down ears of corn every few seconds.

"Hey," he said as he approached. Jeremiah looked over his shoulder and went right back to work. "Need some help?"

"Nope," he said. He peeled down the silks on another ear of corn. "This one's fine. Maybe it's isolated."

"We can still call the dusters," Orion said.

"Yeah, all right," Jeremiah said with a sigh. "But I want a new company. Not the same one. They obviously don't know what they're doing, and we don't need to double-spray our crops."

"It'll be hard to get on someone's permanent schedule. They're full-up by now."

"I know someone," Tripp said, and that got both cowboys to look at him. "Yeah," he said slowly. "Her name is

Marcy Payne. She just took over the crop dusting business for her father."

"A woman flies the plane?" Jeremiah asked.

"Yeah, that's what Ivory said." Tripp looked at Orion. "Payne's Pest-free, or something?"

"I know 'em," he said. "I'll give Martin a call." He nodded at Jeremiah, took the ear of corn he was holding, and walked away.

Jeremiah nodded to Tripp and tried to follow Orion. "Hey," Tripp said, putting his hand lightly on Jeremiah's arm. "Can I talk to you for a second?"

His brother stood statue-still for a moment, and then he only moved his eyes toward Tripp. "All right."

Tripp braced himself, hoping he didn't get slugged after he spoke. "Ivory would like me to ask you if we can have the wedding here."

Jeremiah's eyes widened. "Here?"

"At the ranch." Tripp thought it was a good idea, especially considering her financial situation. "And I'd like to ask you to cook for the wedding. There's no one who does smoked meat better than you, Jeremiah. It won't be a big affair."

His brother's jaw worked against itself, and he looked away. "Have her ask me herself," he finally said. "And yes, I'll cook for the wedding." He walked away then, and Tripp let him go, because his agreement to cater the wedding was as good as an acceptance of Tripp's engagement. Probably better.

Sighing, he pulled out his phone and texted Ivory. *Hey, I need you to text or call my brother and ask him to host the wedding at the ranch.*

Just as quickly as his thumbs had been moving to type out the message, he held one down to delete it. He couldn't send her that in a text.

Best thing to do?

Get her out here to meet his brothers. After all, in six short weeks, they'd be her family too.

"Only on paper," he told himself, facing the corn again.

He lifted his phone to call her and invite her to the ranch for Sunday lunch after church. He'd have to talk to Jeremiah about that too, but now that the ice had been broken, the conversation would be easier.

Before he could dial out, a call came in. From Rhett.

"Hey," Tripp said after swiping open the call.

"You're engaged to Ivory Osburn?" he demanded. "Oh, and you're on speaker with Evelyn."

"Hey, Tripp," Rhett's wife said. "Is this a real engagement?"

Tripp sighed, because he didn't want to admit that the engagement and subsequent wedding would be fake. Not real. Trivial.

So he said, "Yes, I'm engaged to Ivory Osburn."

"How did *that* happen?" Rhett asked. "Last I knew, you weren't even talking to her."

Tripp really didn't want to tell the story, because he'd have to leave so much of it out. So he blurted, "Fine, it's a fake engagement so her ex-husband can't get custody of her son."

Only silence followed, and Tripp hated that more than the thought of lying to his oldest brother. "Say something."

"We all do what we think is right," Rhett said quietly. "Right, honeybee?"

"That's right," Evelyn said. "We'll be home in a couple of weeks, Tripp. When's the wedding?"

"July fourteenth," he said, missing his brother keenly in that moment. "You won't miss it."

"We'd come home from the honeymoon if we had to," Rhett said. "Who else knows?"

"No one," Tripp said.

"Even Liam?"

"I told him the wedding would probably be like yours the first time." Tripp shrugged, though Rhett wasn't there to see. "I did take her to a fancy meal and ask her properly, though. We aren't going to City Hall. Everyone thinks it's real."

"How's Jeremiah handling it?"

"He's the one who told you, right?"

"He may have texted," Rhett said. "Said you want to get married at the ranch?"

The more Tripp thought about it, the more he didn't want to do that. He didn't need to be reminded of how trivial this wedding would be every time he went to saddle a horse. "I don't know," he said. "There are a lot of moving parts."

And he'd never spoken truer. He was glad for Evelyn and Rhett's support, and he finished his conversation with them before turning to face the homestead again. He could see the front porch and the back deck, and he suddenly didn't want to be behind walls.

He headed for the stables, though he had messages to read and scenes to fix for his bosses at Pixelate. But they could wait another hour or two. Tripp needed to clear his head, and the best way to do that was on horseback.

# 10

L iam Walker sat at his computer station, the four screens in front of him sending light right into his brain.

He could not believe he'd asked Callie out, and she'd told him no.

No.

*I'm sorry, Liam.*

Sorry. Right.

He scoffed though he really should be doing something to finish the CGI his boss had sent over yesterday. If only he could get the gorgeous woman at the ranch next-door off his mind.

And now Tripp wanted him to talk to her about using the Shining Star for his wedding. Liam felt knotted from top to bottom, and he practically ripped the headphones off his head and tossed them on his keyboards.

He couldn't work right now, and it wasn't like his boss had given him a deadline. If he had, Liam would meet it.

Instead, he went out to the stables, surprised to find Tripp there, saddling Lightfoot. "I thought you were going to talk to Jeremiah."

"I did."

Liam should've known. Conversations with Jeremiah didn't last long, especially if they were about something his brother didn't want to talk about.

"Not going to use the ranch, then."

"No, probably not." Tripp finished with the reins. "You're riding?"

"Yeah. Wait for me to saddle Pretzel?"

"Yeah, because I want to hear why you're not talking to Callie."

"It's not that interesting," Liam said, though the silence between him and Callie had been torturing him for a week now. He worked quickly to get his horse ready to go too, and then he swung up into the saddle.

"Where to?" Tripp asked.

Liam looked west and then east. "Not west."

"Oh, so it's bad."

Liam didn't want to confirm what his twin had said. He and Tripp had always had a special twin-thing, and he'd be able to feel what Liam felt anyway.

"You said you asked her out," Tripp finally prompted.

Liam reached up and adjusted his cowboy hat. "I did. She said no. Didn't want her feelings to get all confused."

"What does that mean?"

"How should I know?" Liam sighed. "I mean, I apologized for offering to buy the ranch. We were fine."

"You just need a new plan."

"Nope," Liam said. "I'm not asking her out again. She knows how I feel."

"Does she? How did you ask her?"

Liam really didn't want to relive this. He sighed in an exaggerated way so Tripp would know he was asking a lot. His twin just waited, his horse plodding along with a steady clip-clop of horse's hooves.

"I said something like, maybe we could go to a movie together," Liam said. "Get away from the ranches."

"And she said no."

"Yes."

"Dude, that doesn't sound like you told her you like her." Tripp looked at him openly, and Liam stared right back.

"Do you do that? Just blurt it all out?"

"Sometimes," Tripp said. "And it sounds like you just offered her an afternoon off the ranch, like you know, what a friend would do."

"We are friends."

"Yeah," Tripp said. "And she wants to keep it that way, and you don't."

Liam winced, though his brother was right. "So I wasn't clear enough."

"I wasn't there," Tripp said. "But it doesn't sound like it." He took a deep breath. "So you just need a new plan."

Yeah—step one: Get Callie to talk to him again. Even as Liam put that on his to-do list, he knew he was the one who'd initiated the silence between them. Whenever Callie came over to the ranch, he disappeared. He made sure his headphones were on and the music loud, or he physically went down the hall to his bedroom. He knew she wouldn't follow him down there.

"I may have done something else stupid," Liam said, wishing some of his intelligence with computers had been tact or street smarts.

"Oh, boy," Tripp said. "As dumb as asking Jeremiah to host a wedding here at the ranch?"

Liam burst out laughing, glad when his brother joined in. "I think you win that one, bro." Still chuckling, he added, "But I did ask her if she'd go out with Jeremiah if he asked."

Tripp sucked in a breath, his laughter getting cut off. "Oh, boy," he said again, an awed quality to his voice. "No wonder she's not talking to you."

Liam pressed his teeth together. "You have to admit, they spend a lot of time together for two grown adults who don't have any romantic feelings for each other. It's a little... weird." Misery filled him. "I may have told her that too."

"You told her her friendship with Jeremiah was weird? Holy heaven, Liam."

"It *is*," Liam insisted. "I don't get it." Out of everyone, he'd expected Tripp to agree with him.

"Well, maybe it is," Tripp said. "I don't know. But I do know they're just friends."

"How do you really, though?" Liam asked. "They're out on the ranch half the time they see each other. He could be kissing her behind the barn, and we'd never know." The very thought had Liam's fingers tightening around the reins, and he really didn't like this jealousy surging through him.

Tripp laughed again, the sound so carefree. "Trust me, they're not doing that."

"Yeah, yeah," Liam said. "*Miah*'s a mess. He needs a friend. Blah blah blah. That's what she said." He hated that nickname of hers, as literally no one else on the planet called Jeremiah Miah—except Callie.

"You've got to get over this if you have any chance of being with her," Tripp said. "I mean that in the nicest way possible."

"I have no chance with her anyway," Liam said.

"You never know," Tripp said. "Ivory's broken up with me three times now." He shrugged. "We're not home-free yet, but I have a good feeling about us." He looked at Liam. "And a good feeling about you and Callie. You'll find a way."

Liam snorted, because he didn't want to "find a way." That sounded almost creepy, like he was some sort of stalker who couldn't take no for an answer.

But maybe he could send a quick text and open the channels of communication again.

That wouldn't kill him—he didn't think so, at least.

Before he could change his mind, he hurried to type out the two words and send them to Callie.

*I'm sorry.*

He wanted to add *sweetheart* or an invitation for her to meet him at the fence where they talked sometimes. He didn't. If he was going to send her a text, that was all it was going to say.

*In the end, he didn't send the text. Help me, Lord,* he prayed as he and Tripp turned their horses around. *Help me move past these jealous feelings. Help me find the right words to say. Help me to forgive her and..whatever else I need to do to have a chance to be with her.*

Now that Tripp had said he had a good feeling about Liam and Callie, Liam wondered if his brother was right. Maybe he shouldn't give up yet.

He brushed down Pretzel and put the horse back in the pasture. He went back to his office and worked for the rest of the day. He went through the next several days with Callie lingering in the back of his mind.

He ate Jeremiah's cooking, and laughed with Wyatt when he told stories about breaking wild horses out at Bowman's Breeds. He caught sight of Callie out on her ranch, working against that fence where they'd talked, and he really wanted to go out there and say something.

*I'm sorry.*

She came over on Sunday afternoons and ate with him and his brothers. Well, not really him, because she still wouldn't look directly at him. He said nothing to her.

Finally, he realized the giant hole she'd left in his life, and he got down on his knees. He hadn't even started praying yet when he had the very strong feeling that he better get next-door and apologize.

*Now.*

Liam stood up and pulled on his cowboy boots. He prolonged the moment by choosing to walk the half-mile to the Shining Star Ranch, and by the time he got there, his heartbeat was reverberating through his whole body.

He had no idea what time it was or if Callie would even be in the house. She worked from sun-up to sun-down on the ranch, and it was still failing.

Sighing and telling God that He was wrong, that Liam shouldn't be here, he lifted his hand and knocked on the door. He knew the doorbell was broken, and that Callie hadn't likely fixed it in the twenty-six days since he'd last spoken to her.

No one came to the door, but he definitely heard someone walking in the house.

"Callie?" he called. "It's Liam. I need to apologize. Please open the door."

# 11

Callie Foster's heart leapt around in her chest like it had been replaced by a sack of jumping beans. "I can't open the door like this," she said to Simone, who'd gone to the window in the office to see who stood on the porch. Both of them had suspected it would be one of the Walker brothers, but Callie had a secret suspicion.

See, only she knew the dire situation the ranch was in. In the past few weeks, land sharks had been stopping by, offering her half of what the ranch was worth just to "take it off her hands."

They didn't get that she'd do anything she needed to in order to keep the ranch. She'd chased them away every time, and she'd taken to shying away from answering the door.

"I'll get it," Simone said. "We can't just leave him out there. He says he wants to apologize." Her eyes were so round and so worried.

*Imagine how she'll look if you told her you haven't paid the mortgage in four months.* Callie nodded and headed down the hall, embarrassment filling her. She didn't keep secrets from her sisters, and she hardly felt like herself at all these days.

"Hurry," Simone said. "I don't know what to say to him either."

Callie went into her bathroom and turned on the faucet. She could still hear Simone's higher voice and Liam's low one. She'd missed him so much, and she looked into her eyes, desperate to know what to say to him.

Truth was, she'd wanted to say yes when he'd asked her out. But he'd already offered to buy the ranch for her, and his invitation to the movies felt like it might end the same way. And if not that, then he was only going to date her to soften her up.

And her feelings for him were too real to allow herself to go out with him if it wasn't going to be real for him too.

After splashing some water on her face and letting her hair down, Callie went out into the kitchen. Liam jumped up from the kitchen table, where Simone had served him a cup of coffee.

"Heya, Cal," he said, and it wouldn't have mattered if he'd told her she was fat and ugly. She'd missed that voice. Missed the way he called her Cal. Missed *him* so much.

She burst into tears, and Liam rushed toward her.

"Hey, hey," he said, drawing her right against his heart-beat. "It's okay. I'm so sorry. We're okay. Okay? We're okay."

Callie clung to him, her tears drying up quickly. Thankfully. He held her at arm's length, and she noticed that Simone had left. She was such a good sister, and Callie's guilt about the situation at the ranch intensified.

"I'm sorry," he said. "Honest, Callie. I am."

She nodded and took a deep breath. "I know you are." She reached up and touched his face, where he'd been growing a beard for the past few days. "I'm sorry, too."

"You have nothing to be sorry for." He released her and stepped back, putting a proper friendship distance between them.

"I have a phone that works," she said. "I could've said something at lunch yesterday." There was plenty of blame to go around, and she wouldn't have him shouldering it all. "How's the project coming for DesignLabs?"

"Good," he said. "Good."

"Good," Callie echoed, stepping over to the fridge. "Do you want some sweet tea?"

"If you made it, always," he said.

Callie paused, drinking him in. Liam Walker was dashing and charming, and he didn't even seem to know it. He had a dimple in his right cheek that came out when he smiled, as he did now.

"What?" he asked, almost teasing her.

Callie shook her head and got out the sweet tea. "My grandmother would love to take credit for my sweet tea—and she should."

"Yeah? Grandma Elaine's recipe?"

"Yes." She got down two glasses and poured the tea before handing one to Liam. He took it with a glint in his eye Callie had seen before. Liam loved to joke and laugh, and that had captured her attention over the other Walker brothers almost immediately.

Sure, she was friends with his brother. Her and Jeremiah were good friends, as she sensed in him a worried soul like her. She could look at him and see what was bothering him before he said a word. And with Miah, he *wouldn't* say a word. That was the problem.

He kept secrets bottled up, just like Callie did, and he'd needed a soft place to fall a time or two since he'd moved to Three Rivers. It didn't mean they were romantically involved or even wanted to be.

Callie didn't want to be—not with Miah.

Now, the handsome cowboy in her kitchen, sipping her sweet tea, those dark eyes devouring her...yeah, she'd like to be more involved with him.

She just didn't dare. She didn't truly know where his motivations were, and she didn't want to ask. If she could wander into his office when it got too hot on the ranch and watch him work, that was great. If he'd come over and harass her about her pumpkins growing over onto his property, she'd take it. If he'd drink sweet tea with her and tell her they were okay, that was heaven.

"I got a new drone," he finally said. "You wanna come over and watch me fly it tonight?"

"Crash it, you mean?"

"Oh-ho." He chuckled, shaking his head.

"Yes," she said, wishing she could've told him yes when he'd asked her to a movie. "That sounds fun."

"Great." He put his half-finished tea on the counter and knocked next to it. "I have a ton of work to do today, so I have to jet." He actually looked sorry about it, though. "We're really okay?"

"Yes," Callie said. "We're really okay."

Liam embraced her, holding her right where she wanted to be, and then stepped back. "I'm glad. I don't like not being able to talk to you."

"So you have some stories from the past month," she said.

"So many." He laughed. "I'll tell you the best ones tonight." He peered down at her. "You got any?"

"So many," she said with a smile, but she would not be telling him about the land sharks or the calls from the bank. She'd been checking the mail three times a day just to make sure Simone didn't see any late notices.

"I bet yours have barn cats in them," he said, walking toward the front door.

"Yeah, well, we can't all have the best cattle dog on the planet," she said.

Liam laughed, waved, and left the house. Left Callie standing there with the ghost of his laughter in her ears, and the scent of his cologne still wafting on the air. Left her wondering if she could tell him about the financial problems on the ranch and just have him listen.

"No." She shook her head. He'd want to help, and Callie simply couldn't take charity from him, even if his bank account was so big he wouldn't miss the money.

She couldn't, and she wouldn't.

She turned to the back yard and stepped outside. She'd find a way to keep this ranch in the family, and she'd find a way to get caught up. She still had time.

"I will, Mama," she said to the sky. Her mother was buried at the church graveyard, but Daddy had told Callie how much her mama had loved the Shining Star. She'd only been here for a handful of years, but Callie felt her mother wrapping her arms around her in that moment.

"I'm trying," she said. "But I sure could use some help. Anything you've got." She wasn't sure if she was talking to her mom or God. Maybe both.

Definitely both, and Callie had no idea where to get the money she needed, and she absolutely couldn't lose the only home she'd ever known.

# 12

I vory turned down the road Tripp had mentioned, the dirt crunching under her tires. Her heart pounded with every inch she drove, mostly because she was about to meet a bunch of Tripp's brothers and get her engagement pictures taken, all within minutes of each other.

The past three weeks had gone by in the blink of an eye. She'd tailored the dress herself, added a ton of sparkle to it, and removed part of the left sleeve to make it more modern. When she wasn't doing that, she was chasing down clothes for people, or calling on old items to find out what to do with them.

Anything that wasn't claimed, Verona had asked her to put on a special rack, and they'd hold a garage sale at the end of the summer. Ivory was shocked at how many items had gone unclaimed, and when she asked Harmon when the last time they'd gone through their inventory had been, he'd said, "Never."

Never. Some items Ivory had found looked like they were from the eighties, and she couldn't imagine anyone buying them for even a quarter. But Verona and Harmon were the epitome of frugal, and Ivory loved them as if she belonged to them. It had been so long since she had belonged to anyone besides Oliver, and she'd fallen in love with her job and the owners at the dry cleaner.

A massive house came into view, and as she drew closer, she knew it was Seven Sons Ranch. Tripp had told her that he and his brothers all worked around the ranch, and that Jeremiah liked things a certain way.

The gate had WALKER spelled out on it in giant, iron letters, with seven stars to signify each son. Her pulse sounded like a gong now, but there was no going back, because the gate started to swing inward. Someone knew she was here.

"It's Tripp," she said to herself, clenching her fingers around the steering wheel. She'd texted him when she'd left her house. She eased onto the road leading to the house and parked next to his huge truck. Another car stood out among all the other more cowboy-ish items, and she caught sight of Tripp talking to a brunette wearing bright red lipstick.

That would be Whitney Wilde, and Ivory's reservations about getting these pictures taken doubled. Maybe tripled. Number one, she didn't have anything all that nice to wear. Number two, she didn't have a lot of people to send announcements to. Printing them cost money, and mailing them did too.

Tripp, of course, had said he'd take care of all of it. She just needed to give him her address list, which she still hadn't done.

Tripp turned toward her, and Ivory couldn't stall getting out of the car any longer. She wanted to see him; she just didn't want to do the rest of the tasks on their list today.

"Hey, baby," he said easily, and any outsider would've believed they were a normal, loving couple about to be married. He took her hand and led her over to the photographer. "This is Whitney."

"You have beautiful pictures on your website," Ivory said, shaking the woman's hand.

"Aw, thank you," she said in the cutest little Texas drawl in the world. She probably had men lining up to take her out on Friday nights. "Where do y'all want to start?"

They both looked at Tripp, and he said, "You choose us a good spot, Whitney. I need a few minutes for Ivory to meet my brothers."

"She hasn't met your brothers?"

"Not all of them," Tripp said with a perfectly political smile. He nodded at Ivory and led her away from the photographer.

As soon as they were out of earshot, she said, "Are they all in there?"

"All my brothers?" Tripp went up the steps to the front door, and Ivory noticed the large, wraparound porch. She'd always wanted a porch like this. Everything here felt rustic, yet rich at the same time. "Yes, they're all inside. Jeremiah made watermelon granita."

Ivory blinked, unsure what granita even was. "Okay."

"He wants to know if you'd like it at the wedding," Tripp said. "Jeremiah has a very tough exterior, but he's a great guy."

"I'm sure he is," Ivory said, pausing in the doorway. "They're going to like me, right?"

"They're going to love you," he said with a smile. "And you already know Evelyn, and she's here."

"She is?"

"Of course." Tripp tugged on her hand, and she went with him into the house. Once again, the vibrant wood on the floor screamed wealth. The vaulted ceilings. The pale gray walls.

"I work in here," Tripp said, stepping to the right and entering an office. "Liam has the window desk."

"You have three computer screens."

"I do animation," he said. "Trust me, it requires three screens."

She pressed closer to him. "Where are we going to put those at my house?"

"Your house?"

A blip of panic moved through Ivory, and she looked up at Tripp. "Yes, my house," she whispered. "We're getting *married*, Tripp. You'll move in with me."

"Oh." He shook his head as if he'd just now realized he'd

be moving in with her. Could that be true? "I don't know. I haven't seen your whole house."

"Well, we should get that figured out," she said, already overwhelmed and she hadn't even seen another Walker brother yet.

He took her down the hall, which had a bathroom and a coat closet in it, and into the huge kitchen and living area. A hallway ran to her left, leading further into the depths of the house.

"Four bedrooms that way," he said. "Mine included."

Ivory looked down the hall, but the real adventure was in the kitchen. With all the people.

"My twin," Tripp said. "Liam."

"Ivory," Liam said, taking both of her hands. "So nice to finally meet you."

"You've met her before," Tripp said while rolling his eyes.

"Yes, but that was months ago." Liam grinned like he was enjoying this show, while Ivory wished the ground would open up and swallow her whole.

"She's here," Evelyn said, and she came toward Ivory. "How are you?" They hugged, and Ivory wanted to hold onto her friend for a little longer. She had gone to see Evelyn about getting her a handsome cowboy boyfriend— and she'd wanted Tripp himself.

Evelyn had said no, but Ivory had managed to meet him on her own. She'd thought she was ready. She'd been wrong.

"Great," she said instead, stepping back to Tripp's side. "How was the honeymoon?"

"So amazing," Evelyn said. "Relaxing. You remember my husband, Rhett?"

"Of course," Ivory said, as she'd met him before too. So maybe this wasn't a first meeting for everyone.

"I can't believe you roped Tripp into this," Rhett said, a wide smile on his face too.

Ivory choked, her eyes immediately flying to Tripp's. "Rhett," he said under his breath. "Wrong wording, bro."

"Oh, right." Rhett's face colored. "What I meant was, I didn't think Tripp would ever let himself fall in love again."

"Okay, you're done," Tripp said, pushing against his brother's chest. "Do you have to be so embarrassing?" He went with Rhett, still muttering to him while Ivory stood there, sure she'd missed something but unsure as to what it could be.

*He's not in love with you*, she thought. Because he couldn't be. She couldn't shoulder that, along with all the other things she was dealing with. Letting him pay for things was one thing. Having him fall in love with her?

No. She shook her head, and Evelyn linked her arm through Ivory's. "Two brothers to go, Ivory. You've got this." She took a few steps and said, "Wyatt, this is Tripp's fiancée, Ivory Osburn."

"Ma'am," the cowboy said, taking off his hat and tipping it to her. "Great to meet you." He smiled like he was genuinely pleased to meet her, and Ivory remembered

Tripp telling her that Wyatt was the non-drama brother. New to the ranch, as he'd just retired from his rodeo career.

"And Jeremiah," Evelyn said, indicating the cowboy standing at the stove. He wore a black apron over his jeans and T-shirt, but none of the brothers seemed to be able to go anywhere or do anything without those cowboy hats glued to their heads.

"Ivory Osburn," Evelyn said.

"Hello," Jeremiah said, his voice almost cold. Definitely cool.

"Thank you for doing the food," she said. "Tripp talks about your cooking so much."

"Does he now?" Jeremiah cocked his right eyebrow and went back to the pan on the stove. "Well, I have a couple of things for you to try, after you're finished with the pictures."

She'd definitely have to look up what granita was before she stepped back into this homestead. "I can't wait," she said, and it could've been her imagination, but she thought she heard Jeremiah grunt as Evelyn led her away.

"And you know my sisters." She indicated Callie and Simone, who both sat on the back deck, talking with Liam.

"Do you guys do a lot with the Walker brothers?" she asked.

"Yep," Evelyn said. "It's just the two ranches out here, and we've always gotten along great."

"What's Jeremiah's story?" she asked, casting a long look over her shoulder to the cowboy. He was drop-dead gorgeous, and she couldn't believe a woman in this town hadn't snatched him right up.

"Oh, he'll have to tell you that," Evelyn said evasively.

"The light is perfect right now," another woman said, and Ivory turned back to Whitney. "Are y'all ready?"

Tripp was still huddled with Rhett, but he left his brother and started toward Whitney. "Sure thing," he said. "Everyone, this is Whitney Wilde. She's our—"

An earsplitting noise came from the stove, and Ivory gasped as she looked to where Jeremiah stood. He'd dropped the cast iron skillet onto the stovetop, which now smoked.

"Sorry," he said, quickly picking up the skillet and moving to the sink, his head bent. "Sorry."

"We're going to miss the best light," Whitney said, her eyes still on Jeremiah. Ivory didn't blame her, not one little bit. These Walker brothers were a hard nut to crack, and before Rhett had married Evelyn, not a single one of them had even dated anyone in Three Rivers.

"Where are your parents?" Ivory asked as she and Tripp followed Whitney down the hall and out the front door.

"Grand Cayman," he said. "They retired there a couple of years ago."

"Really?"

"Really."

"Will they come to town for the wedding?"

Tripp paused in the doorway and looked down at Ivory. "I didn't invite them. I don't need them to make the trip for something that isn't even real." His features were hard as he spoke, and then he eased outside, full of charm and charisma again.

His words stung, and Ivory didn't even know why. This wedding *wasn't* real. These engagement pictures were a farce. Of course his parents shouldn't fly halfway across the world for a non-real wedding. She hadn't been planning to invite her parents either.

And yet, her chest burned and her heart beat too fast. Why? What was this strange feeling inside her?

"You guys have the cutest little windmill," Whitney said, and Ivory focused on the sweet sound of her voice. "I'd love to bring other brides out here sometime. Are you open to that?"

"You'd need to talk to Jeremiah about that," Tripp said. "He manages the ranch and all of its affairs."

"All right," Whitney said, really making the two syllables into four. "Stand right in front of that bush there, Tripp. Ivory, you're next to him. Get as close as you can. Really press into him."

Ivory did what she said—at least she thought she did.

"More," Whitney said. "Tripp put your arm around her. I don't want to see your hand. Good. Other hand in your pocket."

Ivory brushed her hair off her left shoulder, hoping this could be a smile-and-done photo shoot. They only needed one, right?

"Move in closer," Whitney said. "Actually move your feet closer to his, Ivory."

She shuffled her feet an inch or so.

"Tripp," Whitney said, clearly annoyed. "Grab her and pull her into you."

He did, and wow. Yes, their bodies were now touching at a lot of different points. "Finally," Whitney said. "I mean, you've got to at least act like you like him, you know? You're marrying this man." She backed up a couple of steps, gave Ivory a few more directions, and started snapping pictures.

Ivory felt like crying.

She couldn't even pretend like she liked Tripp? Humiliation filled her, and she caught Tripp shooting her glances every time Whitney paused to give them another direction, move them over in front of the barn, and have them sit on the ground out in the middle of a wheat field.

By the time the photo shoot concluded, Ivory's face felt like plastic, and her stomach complained loudly that she'd skipped lunch.

"Thank you, Whitney," Tripp said as he handed Whitney a wad of cash. "I can't wait to see them."

"I only have one shoot ahead of yours," she said. "I should have these to you within a week." She beamed at Tripp and left. He watched her go before turning back to Ivory.

"Ready for dinner?" he asked.

She wanted to eat, yes. But was she ready for what waited for her inside the homestead? No.

"Sorry about the pictures," she said.

"You did fine," he said, his pleasantness slipping. "We're

a little late for dinner. Jeremiah's texted me twice." He started toward the house.

"Tripp," she said, hurrying to catch him. "Wait."

"Why?" he asked, slowing but not stopping. "So you can figure out how to pretend to like me?" He paused completely. "Better figure it out fast, Ivory. We have to go eat with my family, and it's going to be hard enough to convince them all that we actually love each other, what with one fake marriage behind us already."

Regret tore through her. "I just didn't know she wanted me to get that close," she said.

"Even she knew you don't like me." His head dipped, and she wanted to erase all the pain she felt coming from him.

"That's not true," she said, stopping beside him. She touched his arm. "I *do* like you, Tripp. Too much. It's why I'm so...scared out of my mind."

"I don't think you can tell your fiancé that you like him too much." He met her eyes. "It would be nice if you said it at all."

Shock combined with guilt, swirling through her. "You know what? You're right."

"You spend all of your time telling me how grateful you are. It's fine. Whatever. But honestly, Ivory, I don't need to be thanked. I need you to act like you like me."

"I *do* like you." She liked spending time with him. She liked holding his hand. She liked listening to him sing in the choir on Sundays. She liked the promise of seeing him in the evenings after work. She liked the idea of him in her life—and that scared her. "I'm trying," she said. "You have to understand that I came from a marriage that wasn't great. I made a vow not to let myself be hurt like that again."

And she liked him, sure. But loving him? She wasn't even sure she was capable of that.

He nodded. "Yeah, I know. I've been trying to be patient."

"You are patient." Couldn't he see how great he was? *No*, a voice whispered in her head. *Because you don't tell him.* "You're amazing," she said. "I love seeing you after work, and knowing you'll be there if I call." Her chest shook, because she didn't talk like this. She hadn't with Daniel, and she'd spent so long—so, so long—trying to find who she was again after he left.

"I *really* like you, Tripp, and not just because you're doing all these things to help me keep full custody of Oliver." She gazed evenly at him, feeling powerful for the first time in a long time.

"Thank you," he murmured.

Ivory reached out and touched his chest, quickly moving her hand up to cradle his face. "I've promised the Lord I wouldn't hurt you," she whispered. "Please, tell me if I am."

"I think I just did," he said. "And I appreciate you opening up to me. I know you don't do that with many people."

She leaned her forehead against his chest. "No, not many people," she said. "In fact, no one."

"You must be so tired," he whispered. "I mean, that's a big job to keep everyone out."

He had no idea. "I am tired."

"Well, let's go eat, and let Jeremiah show you all the things he has planned. Then you can go." He put a couple of fingers on her shoulder, and she looked up at him. He bent down and kissed her, and it was the sweetest, most tender kiss of her life.

He didn't move very fast, and he didn't deepen the kiss, but it spoke volumes about how he felt about her. She felt cherished and loved and safe—all things she hadn't experienced in so long.

"Hey," Jeremiah called. "Stop kissing and come taste this granita. It's melting."

Tripp pulled away, a sigh combining with a laugh. "Let's go taste the granita."

Ivory put her hand in his and went with him toward the house, something floating through her she thought she'd never feel again and wasn't even sure existed.

True happiness. And in that moment, she couldn't wait to become Mrs. Tripp Walker.

# 13

Jeremiah Walker felt like every eye in the whole town of Three Rivers had narrowed in on him. Of course, that wasn't true, but Rhett's definitely had, and Jeremiah didn't need that.

He set the frying pan on the burner and turned it on. Tripp and Ivory were taking their engagement pictures out on the ranch, and Jeremiah was feeding everyone afterward. The watermelon granita already waited in the freezer, and he just needed to get the chicken seared and into the oven.

He'd never admit it out loud, but he was grateful Tripp had asked him to do the food for his wedding. He didn't understand why Tripp wanted to get married, but Jeremiah didn't understand a lot of things usually governed by the heart.

His had been ripped out and left on a stage in Austin.

Clearing his throat, he adjusted the flame and poured a

bit of oil into the pan as Tripp entered the kitchen with his fiancée. He started introducing her to everyone, and Rhett's attention got diverted elsewhere. Thankfully.

Jeremiah had already explained why he didn't want Tripp getting married at Seven Sons. Not only was it not necessary, but Jeremiah couldn't handle seeing that setup again, right where he had to work every day.

And he loved this ranch with everything in him, and Tripp could find somewhere else. Heaven knew they could all afford whatever they wanted. Heck, Jeremiah would pay for a venue if he had to.

*You don't own the ranch*, Rhett had said, and he was right. But Jeremiah certainly had a say in what went on there, and he couldn't help it if his voice was loud.

Tripp had said he understood, so Jeremiah wasn't sure why Rhett was making it into a capital case.

He turned back to the chicken sitting in the buttermilk as if he didn't see and hear all of the introductions going on in the kitchen. Evelyn was just presenting Ivory to Wyatt when Jeremiah realized the flame was much too hot for browning.

He moved the pan to a cool burner and turned the flame off, already annoyed, and his turn to meet his brother's fiancée hadn't even come yet.

"And Jeremiah," Evelyn said, indicating him, and Jeremiah couldn't even get himself to smile. He was sure Ivory was nice. Tripp sure did like her, and Jeremiah did want Tripp to be happy.

He just didn't understand how his brothers had healed so quickly. He still felt like the gash on his heart had happened yesterday, and if he didn't get to the hospital in the next ten minutes, he'd bleed to death.

"Ivory Osburn," Evelyn said.

"Hello," Jeremiah said as kindly as he could, which he knew was about the level of an ice cube.

"Thank you for doing the food," Ivory said. "Tripp talks about your cooking so much."

"Does he now?" Jeremiah cocked his right eyebrow and returned his attention to pan on the stove. It should be cool enough now, and he twisted the knob to put a new flame under it. "Well, I have a couple of things for you to try, after you're finished with the pictures."

She looked like he'd hit her with the frying pan, but she said. "I can't wait," and Jeremiah grunted as she turned away from him.

He relaxed slightly now that he'd met the woman, and he opened a drawer to get out a pair of tongs while Evelyn and Ivory moved back over to Rhett and Tripp.

He moved his bowl of uncooked chicken to the counter beside the stove, where his flour, egg, and breadcrumbs waited. He started coating the first piece of chicken, the oil talking to him in a way that said it was ready for the protein.

"The light is perfect right now," an unfamiliar voice said, and Jeremiah looked up from the bowl of chicken. A gorgeous woman with dark hair stood in the homestead now, and everything around him stilled.

Who was she?

She had a smattering of freckles across her face; she had a camera looped around her neck, and she'd painted her lips bright red. Jeremiah sure did like them. In fact, he couldn't tear his eyes from her mouth, and he wondered what it would be like to kiss her.

Heat filled his body, because it too was now betraying him.

He was not interested in getting to know this woman. Oh, no, he was not. His heart expanded about six sizes, and it no longer fit in his chest as it sent out heavy beat after heavy beat.

Why couldn't he look away?

He finally did, realizing that he'd let the pan get too hot again. He reached for it at the same time Tripp said, "Every-one, this is Whitney Wilde. She's our—"

Jeremiah dropped the cast iron skillet as the woman's name screamed through his head.

*Whitney Wilde.*

Now he knew how to get in touch with her again. With her name and the fact that she was Tripp and Ivory's photographer, she wouldn't be that hard to track down.

Which was absolutely ridiculous.

The stove smoked where he'd spilled the oil against the flame. If he didn't pull himself together, he could start this whole place on fire.

He had a vision of the homestead and ranch he'd spent so long perfecting turning into ashes—the same way his life had when Laura Ann had left him standing there by himself.

"Sorry," he said, quickly picking up the skillet and moving to the sink, his head bent. "Sorry." His cowboy hat kept his eyes concealed, but wow, everyone was surely staring at him now. Full-blown staring—and the heaviest gaze belonged to one Whitney Wilde.

For some reason, Jeremiah could feel her stare differently than the others.

"We're going to miss the best light," she said in the perfect feminine Texas twang, and Jeremiah cut a glance at her out of the corner of his eye as she led Tripp and Ivory down the hall toward the front door.

The relief that moved through him was immediate and strong, and he ignored Rhett when his brother stepped into the kitchen.

"I don't need help here," Jeremiah said, probably a little too gruffly. Didn't matter. Rhett would just think he was in a bad mood because of the pictures. Which he kinda was.

"You sure?"

"You can get the table set, if you want," he said. "I need to get this chicken going or we'll be eating potato skins and granita for dinner."

"All right," Rhett drawled, and Jeremiah wanted to roll his eyes. His brother was barely a cowboy, for crying out loud.

He re-set the pan on the burner and turned on the flame. He re-oiled it and went back to the chicken pieces.

Frying and browning went smoothly from there, and he slid the pan in the oven a few minutes later.

He wiped his hands down the front of his apron, his mind still circling the brunette who may have just re-started his heart.

*Impossible*, he told himself. He didn't feel anything for Whitney, because Jeremiah didn't feel anything at all. And a pretty set of eyes and a bright pair of lips wasn't going to change that.

———

"Fake fried chicken," he said later, with Ivory and Tripp sitting together at the table. Everyone else had stayed for dinner too, and Jeremiah was glad.

Well, everyone but Whitney. He'd wanted to ask Tripp why he hadn't invited her to stay, but that would be way too obvious. And Jeremiah didn't need any questions about why he'd really dropped that pan earlier.

Ranching and cooking were what made him happy, and neither of those could leave him standing at the altar, everyone staring at him with sympathy in their eyes.

The publicity had been the worst part of being left by Laura Ann. The way everyone looked at him like he was completely broken. At the same time, everyone wanted to know how he was going to react.

Thankfully, the twins had stood up and blocked the crowd that had dressed up and taken time from their lives to come celebrate with him and who was supposed to be his wife.

"Fake fried?" Ivory asked, and Jeremiah focused on the here-and-now. It was never good to look back anyway. But somehow, his reaction to Whitney had opened all kinds of doors he'd thought he'd dead bolted shut.

"Yes," he said. "I just fry the outside, the coating. It's the best part anyway. But by finishing it in the oven, I can literally make three times as much food in the same amount of time."

"Amazing," Tripp said, as he'd already taken a bite. "This is delicious, Jeremiah." He grinned and looked at Ivory. "Do you think we could serve this at the wedding?"

"Sure," she said, focusing on the dipping sauces.

"That one's honey mustard," he said. "I raise the bees for the honey right here on the ranch." Jeremiah didn't mean to sound prideful, but he sure did love his beehives. "The second one is a sweet barbecue sauce, and the last one is a chipotle ketchup. I can make all of those too, as well as something creamy too. Maybe a garlic aioli or an herb ranch?" He looked at her for confirmation, but Ivory wore that wide-eyed look again.

"All of them," Rhett said, dipping his chicken in the sweet barbecue. "We need to get re-married and have Jeremiah cook for it." He laughed along with several others at the table, and Jeremiah finally settled into his own food.

He did enjoy watching others eat his food and enjoy it. That was how he experienced joy now. *Nothing wrong with that,* he told himself as they ate. He let everyone else carry the conversation, as he usually did.

"I love all of this," Ivory said when they'd finished eating, her eyes shining when she looked up at Jeremiah. "Thank you. Really."

"You haven't even tasted the best part yet," he said, tossing his napkin on the table. "The watermelon granita." He got up and retrieved the pan of flavored ice from the freezer. "It's going to be hot when you guys get married. This should keep everyone cool."

He scraped the ice with a fork, which he'd already done a few times, and served it with a sprinkle of crushed mint leaves.

Ivory looked at it in wonder. "It's beautiful."

"Wow, yeah," Tripp said, accepting his glass and picking up his spoon. He tasted it, and a groan came out of his mouth. "And it's great."

Jeremiah allowed himself a small smile as he kept serving the watermelon granita, and then he took his out onto the deck.

Callie joined him, which was no surprise. "This is amazing, Miah," she said.

"Thanks." He did smile fully at her then. If there was anyone who could maybe restore his faith in the female half of his species, it was Callie Foster.

Maybe.

She had been pretty rough on Liam, and while Jeremiah thought she was a nice woman, in the end, she was still a woman, and Liam hadn't spoken to her for much of the past few weeks.

Jeremiah hadn't asked her why. He didn't get in between Liam and Callie, and he wanted that to be very clear.

"I heard you met Whitney and started throwing pans," she said, a twinkle in her eye.

"You heard wrong," he said, not caring that he'd practically barked the words. "The pan was too hot, and I picked it up with my bare hands when I should've used a towel. So I dropped it."

"Mm." Callie put another bite of the granita in her mouth. "Whitney Wilde is very pretty. And nice."

"I'm not interested in Whitney Wilde," Jeremiah said, his voice a monotone. And while he'd felt removed from the Lord since the day he was supposed to get married, he'd kept going to church. He'd kept trying to feel something. He kept trying to work hard, and be a good person.

He didn't lie.

But as the sentence ran through his mind again—*I'm not interested in Whitney Wilde*—Jeremiah had the feeling he'd just told a bold-face lie.

# 14

Whitney Wilde culled the pictures of Tripp Walker and Ivory Osburn, her mind on auto-pilot. She'd taken so many pictures and done so many weddings, she barely had to think when she went through the shots for the first time.

One to keep, two to throw away. Then she'd go through all the ones again, remarking the best shots, the one with the sharpest focus, the best light, the cutest smiles.

But right now, all she could think about was that man in the kitchen at Seven Sons.

Jeremiah Walker.

She apparently needed to talk to him if she wanted to shoot at Seven Sons Ranch again.

And, oh boy, she did.

But that wasn't the reason the drop-dead gorgeous

cowboy was on her mind. When he'd met her eyes earlier, an instant tether had formed between them. Everyone else in the homestead had disappeared, and it was just her with her camera, and that dreamy cowboy in the black apron and matching cowboy hat.

Then the smoke had obscured their connection, and he'd hopped into action to get the almost-catastrophe handled.

Wow, she wanted him to handle some of her problems too. Unconsciously, she scoffed. She didn't know Jeremiah personally, but she knew all about the Walker cowboys out at Seven Sons.

Well, she'd listened to the rumor mill around Three Rivers. Jeremiah hadn't been out with a single woman in town since moving to town a couple of years ago. Hardly any of the Walkers had, though they seemed normal enough.

She'd heard Jeremiah and Callie Foster might have something going on, as it seemed like the Fosters were chummy with the Walkers. Whitney normally didn't care about the gossip, and she just liked getting her hair deep conditioned at the salon.

But she sure was glad she had ears and could hear as she sorted through the pictures. Another scoff, and Whitney asked herself, "What are you going to do? Get Jeremiah to fall in love with you?"

The idea was actually laughable, as he clearly had walls

around himself that rivaled those she'd find surrounding a refuge after a zombie apocalypse.

Her phone beeped, and it was the sound she'd assigned to her baby photography. She immediately abandoned the sorting of Tripp and Ivory's engagement shots—which had been wow-hard work—and picked up her phone.

She shot brides and weddings and families to pay her bills. She was the premier wedding photographer in Hutchinson County, and she traveled to Oklahoma, New Mexico, and all over the Panhandle to make sure couples had gorgeous wedding pictures.

But her love really lay with babies. Well, babies and vegetables.

Sure enough, Lake Winters had gotten a message, and Whitney's heart leapt. No one in Three Rivers knew she was Lake Winters.

Well, her clients did, but she had them sign a confidentiality agreement before she ever met them. She could actually pursue legal action should one of them say who she really was.

Thankfully, she hadn't had to do that yet, and she read the message with gratitude in her heart. Boone Carver had heard about her from a friend, and he wanted to book something as a surprise for his wife, Nicole.

*I heard you do consultations over the phone,* he said. *And there's paperwork before you'll meet us in person. When are you available?*

*Thank you, Lord,* she thought as she clicked away from her editing software and opened her calendar. Even though Texas was a sauna from April to November, people still wanted to get married.

But she prayed daily for more opportunities to sneak into the organic grocery store her parents owned and lay sleeping babies among ears of corn or bunches of radishes. And she'd been dying to try a cabbage cap on a perfectly bald baby.

Not that she knew if Boone and Nicole would have a bald baby. But still. Her baby photography was her passion, and she was grateful the Lord had brought her another client.

*I can do a consultation anytime,* she tapped out. *When will the baby be born?*

*End of July,* Boone responded.

Whitney went back to her calendar, knowing she had the Holmes wedding at the end of July.

*July 30, Boone said. Very end. I've seen your work. Tracey said you like to do the pictures in the first ten days.*

"Yep," Whitney muttered to herself, looking at her calendar. "And I can do August fifth." If there weren't any problems with the birth or delivery, that was.

She told Boone as much, and they scheduled a call for tomorrow night. Whitney didn't mind talking on the phone, and she actually looked forward to interacting with other people. She didn't like being home alone for long stretches of time, and a photography career had been perfect for her. She met lots of new people and had lots of opportunity for conversing.

After scheduling her phone call with Boone for six-thirty the next night, she paused, still looking at her calendar.

"I wonder what time Jeremiah comes in off the ranch." He'd been in the homestead, cooking dinner already tonight. But she knew that was a special circumstance. Still, she wondered how hard it would be to get his number and if he'd answer when she called.

Feeling adventurous, she clicked to open a new event, and she added *Call Jeremiah about shooting at Seven Sons Ranch* to her agenda for tomorrow night.

That was all she wanted from the man. A spot to shoot a bride by that absolutely cute windmill again.

*Sure*, her mind said in a super-sarcastic tone, but Whitney ignored it. If she had to talk to the best-looking man on the planet to schedule a location, that wasn't her fault.

As she went back to culling pictures, her brain now moved through ways to get Jeremiah Walker's phone number. She had a number of friends in town, and if she got the ball rolling, Whitney didn't think it would take that long until she had the digits in her possession.

The problem was, she didn't want anyone to know. So involving friends was out.

"He's a foodie," she muttered to herself. And she knew

what that meant—he probably shopped at Wilde & Organic. And if he did that, he might have a loyalty card. And loyalty cards had names and phone numbers attached to them.

Feeling devious and a little bit like she was coloring outside the lines, Whitney smiled at her plan to get the cowboy's phone number.

*He'll be mad*, she thought. But he didn't have to know, and she finally had a reason to enjoy going to work early in the morning to stock organic bananas and loaves of carrot and walnut bread that weighed as much as a sack of flour.

---

THE NEXT MORNING, Whitney tied the green apron around her waist. It had been dyed organically with spinach, and she set to work putting out the green beans that had come in off the farms that morning.

Everything in the store was grown in Texas, something her parents were adamant about. Whitney worked at the grocer, because it was expected that all the Wilde siblings would, no matter what other jobs they had.

Her oldest brother would take over the operation when her parents were ready to retire, so Whitney left the details about which farms, orchards, and ranches they bought from to Michael. He was a stickler for details, and if he knew Whitney was going to go into the loyalty card program and use one of the numbers for her personal gain, he'd lose his mind.

She swallowed, because she didn't feel quite right about it either. And Jeremiah may have high walls up, but that didn't mean he was stupid. He'd ask her how she'd gotten his number.

*Loyalty program is out*, she told herself as she moved from green beans to tomatillos. On the other side of the produce section, her sister Patsy worked putting out oranges and grapefruits. Patsy was married and actually worked at Wilde & Organic full-time as the business accountant.

Johnny worked the family farm that brought in a lot of their kale and heirloom tomatoes, and Whitney was the only one who didn't work for their family full-time. She did take pictures for their signage, and her mother had even let her put up her baby pictures in the store. Whitney had chosen the one with the newborn snuggled among a variety of peppers and leeks, and she switched out the picture every season.

She'd gotten a fair few jobs from the pictures on the community announcement board, and she replenished the business cards every so often too.

She finished stocking the tomatillos and opened a box of Brussels sprouts. Her sister's phone rang, and Patsy paused in her stacking of fruit to answer it. She kept her back to Whitney, but the annoyance and anxiety rolled off her sister's shoulders.

So she was dealing with Dalton again. Her fifteen-year-old son had been giving her some problems for the past six months or so, and he was supposed to be at the store working this summer. Whitney hadn't seen him yet today, though.

The conversation lasted through her unpacking of the sprouts, and she tossed the box to the floor. One more vegetable, and Whitney would be done for the day. She had a ton of photo editing to do today before her phone calls that night, and she was already tired.

And she still didn't have Jeremiah's number.

"Whitney," Patsy said, and she looked away from the jalapeños in the box she'd just opened.

"Yeah?"

"Do you have anything for Dalton to do?"

"Sure, yeah," Whitney said, the idea of spending the day with her nephew better than sitting in front of the computer in the house by herself. "Tons of yard work, and my fridge needs to be cleaned out, and my cats need a bath, and—"

"She has a ton of work," Patsy said, her dark eyes firing lasers meant for her son. "So you'll go over to her house in an hour. She's almost done here, and you'll work for her all day." Her sister smiled at Whitney and moved away, the words, "I don't care if you want to or not. You don't come in to work here, you'll be working somewhere else. That was our agreement," going with her.

Whitney smiled, though she didn't envy her sister. Of course, she was the only Wilde who wasn't married with children, and she often felt like she didn't quite fit in her family.

She finished the peppers, broke down her boxes, and put

them in the recycler in the back room of the grocer. She still didn't want to involve her friends, so she pulled out her phone and texted Tripp Walker.

*Can I get your brother's number so I can ask him about shooting at the ranch?*

*Sure thing,* Tripp said within seconds. A moment later, the contact appeared on her phone, and Whitney smiled. That had been easier than she'd thought. And Tripp obviously hadn't felt the tether between her and Jeremiah yesterday, or he wouldn't have given her the number quite so fast.

Whitney had it on her schedule to call him that night, but she hurried to her car and turned it on so the air conditioning would blow.

Then she dialed.

"Yep," Jeremiah answered, and Whitney's pulse scattered through her body.

"Jeremiah," she said, really drawling out his name. "It's Whitney Wilde. You know, the photographer from last night?"

Maybe she'd imagined the tether. The shower of sparks that had filled the space between her and him. If he couldn't remember her....

"Yeah?" he asked, his voice a bit lower. "Did you need something?"

Oh, she needed something, and she turned up the AC so it was blowing harder. Because, wow, she was suddenly so hot, and they weren't even in the same room together.

"Yeah," she said. "I want to shoot out at your ranch again sometime."

He started laughing, and while the sound was delicious and rich, she couldn't label it as happy. "I don't think so," he said. "But you have a nice day, ma'am."

The line went dead, and Whitney stared at her phone. He'd honestly just hung up on her. Too bad he didn't know she didn't give up so easily.

# 15

Tripp finished washing the cookie sheet and put it on the counter next to Ivory's sink. He turned, looking for something else to do.

"Relax," she said from her position at the kitchen table, but Tripp didn't know how to do that.

Oliver would be home any minute now. Tripp was meeting the boy for the first time. His marriage to Ivory was six days away, and Tripp felt like someone had poured honey in his veins, complete with the entire hive of bees, queen and all.

He swallowed. "Okay, peanut butter chocolate chip cookies. Chocolate milk. New soccer ball."

"You can't bribe a kid to like you," Ivory said, glancing up from her laptop. "And I just got three new necklace orders." She grinned and closed her computer.

"That's great," he said, receiving her into his arms when

she stepped into him. The last few weeks since they'd gotten their pictures taken had been pretty easy breezy. Ivory worked at the dry cleaner. Tripp brought her lunch or took her to dinner. Or both.

They spent time together, planning the wedding, and if Tripp were being honest, he'd been falling in love with Ivory Osburn. He wasn't sure where she was on the path, and he was too afraid to ask, just in case she got cold feet about marrying him.

Although, she was the one who needed the favor. Tripp couldn't help feeling like she was doing him the favor, though.

*Can't think like that,* he told himself. But Ivory tipped up and kissed him, and Tripp actually felt himself slipping down that slippery slope toward love.

He felt like he'd cracked open his heart and invited her to take big handfuls of it. If he ended up hurt, he wouldn't blame her, despite her promise to the Lord that she wouldn't hurt him.

No, if after all of this, if Tripp ended up hurt, it would be one hundred percent his fault.

"Mom!" The front door crashed into the wall behind it, and a tow-headed boy came running into the house. He dumped his backpack on the floor and flew into Ivory's arms.

She laughed and said, "There's my baby. How are you, snuggles?"

"Mom." He laughed as he hugged her. "Don't call me that."

"Why not?" she teased. "You're my little snuggle bunny."

Tripp wiped his palms down the front of his jeans, knowing that every eye was about to land on him. A man Tripp recognized came through the front door of Ivory's house, and he wasn't as excited about the reunion as Ivory and Oliver were.

Their eyes met, and Tripp realized where he'd seen this man before. At the dry cleaner. He pulled in a breath, his mind spinning now.

What had Ivory's ex-husband been doing there? Weeks ago, no less. One of the first days she'd worked at Verona's.

Ivory rose, saving Tripp from having to introduce himself. She positioned herself between him and Oliver and Daniel and tucked her hands in her back pockets.

"How was the drive?" she asked.

Whatever Tripp had expected her to say, it wasn't that.

"Fine," Daniel said, dropping the suitcase he held in his hand on the floor. "He has another bag."

"I'll go with you," Ivory said. Daniel left without acknowledging her, and Ivory turned back to Oliver. "Baby, stay here with Tripp, okay? I need to talk to Daddy for a minute."

Oliver looked up at Tripp, who smiled at him. "Hey," he said.

Ivory straightened and looked at Tripp too, clear anxiety in her expression. "I'll be right back, okay?"

"Okay." Tripp watched her walk out, and he flinched slightly when the door closed behind her. "So, Oliver," he said. "How was your summer at your dad's?"

"Boring," Oliver said. "He works all the time, and I just sit in the house."

"Alone?"

"No, he has a nanny."

"Oh." Tripp nodded and turned back to the kitchen counter. "Do you want a cookie? Your mom said you liked peanut butter chocolate chip the best."

Oliver's whole face lit up, and Tripp was sure Ivory was wrong about being able to bribe children. "Yeah."

"I made them," Tripp said, not trying to be boastful. "And I got you some chocolate milk."

"Thanks," Oliver said, looking at him again, this time with more curiosity in his face. "Are you my mom's friend?"

He glanced over his shoulder, wishing Ivory was here so she could use the right words to explain this to her son. "I'm...." He let his voice trail off, because he heard shouting coming from outside. "Stay here for a sec, okay, bud?"

"My mom won't let me have a hat like yours," Oliver said, climbing up on the barstool and reaching for a cookie.

Tripp wanted to go back and ask the child why, but his feet carried him toward the front door. He opened it, and the yelling was definitely coming from Ivory's driveway. From Ivory.

He stepped outside quickly and closed the door behind him. "Ivory," he called as he went down her steps and then her sidewalk.

"And this is real, so you can climb in your luxury SUV and go back to your free lifestyle in Amarillo," she said. Tripp reached her side to find tears sliding down her face. "And you won't have to think about your son for another six months."

Daniel's face was a mask of rage, and Tripp wanted to put some distance between her and her ex. His jaw jumped, but his lower-pitched voice had definitely been yelling before Tripp had come outside.

"Ivory," he said again. "Let's go inside."

She looked at him then, and she seemed utterly wild and out of control. And Tripp wanted to tame her. He slipped his hand into hers, and realization came into her face. He nodded at her. "Let's go inside."

He glanced at Daniel, who fumed, the steam practically showing in wavy lines as it came off his face. Tripp wanted to tell him to go. Puff up his chest and make sure Daniel knew Ivory wasn't going to put up with anything from him.

Tripp said nothing, instead guiding Ivory away from her ex-husband and back toward the house.

"This isn't going to stand," Daniel called after them. "I have an entire legal team examining everything about both of your lives."

"Ignore him," Tripp murmured, tensing as Ivory did. "Oliver is inside. You have two neighbors watching." Ivory kept going, and they went up the steps and into the house together. Tripp locked the door behind them and wanted to sag into the door with relief.

But he had to be strong. For himself. For Ivory. For Oliver.

"Mama, can I get a hat like his?" Oliver still sat on the barstool, a smear of chocolate on his face by his mouth.

Ivory half sobbed and half scoffed. "No, baby. No cowboys, remember?"

"What's wrong with cowboys?" Tripp asked, his pulse skipping around. He felt like he was being whiplashed around, first meeting Oliver essentially on his own, dealing with a yelling match on the front driveway, and now—no cowboys?

"Nothing," Ivory said with a watery smile. "There's nothing wrong with cowboys."

"So why can't he have a hat?"

"Yeah, Mama," Oliver said. "I've always wanted one of those hats."

"Maybe he could get one for the wedding," Tripp said. "I could take him to get it."

Ivory looked at Tripp and said things with her face but without her mouth. He knew she'd protest about the cost, and that was one of the very biggest reasons he couldn't wait to marry her. Then maybe she wouldn't question him every time he walked in with a gallon of milk.

"Ollie," Ivory said, walking over to him. She wiped her

eyes as she went. "Did Daddy tell you anything about me and Tripp?"

"He said you guys were faking."

"Faking what?"

"I don't know. Just faking. He said he wasn't going to let you get away with it."

Ivory looked over her shoulder at Tripp, but he had no idea what to say. Daniel Osburn *was* a lawyer, and he was probably very good at what he did.

"Baby," Ivory said, picking up her son and bringing him into the living room. She looked at Tripp and he joined her on the couch. "Tripp and I are going to get married. Soon. This Saturday."

Tripp wasn't sure how much seven-year-olds knew about time, and Oliver's jaw didn't drop or anything. "Is he your boyfriend, then?"

"Yes," Ivory said with a giggle. "He's my boyfriend."

"The real term is fiancée," Tripp said with a grin. "And if your mom says yes, I really do think you should wear a cowboy hat to the wedding. All of my brothers will be wearing one."

Oliver looked up at Ivory, and Tripp could never say no to the child if he looked at him with those puppy dog eyes. "Mama? Please?" And he could beg too.

Ivory rolled her eyes, but Tripp could tell she wasn't going to say no. "Fine," she said. "But it has to match your suit."

"Great," Tripp said. "We'll go tomorrow." He stood up

and went into the kitchen, suddenly ravenous for a peanut butter chocolate chip cookie.

———

THE FOLLOWING MORNING, Tripp waited on the front steps of the homestead. He'd told Ivory a dozen times that he could come to her house, but she'd insisted on driving Oliver out to Seven Sons. The trip added a half an hour to her day, but she wouldn't see reason in this instance.

In the past seven weeks, he'd learned when to argue with Ivory and when not to, and when it came to her son, he didn't argue.

She was late driving through the gate and under the huge branches of the oak tree in the front yard. By the time she pulled to a stop, he stood at the bottom of the stairs.

"He really is a cowboy," Oliver said as he got out of the backseat.

"I told you he was," Ivory said. "Hey."

"Hey." He leaned down and kissed her quickly. "You ready for this, bud?" he asked Oliver.

Penny barked from somewhere on the ranch, and in the next moment, the black and white cattle dog came tearing around the corner of the house from the backyard. "Whoa," Tripp said, glad the dog listened to him sometimes.

She barked again, and Tripp added, "He doesn't need to be herded, Penny."

"Is this your dog?" Oliver asked, skipping over to Penny. He crouched down and started rubbing behind her ears.

"My brother's," Tripp said, slinging his arm around Ivory's waist and keeping her close to him. "You better go, sweetheart. You're late."

"I know." She cuddled into him for another moment, and then she hurried back to her car, waved as she backed up, and then she was gone.

Terror hit Tripp right in the chest. For the next nine hours, he was responsible for this child. What in the world would they do all day?

"So," he said, taking in a deep breath. "The hat store doesn't open until ten. You want a tour of the ranch?"

"Sure," Oliver said, standing up. "Can Penny come?"

"Oh, she'll do what she wants," Tripp said. "She'll probably come with us for a little bit." He walked over to the boy and nodded toward the backyard. "Let's go see the horses."

Oliver started talking before they'd even reached the corner of the house, and Tripp just let him talk about the park in Amarillo with "the big statue."

"We have a big statue here," Tripp said. "I mean, not on the ranch, but in town. With a fountain."

"Yeah?" Oliver asked. "Can we see that today?"

"Yeah, sure," Tripp said. "There's a bark park right by it, but Penny doesn't like it."

"Why doesn't she like it?"

"Oh, she's a ranch dog, not a pet."

"She liked it when I scratched her ears."

"Yeah, she sure did." He smiled at the boy. "So there's the barn."

"Wow, look at that flag!" Oliver exclaimed. "It's huge."

The American flag painted on the side of the barn was huge, and Tripp loved it. Absolutely loved it. "There's a Texas one on the other side."

"Really?"

"Yep," he said. "I helped my brothers paint them on when we first moved here."

"Can I go see?"

"Go ahead." Oliver ran ahead, Penny barking as she went after him.

"He's cute," a man called, and Tripp turned to find Liam standing on the deck. He detoured that way, casting another glance at Oliver as he went around the barn.

"Yeah, that's Ivory's son," he said, climbing the three steps to the deck and joining his twin. "I'll bring him around to meet everyone."

"You're really going to marry her on Saturday then," Liam said, and it wasn't a question.

"Yes," Tripp said without hesitation.

"I'm happy for you," Liam said, clapping Tripp on the shoulder.

"I'm heading over to talk to Callie tomorrow," he said. "About the cake. You want to come?"

"I don't know, bro," Liam said. "She's still not very happy with me."

"Just don't offer to buy her ranch again," Tripp said. Or maybe he should tell his brother to ask Callie Foster to marry him. That way, the Shining Star would have the money it needed, and Liam would have the woman he'd liked for so long.

"I know, I know," Liam said, rolling his eyes. "That was stupid. Rhett's already tried it, and I shouldn't have brought it up. I just want her to be...happy."

"I understand," Tripp said, because he felt the exact same way about Ivory. He couldn't believe that their relationship these past seven weeks hadn't meant something to her—and something more than a favor. But he honestly didn't know how she felt about him.

"Tripp," Oliver called. "Come see this horse."

"I gotta go," he said.

"Bring the boy in for waffles after you see the horses," Liam said. "I'll heat up the syrup."

"Yep," Tripp said, heading down the steps and down the path to the barn. He walked Oliver around the ranch, giving him peppermints to treat the horses and introducing him to Wyatt and Jeremiah, as well as the ranch hands that worked Seven Sons.

He did take the child back to the house for waffles, and by the time they left to go buy a cowboy hat, Tripp was pretty sure he wasn't the only one who'd realized the magic of a seven-year-old.

"All right," he said. "Let's go get you a cowboy hat."

Tripp felt like the past few weeks had been filled with

prayer, and he kept the stream going so he could find the right cowboy hat that would make Oliver—and his mother—happy.

# 16

"Mama, look at me!" Oliver burst into the house, and Ivory stood up from the kitchen table where she'd been staring at her laptop.

Seven more necklace orders. Why hadn't these come in when she was desperate for them? She left the computer and turned toward her son.

He galloped toward her as if he was riding a horse—and he certainly looked the part. "Wow," she said, laughing. "Look at you, my little cowboy." She reached down and tickled him, causing him to giggle in his high-pitched voice.

Tripp came inside and closed the door, carrying two boxes of pizza. Her personal savior.

"Hey," he said, drawing out the word and putting a lot of happiness into it. She wasn't sure what that meant. Had today been hard for him with Oliver all day? "How was work?"

"Great," she said, taking the pizza from him. "I missed you at lunch."

"Well, we went to the pancake house for lunch. Did you know this kid can eat *two* cheeseburgers?"

"Hey," Oliver said. "You said you wouldn't tell her."

"They were sliders," Tripp said. "And then he ate a bunch of Jeremiah's Christmas crack."

"Christmas what?" Ivory asked, setting the boxes on the counter and opening one. All cheese. Which meant Oliver had already gotten to Tripp. One day, and the child had the big, burly, broad-shouldered cowboy wrapped around his little finger.

"It's toffee, but only kind of," he said. "Made with—"

"Crackers," Oliver interrupted. He sat at the bar and took a piece of pizza out of the box.

"Hey," Ivory said. "Plate."

"Daddy doesn't make me use a plate."

Ivory's motion stuttered as she got out three plates from the cupboard. She faced Oliver and cocked her eyebrows. "I'm not Daddy. This is our house, and we eat like civilized people here."

Tripp opened the other box and took out two pieces of supreme pizza and put them on a plate. He sat beside Oliver and looked at the boy, who put his pizza on a plate too.

"Crackers and toffee?" Ivory asked when no one said anything else.

"It's *so* good, Mama," Oliver said. "It had chocolate on top, with all these nuts."

"Almonds," Tripp said.

"Sounds delicious," she said, taking her own pizza and sitting on the other side of Oliver. "What else did you guys do today?" The weight of her jewelry orders wouldn't go away, and once she got Oliver going, the boy could talk, and talk, and talk.

He told a great tale about the ranch, and no, she hadn't known about the American flag on the barn, or the "huge" Texas flag on the other side. She wasn't surprised by them. Texans were some of the most patriotic people on the planet, especially the cowboys.

Oliver told her about the waffles he'd eaten for breakfast. "They didn't taste like yours at all, Mama," and Ivory looked over his head to see Tripp shaking his head and smiling.

"My brother makes them from scratch," he said.

"Ah." She nodded and picked up another piece of pizza. Maybe she could make one necklace tonight after Oliver went to bed.

"Then we went to the hat store, and I tried on so many hats. There were like, a hundred of them there."

Ivory laughed. "Probably more than a hundred," she said.

"And Tripp got a new hat too," Oliver said.

"He did, huh?" Ivory looked at the handsome cowboy who had turned her whole world upside down. "What kind of hat?"

"It's a secret," he said. "For the wedding."

"I thought it was the bride who wasn't supposed to be seen before the wedding."

"And apparently, the cowboy," Tripp said.

"After that," Oliver continued as if Ivory and Tripp weren't having another conversation. "We went horseback riding, and Tripp showed me how to throw this rope." He made a motion with his arm that didn't look anything like what Ivory had seen the cowboys do in the rodeo.

"Wow," Ivory said. "A real cowboy afternoon."

"And now we're here," Oliver said. "And he said tomorrow, we can go to the water park."

"Oh, is that what he said?" She raised her eyebrows at Tripp, who only shrugged. Yes, she'd asked him to watch Oliver during the day this week while she worked. Next week, while she and Tripp went on a honeymoon, Kate was taking him.

Ivory's pulse started bobbing beneath her breastbone at the very thought of a honeymoon with Tripp. But he'd suggested that if they wanted Daniel to think this relationship and marriage were real, they better take all the steps.

So she had the engagement story, and all the pieces she needed to make a real wedding, and now the forthcoming honeymoon. They'd only be gone for a week, because she had to be in court the following Monday.

Ivory put the last piece of pizza in her mouth while Oliver asked Tripp about something. It felt nice to let her mind wander and not be the only one focused on her son.

She got up and put her plate in the sink, honestly wondering why she insisted on using something that created more work for her.

"Bath time," she said. Oliver ignored her, and she cocked her hip. "Come on. You stink. I can actually smell you from here."

"Go on, bud," Tripp said. "We can't do fun things if we don't bathe afterward."

"Okey dokey," Oliver said, jumping down from the barstool and skipping down the hall.

"Okey dokey?" Ivory repeated. She looked at Tripp, slightly annoyed that he'd gotten her son to head to the bathtub without an argument.

"It's something Liam says," Tripp said. "My brothers all really liked Oliver."

Ivory nodded. He was a great kid, and hey, if they only had to feed him waffles once or twice....

*That's not fair*, she told herself. Tripp had spent all day with her son, and he wasn't getting paid. Tears filled her eyes unexpectedly, and she spun around and started rinsing the dishes.

She'd just composed herself when Tripp came up behind her and wrapped his arms around her. His lips landed against the back of her neck. "It was a great day," he whispered. "Thank you for letting me have him."

Ivory couldn't help leaning into his touch. She couldn't help how soft her feelings for him had become. Seven weeks was the longest she'd kept Tripp in her life, and she couldn't push him away now. Not when Daniel suspected the relationship wasn't real.

And in that moment, with Tripp's strong body behind her, and his soft lips kissing her, she realized she didn't want to push him away.

She turned in his arms and kissed him, hoping he would get that message without her having to say a word.

"I can't wait until Saturday," he whispered, breaking the kiss for a moment and then starting it again.

*Me either*, Ivory wanted to say.

So she did.

———

"I CAN'T BELIEVE I'm doing this," Ivory said, sliding her hands down her stomach. She felt like throwing up.

She couldn't back out now.

"It's okay," Kate said. "You look beautiful. This place is perfect." She grinned at Ivory with such light in her eyes, and Ivory took a deep breath.

This was her wedding day. She should be happy—and look it—and she smiled at her best friend. "You're the best." She hugged Kate and took the bouquet from her.

"Don's ready for you," she said. "I'm going to go sit down." She squealed and hurried out of the room where she'd helped Ivory get dressed.

She looked at herself one more time in the mirror, and she really liked how the wedding dress had turned out. She'd bought a hat with part of her dry cleaning paycheck, and it had a nearly transparent veil that fell to her chin.

Daniel had called that morning, but she'd ignored him. He wasn't going to ruin today, and he wasn't going to win the custody hearing.

*Please*, Ivory prayed.

Then she took a deep breath and stepped out of the room. Don, Kate's husband, stood there, and he offered her his arm. "Thank you," she said to him. She had not invited her parents to the wedding, and she'd needed someone to walk her down the aisle. Tripp had said one of his brothers would do it, but Ivory wanted to keep some distance between them and herself. Why, she wasn't sure.

Because Tripp was going to be part of her life for a while now.

*Permanently?* she wondered to herself, burying the thought deep as she left the house where the Foster sisters lived. She knew who they were, of course, though she'd never been out to their ranch. She'd met with Evelyn about meeting Tripp at a cute house on Quail Creek Road.

She wasn't sure why Tripp had suggested the Shining Star Ranch over the one he and his brothers owned, but Kate had been right. This place was perfect, as evidenced by the aisle leading from the back deck to the gazebo in the corner of the yard, which was decorated with ribbons and flowers and tea lights.

Only about twenty people sat in the chairs, and the most important one waited at the top of the steps in the gazebo. Before she knew it, Don passed her to Tripp, who gazed at her with the most adoring look of...love.

Fear gripped her heart and squeezed. Squeezed hard.

She supposed she loved him too, on some level, but not the one she should as a wife. She honestly wasn't sure she could love a man like that again. Because love like that took everything from a person. Ruthlessly and without care.

"Wow," he said quietly, and she could say the same about him. He wore a midnight black suit, a bright blue tie, and those delicious cowboy boots—and his hat. A new one she hadn't seen before.

"Is that the hat?"

"My brand-new dress hat," he said. "My wedding hat."

"I like it." She looked down at Oliver. "And you look dashing too." His black hat matched Tripp's, and Ivory had to admit she liked that. Liked the pair of them a lot. Liked that they got along. Liked the idea of a family with the two of them.

Such things had kept her from dating for years. She didn't want to repeat her mistakes with Daniel. She didn't need a man to babysit in addition to Oliver. Didn't need a man choosing literally everything under the sun over his wife and child, as he searched for "his own happiness."

But Tripp wasn't anything like Daniel, and maybe if she'd allowed their previous relationships to go beyond her fear, she might have known that before standing at the altar with him.

"Good evening," Pastor Daniels said, drawing Ivory's attention to the man of God that was going to marry her and Tripp. "What a beautiful night for a wedding. Am I right?" He spoke in the same animated, joyful tone he did while standing at the pulpit, and Ivory's spirits lifted.

Marrying Tripp was the right thing to do.

She squeezed Tripp's hand, and he squeezed back.

And while this idea had started out trivial, Ivory felt like this tie to Tripp was very, very real. She just wished she wasn't so nervous for what came next.

*The I-do.*

*The honeymoon.*

*The married life.*

*The court hearing.*

"Ivory?"

She startled and looked at Tripp. "Mm?"

"It's your turn to say I do." He glanced at Pastor Daniels, and embarrassment filled Ivory.

"Oh, right. I do."

Pastor Daniels smiled at her and asked Tripp if he'd love and cherish her, protect her, and take care of her for the rest of her days. The words sure were nice, but she'd heard them before.

"I do," Tripp said, and they faced each other.

"You may kiss your wife," Pastor Daniels said.

Tripp chuckled as he held her close, swayed with her, and then kissed her.

And wow, what a kiss—with her husband.

Now if she could only get her brain to stop revolving through the list.

*The honeymoon.*

*The married life.*

*The court hearing.*

# 17

Tripp hefted his suitcase into the back of his truck, sliding it next to Ivory's. He paused for a moment, the brutal Texas heat still hanging in the air though the sun had sunk an hour ago.

The wedding was done. Over.

The dinner had been successful, and Jeremiah's face could've lit the entire state for a week with how much he'd beamed.

Daniel had not showed up and caused a problem. Oliver was adorable in his suit, and Ivory....

Wow, Ivory made Tripp's mouth dry.

And she was legally his now.

"Ready?" she asked, joining him at the tailgate.

"Uh." He lifted his hand and wiped his forehead. "I think so?"

"We're going on a cruise," she said. "If you forgot something, you can buy it." She looked at him and laced her arm through his. "Right?"

"Right." He looked back toward her house, where her son sat on the front steps, his face illuminated by a video game machine screen. "So we're ready to take Oliver down to Kate's?"

"I think so."

"And he'll be okay?"

"He'll be more than okay," she said. "She has kids the same age, and they get along great."

"So she's a better babysitter than me," Tripp said in a teasing tone. "I get it."

Ivory giggled, put her hand in his, and they walked back up to the steps. "Where's your bag, bud?" Tripp asked. "It's time to go."

"In my room," he said without looking up.

"Turn it off, Ollie," Ivory said as Tripp started climbing the steps. Today had been a very long, very wonderful day. Wyatt had filmed the ceremony and streamed it for their two brothers and their parents who hadn't come. Everything had looked very real on the outside. At least Tripp hoped so.

Once they dropped off Oliver, they were driving to Amarillo and flying to Seattle. They'd be there for less than fifteen hours before the cruise ship boarded and they went north to Alaska.

Tripp hadn't done a ton of traveling, but he knew how to fly from Texas to Seattle. The company he worked for was stationed there, and he'd made the trip several times. He'd seen the huge cruise ships docked along the coast, and when he'd suggested the idea of an Alaskan cruise to Ivory, she hadn't protested.

Which was surprising.

Tripp hadn't let it trouble him, and he couldn't wait to be alone with her. Yes, they'd had plenty of alone-time while Oliver was with his father, but the first few weeks had been strained. Spent arguing about money or what they did and didn't need at the wedding. Making plans, and for Tripp, hoping, hoping, hoping that things would get to this point.

And now he was here.

He grabbed Oliver's bag from his bedroom and went back outside. "All right, partners. Let's go."

Oliver started to giggle. "It's not partners, Tripp. It's pardners. With a D."

"Oh, of course," he said, grinning at the little boy. They moved out of the halo of the porch light at Ivory's house, and Oliver slipped his hand into Tripp's free one. Surprise moved through him, along with a feeling of complete satisfaction. Contentment. Joy.

He looked at Ivory to find her watching him too, and he smiled at her. She ducked her head, but the smile was already on her face, and Tripp had already seen it. He wasn't sure what to pray for in that moment, so he just bowed his head too and thought, *Thank you.*

"Swing me," Oliver said, and Tripp barely had a tight enough hold before the boy launched himself off the ground.

"Baby," Ivory said, clearly not amused. "You've got to give Mama more warning than that."

Tripp agreed, but he didn't say anything. They walked down the street like they were a real family, and he was having a hard time not believing it himself. At the same time, he wondered where this relationship was going to go. Could she grow to love him if he stuck around long enough?

Did he love her?

Tripp certainly felt like he did, and he didn't know what to do with the emotion. It felt too big for his body to contain, too big for the sky surrounding him, too big for the enormity of the universe. His breathing hitched as he realized his love for Ivory, and he desperately didn't want to be the only one who felt this way.

But in that moment, he knew he was.

*Hold on.* The words just came to him, and he decided to do that. He'd hold on to Oliver's hand. And he'd hold on to the vows he'd made that night, even if they were supposed to be trivial. And he'd hold onto his hope that he and Ivory could find a way through this confusing relationship they'd built for themselves.

———

A couple of hours later, he stood up as they called his zone for boarding. His eyes felt like he'd rubbed sandpaper across them, but he managed a smile in Ivory's direction. "Ready, sweetheart?"

"Yes," she said, standing with a sigh. She looked completely worse for the wear, but Tripp knew better than to tell her that. His mother had made sure all seven of her sons knew how to interact with a woman, and a fondness for her moved through him.

"Why do you call me sweetheart?" She looked at him like she really wanted to know.

Tripp simply blinked. "We got married today." He glanced around as if he should be embarrassed by what he'd said.

"I know," she said. "I'm just....never mind."

"No, what?" He inched forward, his muscles suddenly too tight.

"I think you actually think of me as your sweetheart."

"I do," he said. "Is that a problem for you?" He searched her face, but she wouldn't look at him fully.

"I guess not."

"I don't have to use the pet names if they bother you." He wanted to, but he also wanted to keep Ivory in his life long enough to fall in love with him for real.

"They don't bother me," she said. "I just...wonder at their authenticity."

"Ma'am?" The counter clerk gestured for her to move forward, and Tripp nodded in the right direction. Ivory stepped in front of him while Tripp tried to figure out how to tell her what he'd realized himself earlier that evening.

No way he could say *I love you* right now. She'd run to the next departing airplane, luggage or not.

She yawned, and Tripp suddenly felt the urge too. He didn't want to have hard conversations tonight. He just wanted to get to Seattle and rest. They had plenty of time to talk while they were trapped on a cruise ship off the coast of Alaska.

"We can sleep on the plane," he said. "And I checked into the hotel with their app, so we can sleep when we get there too."

"I can't believe you got a hotel in Seattle." She shook her head as she stepped closer to the scanner to board.

"Where else would we go?" he said. "Loitering on the beach in the middle of the night is against the law. Don't ask me how I know that."

"Ooh," she said, her face brightening. "Are you a naughty cowboy?" She laughed as she tipped into him, and Tripp chuckled with her. She scanned her boarding pass and he did too, right behind her. He still wasn't sure this was his life, but surely he wouldn't feel this trashy if he were dead.

"First class is to your left," a flight attendant said, and Ivory turned back to him.

"We're in first class?"

"To your left," he said, smiling at her. She turned and found her seat. They got settled, and Tripp put in his earbuds. He'd be lucky if he was awake when the plane took off, and he asked for another pillow and an extra blanket.

"Anything to drink?" the flight attendant asked.

"Not for me," he said. "Baby?" He looked at Ivory, realizing too late that he'd used another pet name. She blinked first at him and then looked at the flight attendant.

"Nothing for me either. Can I get another pillow too, though?"

"Of course. Headphones?"

"You give out free headphones?"

The flight attendant smiled and stepped away. She returned a moment later with the headphones and the pillow, and Ivory started really settling in. Tripp lifted the armrest between them and said, "You can lay on me if you want. You won't be able to put your seat back until we take off."

"How far does this thing go back?" She reclined the seat, a smile filling her pretty face. "This is amazing. I've never flown first class."

Tripp just smiled at her, fiddled with his phone to find the classical music he wanted to fall asleep to, and watched her put her seat back up. She did build herself a little bed against his body, and Tripp didn't mind one single bit.

In fact, he lifted his arm around her shoulders so she could snuggle in further, and once she did, Tripp knew he'd died and gone to heaven.

———

WOKE SOMETIME LATER, the violins in his ears blocking the other noise on the airplane. Not that there was other noise. Everything was mostly dark. His mouth felt stuck together, and he needed to use the bathroom. He glanced at Ivory, still nestled into him, and carefully eased her over against the window.

She didn't wake, and he got up and moved toward the back. "Everything okay?" the flight attendant asked.

"Yes, just need to use the bathroom," he said, his eyes fully adjusted to the darkness now. "Could I get some water on my way back to my seat?"

"Of course. I'll get you a little bottle."

"Thanks." He checked his phone for the time, took care of his business, and returned to his seat to find Ivory awake. "Hey," he said, sliding into his seat. "Sorry to wake you."

She gave him a sleepy smile, and he lifted his arm again, a clear invitation for her to rest against his side again. She did, and Tripp managed to get his water bottle open with one hand, take a long drink, and offer the rest to Ivory.

She sipped it and whispered, "Tripp, you're the best guy I've ever been with."

"You must've been with some real losers, then," he said, adding a quick laugh.

"You met Daniel."

"Yeah," Tripp said. He'd always wanted to ask her what she'd seen in him, because there must've been something. She'd married him when she wouldn't even date Tripp for longer than a month. She'd had a child with him. She was forever linked to him, whether she wanted to be or not.

"He was very charming when we met," she said. "When I first started dating you, you reminded me a lot of him."

"Oh." Tripp didn't like that at all.

"But you're the sun, and he's the moon. Just because you have a lot of charisma doesn't mean you're a jerk."

He pressed his lips to her forehead and leaned his head back, his eyes drifting closed. "Thanks, baby." He started falling asleep, the vibration of the plane very soothing. With his thirst quenched and Ivory in his arms, everything was perfect.

*I think I'm falling in love with you.*

The words wafted through his mind, but he wasn't sure if he'd thought them or if Ivory had said them. He was warm, and content, and a sense of peace took him all the way into unconsciousness.

He woke next when Ivory said, "Tripp, we've landed and it's time to get off the plane." Tripp blinked a couple of times, the cabin now filled with too-bright light.

Clumsily, he gathered his earbuds and his phone, the empty bottle magically gone. He stood and shouldered his backpack and looked at Ivory. "Okay," he said. "Leg one is done."

# 18

I vory actually felt pretty decent as Tripp collected their baggage from the carousel and led her outside to get a car. "The hotel isn't very far," he said, joining the taxi line.

She didn't know how to answer. She hadn't asked him if he'd booked two rooms, because why would he? They were married, for crying out loud.

*Married.*

Horror struck like lightning, and everything inside of Ivory felt like it had been encased in plastic. She'd promised herself she'd never get married again. She didn't want to be tied to someone like that. Didn't want to be micromanaged and made to feel like she couldn't make her own decisions.

*Tripp doesn't do that,* she told herself as he stepped up to the podium and gave the hotel name to the man there. Sure, he took care of business, but that didn't mean Ivory couldn't do things herself.

"Here we go," he said, handing his suitcase to the cab driver. Once everything was in, the car sped away from the airport. Ivory relaxed slightly, but all she could think about was the sleeping arrangements. She and Tripp hadn't really talked about their life after the wedding. Everything had been so wrapped up in making it look and feel real to everyone in Three Rivers. To Daniel.

And after that, all she'd been able to focus on was the hearing. "Tripp?" she asked, and he turned his head toward her as if in slow motion.

"The Crowne," the driver said, turning before Ivory could say anything.

*I think I'm falling in love with you.*

She'd spoken those words on the airplane, but Tripp obviously hadn't heard her. He hadn't responded, and she'd found him asleep a few seconds later. She wasn't even sure they were true, which meant she had no right to say them out loud.

She folded her arms as the taxi came to a stop. She wasn't even sure she was capable of loving another man, but if she was, she wanted it to be Tripp.

*Wanting something doesn't make it true,* she told herself. She'd learned that from Daniel, because she had desperately wanted him to love her, to stay in Three Rivers with her and Oliver, to keep their family together.

None of that had happened, despite her best efforts.

Tripp got out of the car, and Ivory pulled herself out of her thoughts. He paid the driver and started toward the entrance to the hotel. Even in the middle of the night, a doorman stood there to open the door for them, guiding them over to the front desk to check in. As sleep-deprived as Ivory was, she still noticed the grandeur of this hotel. Everything glinted with gold and light, and Tripp barely seemed to see it.

She stood half a step behind him while he collected their key, and he led her to the elevator like he'd stayed here before. When she asked him if he had, he said, "A few times, actually."

"Why?"

"Planes getting delayed, stuff like that," he said. "Seattle has some terrible ice storms in the winter."

"Do you travel a lot for work?" she asked as the elevator shot up toward the twenty-first floor.

"Very little, actually," he said. "I usually only come up here for our big mastermind meeting at the beginning of a project. A few times a year."

She nodded, flinching when the elevator dinged. They were on their floor. He only had one key. He didn't seem to be worried about the number of beds in the room, or changing in front of her, or anything.

But Ivory's mouth felt like she'd stuffed it full of rice cakes and sawdust—which were about the same thing, in her opinion. He keyed his way into the room and sighed as he dropped their bags to the floor.

He switched on a couple of lights. "Here we are."

Ivory followed him inside, finding the bathroom on her

left right inside the door, and a huge room spreading in front of her. A couch. A desk with a chair. A huge TV.

One bed.

He went over to the window and closed the black-out curtains, saying, "I know our marriage wasn't really a thing, Ivory. I'll sleep on the couch."

"You don't have to do that." She wasn't even sure where the words had come from. Of course she wasn't going to sleep with him.

He turned toward her, his eyebrows raised. "What?"

"That's a king-size bed," she said. "Plenty big for both of us." If she crammed way over on her side, there'd be feet between them.

He walked back toward her. "I'll sleep on the couch." He bent, picked up his bag, and went into the bathroom. Ivory felt like someone had filled her body with jumping beans. She hurried to haul her bag to the bed and open it too, changing out of her clothes and into her pajamas as quickly as she could.

She had her suitcase laid out on the luggage holder and was walking around the bed, untucking all the sheets when Tripp came out of the bathroom. He wore a pair of basket-ball shorts and a T-shirt, and sans cowboy hat, he was still the sexiest man Ivory had been with, ever.

He opened the closet and pulled out an extra blanket and moved over to the couch without looking at her.

Her chest cavity seemed too small for her heart. Desperation clogged her throat, and she said, "Tripp, really."

Without looking at her, he spread the blanket over the cushions and started pulling off the pillows. "Really what, Ivory?"

"You'll never fit on that thing. You're too tall."

He straightened then and looked at her. Really looked at her. "I'm in love with you." He said the words without any stutter at all. His dark eyes burned with emotion, and Ivory felt the truthfulness of how he felt about her way down deep in her soul.

"And we're married," he said. "If I get in that bed with you, I'm going to want to do a lot more than sleep." He kept the bed between them as he went over to the side by the nightstand and picked up a pillow. "The couch is fine. I'll be asleep in five seconds anyway. I'm beat."

If he was so tired, maybe he could sleep in the bed with her and not do anything. She didn't suggest that though, because she was still processing what he'd said.

*I'm in love with you.*

He lay down on the couch and pulled the blanket over him. "Good-night, baby," he said, reaching up and snapping off the lamp above him. The other two flanking the bed stayed on, so Ivory could still see his face.

She appreciated this man and everything he'd done for her. She enjoyed spending her time and her life with him. She needed him to help her win the custody hearing.

But could she love him too?

She knew she wasn't ready for a physical relationship with him, whether they were married or not, so she simply

199

said, "Good-night, Tripp," turned off her lamps too, and climbed into the big, king-sized bed alone.

*Dear Lord,* she prayed into the darkness. *Help me see clearly how I feel about this man and be brave enough to tell him, the way he just told me.*

With that prayer running through her mind, Ivory fell asleep.

———

"It's so BLUE," Ivory said, leaning against the railing. Tripp joined her, one arm slipping easily around her waist. Everything with Tripp was easy—except navigating their sleeping arrangements. He'd booked the Norwegian suite on the ship, and it actually had two twin mattresses they could push together and convert into a king-sized bed.

They hadn't done that, but the four feet between them felt very close and yet extremely far away.

"I think it's beautiful," he said.

"It is." She leaned into his body, appreciating the warmth from him. While it was summertime, the temperatures this far north were still quite cool to her. Especially compared to Texas.

"What's been your favorite part of the cruise?" he asked.

"The blue whales," she said immediately. "I've never seen anything like that." And she hadn't. The day the ship had come across two whales had opened her eyes to a whole new world.

He smiled out at all the water, also something that intrigued her. "I liked the whales too," he said. "I think I liked that band that played the first night."

"Really?" she teased. "You're going to go with a band when we're surrounded by glaciers and mountains that rise right out of the ocean?" She pushed against his chest, laughing. "That's just lame."

He laughed with her. "I also liked that key lime pie they have on the buffet. Good thing we have one more dinner on this ship. I might eat only pie tonight."

"Yeah, and then I'll have to listen to you complain about how sick you are all night long." She rolled her eyes. The man certainly liked food, and he could eat a lot.

"I haven't complained," he said. "Not even one night."

"No, you just toss and turn and groan."

He stepped away from her and leaned his hip against the side of the boat, looking fully at her now. "You're awake for that?"

She shrugged, because she didn't want him to know she couldn't fall asleep until he did. "Sometimes."

"I've talked to you, and you haven't responded."

"Maybe I didn't hear you."

"Maybe?" He cocked his eyebrows at her.

"I think I heard you say one night that you wished you hadn't eaten three pieces of chocolate cake."

Tripp's eyes danced, and oh, Ivory loved this game. So she was completely unprepared when he said, "Yeah, and last night, I said I hoped you could fall in love with me too."

He swept his gaze back out over the open water. "Did you hear that?"

Yes, she'd heard him say that. Her first instinct was to deny it. But her voice said, "Yes."

"How *are* you feeling?" he asked. "If I can be so bold as to ask. You never really...say anything about how you feel."

Tremors shook her body, and the breeze coming off the water now felt like a gale. "Uh, I'm...."

*Falling in love with you.*

She'd said it once. He hadn't heard her. Could she say it again?

"I think I'm falling in love with you," she said, the words barely meeting her own ears. "But I'm scared, and I just need to go slow."

Tripp took her into his arms, the strength of him so comforting and sure. "Slow I can do, sweetheart." He leaned down and kissed her, and there was no "think" in Ivory's statement. She was definitely falling in love with him.

And falling always hurt, so how was she going to survive this?

———

LATER THAT NIGHT, Tripp did indeed eat too much pie for dinner. He tossed and he turned and he groaned. "Did you hear that?" he asked.

Ivory giggled, because yes, she'd heard it.

She also heard him when he got out of bed, and she felt

it when he peeled back her covers. Nerves had paralyzed her, but the moment he slid into bed beside her calmed her. Soothed her. "Ah, yes," he said, sighing into her hair. "This is better."

"This is a twin-sized bed," she whispered. She wasn't exactly uncomfortable, but she liked to spread out while she slept. Have all the blankets untucked and ready to be bunched up around her legs if that was how she wanted them.

"Then let's push the beds together," Tripp murmured, kissing her ear and then down her neck. Ivory liked the showers of sparks moving through her, though her muscles felt tight and her stomach was writhing—and not because she'd eaten too much pie.

"Okay," she whispered.

"Okay?" Tripp asked.

She turned in his arms and kissed him, this gentle, kind cowboy she'd grown very, very fond of. Maybe she didn't need to be so afraid of him. Maybe their love story wouldn't end in a tragedy. Maybe she needed to trust herself more than she currently did. Maybe love didn't always shatter hearts and lives and promises.

He deepened the kiss, and Ivory went with him. As quickly as he'd slid into her bed with her, he slipped away. In the next moment, he'd pushed his bed flush against hers and was sitting on his side of the mattress.

She watched him take a deep breath, and then another, and she smiled though he couldn't see her. He adjusted his pillows and lay down, and this time, Ivory was the one to slide over toward him and ease into his embrace.

"I love you," he whispered, and Ivory accepted his kiss, accepted that he wasn't anything like Daniel, and accepted that perhaps he really did love her.

After all, no one was that good of a liar. Were they?

# 19

Tripp sat in his ergonomic chair, the moment of truth in front of him. "All right," he said. "Let's see if I got everything hooked up right." He pushed the button to turn on his computer, which should make a chiming noise as it started and light up all three screens he'd arranged on the desk in Ivory's jewelry studio.

Her house was on the smallish side—only three bedrooms and two bathrooms—and there hadn't been enough space to put his animation setup in the dining room.

And nothing happened. "Hmm," he said, looking at Oliver. "Did you get that power cord plugged in?"

"Yeah," Oliver said, kneeling down to get behind the desk again. "Oh, just into the power strip."

Tripp stood up and looked over the equipment to find the bright orange power strip not connected to the wall. "Okay, that has to be plugged in too."

Oliver did it and backed out from behind the desk. "Done."

Tripp pushed the button again, and this time the chime sounded and the screens brightened. "All right," he said, grinning at Oliver. He lifted his hand so the kid could give him high five, which he did. "Let's see how everything fared in the move."

His brothers had brought over Tripp's belongings while he and Ivory were on their cruise. Church was in a couple of hours, and the custody hearing tomorrow, so Tripp wanted to get his workstation up and ready so he didn't fall too far behind on his work. He clicked around, and all of his files and projects were there, and he leaned back in his chair. To his surprise, Oliver climbed right into his lap. He smiled to himself as he held the boy, pure love flowing through him.

"Can you watch movies on this?" Oliver asked.

"I *make* movies on this," Tripp said. "That's what I do for a job."

"You make movies?" Oliver sounded like Tripp had told him he was Santa Claus.

"Yeah. Look." Tripp clicked open a project he'd worked on last year. "For this one, I animated all of the gnomes." He started the movie, and it began playing on the middle screen. "I have to do it one character at a time." He opened the files just for Linus, the gnome with glasses. "One movement at a time. I do all the coloring and shading. All the facial expressions." He showed Oliver the stills of the gnome and then set him in motion. He moved identically to the gnome in the movie, with the human actors around him.

"How do they talk to him?" Oliver asked.

"They don't," Tripp said with a laugh. "They interact with a puppet or something, in front of a green screen. It looks like this." He opened the footage he got from the movie studio in LA. "See?" He played the raw file of the man talking to the gnomes. "He's got a cardboard box there for the gnome. That's how he knows where to look."

"Cool," Oliver said.

"Yeah," Tripp said at the same time Ivory called, "It's time for breakfast," down the hall.

He tipped Oliver forward so the boy would slide off his lap. "Come on, bud. I think I smell bacon." His brothers had brought food to the house too, and Tripp had specifically requested a lot of bacon.

Sure enough, Ivory stood in the kitchen in her silky pink pajamas, a pair of tongs in her hand as she took bacon out of the pan and laid it on a plate of paper towels. Tripp stalled while Oliver skipped into the kitchen, watching this woman he was married to.

He could hardly believe this was his life, and he pressed his eyes closed to give thanks to God. He'd never been this happy before, even when he'd thought he had everything he wanted in Austin.

Thoughts of Maddie crept into his mind, and he shoved them right back out. He'd dreamt of marrying her too, and he'd even bought her a ring. The night he was going to ask her to marry him, she'd broke up with him.

Through a text.

Her sudden ending of the relationship without any explanation at all had prompted his move from Austin to Three Rivers, where Rhett had just bought the ranch. Jeremiah had just been stood up at the altar, and Liam had been suffering from an on-again, off-again relationship for about a month.

All four brothers were so much happier now—at least in Tripp's opinion.

"Are you going to stand there all morning?" Ivory asked, and Tripp blinked to find her teasing smile only inches away from his face. "Come eat." She tipped up onto her toes and kissed him, and Tripp suddenly wanted to eat quickly and go back to bed. With her.

But with Oliver here....

"Smells good," Tripp said, following her to the kitchen table, where Oliver already sat.

Ivory put a pitcher of apple juice on the table and sat down too. "Let's say grace, baby," she said, looking at her son. Oliver put his forkful of scrambled eggs down and waited. Ivory looked at Tripp. "Will you?"

"Yeah, sure," Tripp said, closing his eyes as he reached for Oliver's hand and then Ivory's. "Lord, we're grateful to be here together this morning. Help us to do what's right. Help us to listen at church today. Bless this Sabbath for Thy good. Amen."

Oliver went right back to scarfing down his eggs, and Tripp chuckled as he spooned some onto his plate and took a healthy amount of bacon too.

"So the hearing is tomorrow," Ivory said. "Are we ready?"

Tripp met her eye, and he could easily see how nervous she was. "I'm ready."

"Ready," Oliver said.

"You get to meet with the judge beforehand," Ivory said, reaching over and smoothing her son's hair off his forehead. "Remember?"

"Yep."

"You can tell them whatever you want." She smiled at him, but it was shaky, and Oliver didn't even seem to notice her emotion.

"I know, Mama."

She nodded and lifted her coffee mug to her lips. She hadn't taken any food yet, and Tripp lifted his eyebrows at her. "You're not eating?"

Ivory picked up a piece of bacon and took a bite. "I'm not very hungry."

Tripp didn't know everything about Ivory, because their romance had been a bit accelerated. But he knew her declaration of non-hunger had everything to do with her anxiety. He wished he could erase it from her life. Wasn't that why he'd married her?

*Tomorrow*, he told himself. She'd eat a lot tomorrow, because she was going to win the custody case against her ex-husband.

———

"Right through there, bud," Tripp said, gently pushing on Oliver's shoulder so he'd go with the court-appointed escort. "We'll be right here when you come out."

Oliver took a step and then turned around, something on his face that made Tripp's heart hurt. He crouched down, and Oliver flew back into his arms.

"Hey, it's okay," Tripp said. "You just answer the questions. It won't be hard." He held the boy tight, tight, very aware of Ivory's sniffling beside him. He wasn't sure what he'd done to make Oliver like him so much. Maybe it was all the times they'd gone to lunch. Or the splash pad. Or out to the ranch, where Oliver could play with Penny and eat his brother's desserts. No matter what it was, Tripp found himself desperately praying that God would allow this child to stay with him and Ivory full-time.

He separated from Oliver and held the boy by the shoulders. "You tell them the truth, okay? That's all that matters."

Oliver nodded, turned, and went with the woman in uniform. He twined his fingers through hers, and she smiled at him, and then Tripp and Ivory. "We'll be about fifteen minutes is all."

Ivory lifted her hand in a wave, and she crumpled into Tripp as the door closed behind the escort and her son.

"It's okay," Tripp repeated, but he wasn't sure if he was

trying to reassure her or himself. "We have to be calm for the hearing."

"I know." Ivory reached into her purse and pulled out a small packet of tissues. "I'm going to pull myself together." She gave him a watery smile and slipped into the restroom. Tripp looked both ways down the hall, this being his first time in family court. Everything felt wide and tall and sterile, with white tile on the floor and rich wood on the walls.

He caught sight of Daniel Osburn, and Tripp turned away from him. But Daniel wouldn't miss him. Whether he'd say hello or not was a different story, and Tripp reached up and adjusted his cowboy hat. He should say hello. Daniel was part of his life now, whether he liked it or not.

Turning, he came face-to-face with the man. "Hello, Daniel," Tripp said, glad his voice didn't betray how he felt about this man though a river of distaste and nerves ran through him. He stuck out his hand for Ivory's ex to shake.

Daniel looked at his hand and then back at Tripp. "Tripp." They shook hands, and the motion was quick and then over and done. "Oliver's in with the judge?"

"Yep."

"And Ivory?"

"She's in the bathroom."

If Daniel felt bad about making his once-wife cry, he didn't show it. He simply moved the folder he held from one hand to the other and shifted his weight. "Okay, well, I'll see you in there."

"Yep." He watched Daniel walk away, wondering what

was in that thin folder. It couldn't be holding much, and Tripp told himself there was nothing to find. He and Ivory had gotten engaged and then married. Their wedding had taken seven weeks to plan; it wasn't like they'd run off to the first spot that would marry them.

He drew in a deep breath and pulled his phone out of his back pocket. *The hearing is about to start,* he tapped out on his brothers text string. *Prayers would be great about now.*

Rhett sent back a pair of praying hands, and Liam said *You got it, bro.* Wyatt and Jeremiah didn't respond immediately, because they were probably out on the ranch, but Micah, Tripp's youngest brother, said, *Good luck, Tripp.*

Skylar sent the same emoji as Rhett, and Tripp looked up when Ivory came out of the bathroom. She looked fantastic, with all the proper pieces in place. "Verona called," she said, stepping back into his side. He slid his arm around her and held her close. "She wants me to come by the dry cleaner this afternoon if I can."

"Can you?" Tripp asked.

"I think so." She looked up at him, and Tripp hoped he'd get lost in her eyes for the rest of this life. "Thank you for being here."

"Of course." He pressed his lips to her forehead, and the door in front of them where Oliver had gone opened. He came skipping out, and the judge stood in the doorway, a smile on her face.

Ivory bent to scoop Oliver into her arms, asking, "Heya, baby. How'd it go?"

"Good," Oliver said, looking from her to Tripp. "I told the truth."

"Good boy, bud," Tripp said with a smile.

"Okay." Ivory set her son down. "Let's go see what happens." She took Oliver's hand in one of hers and Tripp's in the other, and they turned to go into the courtroom.

*Please*, Tripp prayed, because he figured if he was going to ask his brothers to pray for him, he could do it too.

# 20

I vory wanted to squeeze all the nerves out of her body. But she held Oliver's hand lightly and let Tripp hold hers. As insignificant as she was in the universe, she couldn't change what was about to happen. She'd spent most of the flight home from Seattle praying for the outcome she wanted to have today, and the Lord knew what she wanted.

Didn't mean she was going to get it, if her past track record was any indication. But she also knew she'd come out the other side okay, just as Tripp had said. No, she didn't want to deal with Daniel more than she had to. She didn't want to drive Oliver back and forth more than she currently did—and that was only twice a month.

*If that*, she told herself, as Daniel sometimes cancelled the weekends he got with his son. She had all the dates for the past year in a folder, but she wouldn't be speaking today unless the judge asked her a direct question.

"Good morning," Byron said just inside the courtroom, and Ivory almost burst into tears again. She was so happy her lawyer was here, that she wouldn't have to face the judge alone. She didn't even know how.

"Morning," she said, making her voice as strong as possible. "You remember Tripp?"

"Of course." Everyone shook hands, and Byron carried a black briefcase as he led the way to their table. "I have a good feeling about today," he said with a smile.

"My mama got me a cowboy hat," Oliver said. "Kind of like yours."

"Is that right?" Byron smiled down at Oliver. "How did your meeting with Judge Tomlinson go?"

"Fine," Oliver said. "I told the truth."

"Always good," Byron said, glancing at Ivory and then Tripp.

Ivory wished she had a good feeling about today, but one glance over to Daniel's table, and she felt like crumbling again. She squared her shoulders as she sat down. She would not let that man influence her anymore. She'd spent a year after their divorce in therapy, building up her self-confidence again, learning how to trust herself and her thoughts, and rebuilding her self-worth.

He wouldn't win this custody complaint, and Ivory popped right back to her feet as Judge Tomlinson entered.

"Good morning," she said, and both Byron and Daniel responded. "Be seated."

Only she, Tripp, and Oliver sat while the judge looked

down at her papers. "All right, Mister Osburn. You've filed for full custody on the complaint that your ex-wife, Ivory Osburn—now Ivory Walker—can't provide for your minor son, Oliver." She peered up over the edge of the case file. "I'm assuming you have proof."

"Right here, Your Honor," he said, lifting a folder. Ivory's stomach clenched with the thought of what was in that folder. He handed it to the bailiff, who took it up to the judge. The silence as she leafed through the paperwork felt deafening and crushing, and Ivory fidgeted.

Byron glanced at her, a stern warning to stop. Hold still. She managed to do it, but only when Tripp reached over and took her hand in his. He wore a suit and tie with his cowboy hat today, as if they were getting married all over again.

Ivory suddenly felt like she was drowning. She owed him so much, and there was no way she'd ever be able to pay him back.

"Mister Hammond?" Judge Tomlinson asked.

"We have what I'm sure will counteract everything in Mister Osburn's file right here," Byron said. "My client is now employed by Verona's dry cleaner, right here in town. It's a full-time position with benefits. Verona and Harmon love her. She's current on all of her bills, debts, and mortgage. And in fact, Miss Osburn has just married Tripp Walker, and the couple is looking forward to continuing to raise Oliver and perhaps expand their family."

Ivory almost bolted from the courtroom. She and Tripp

had been intimate, but she'd honestly given no thought to having another baby.

His baby.

Her panic must've put off a scent, because the pressure from Tripp's hand increased. She couldn't get her pulse to quiet though, and she could barely hear the proceedings of the case. Not that anything was happening. Byron had handed over their evidence, and the judge was now looking at it.

A few minutes felt like a few hours. "Mister Walker," Judge Tomlinson finally said, and Tripp let go of her hand so he could stand up.

"Your Honor." He was pure perfection, and Ivory wondered how in the world she'd caught his eye.

"You married Miss Osburn of your own free will?"

"Yes, Your Honor."

"Do you love her?"

"Completely."

"And you're ready to take on the role of step-father?"

"Yes, Your Honor." He buttoned his suit coat and faced her brazenly, evenly, despite the eyes on him.

"Have you consummated your relationship?"

Ivory's face burned, but Tripp simply said, "Yes, Your Honor."

She closed her folders and looked at Daniel. "Sir, I find no merit to your claim that your ex-wife's new marriage is false. Your ex-wife is employed and has child care. There are no outstanding balances on any of her accounts." She took a deep breath and frowned at Daniel. "You've missed four of the last twelve weekends with your son. That's one-third, sir. And furthermore, my interview with your son indicates that he would like to stay with his mother and Mister Walker, right here in Three Rivers. Your motion for full custody is declined. The current custody agreement stands."

She nodded, handed the folders back to the bailiff, and stood.

Ivory scrambled to her feet too, gratitude right at the tip of her tongue. She wouldn't blurt it out, but she hoped Judge Tomlinson would feel it all the same. Relief filled her and filled her until she couldn't hold her tears back, and as soon as the judge left the courtroom, she let them slide down her face.

She hugged Oliver, and then Byron, and then Tripp, who held her tight. "Thank you," she whispered. Their marriage had certainly looked and felt real to everyone else —now Ivory just had to figure out if it could be real for her too.

"This isn't over," Daniel said.

"Sir," the bailiff said. "You need to exit the courtroom."

"I know this marriage wasn't real," he said anyway. "I'm going to keep an eye on you two."

"Sir," the bailiff said again.

Daniel glared for another moment and then he stalked out of the courtroom. Ivory watched him go, so many things to say piling up at the back of her throat. She swallowed them back, because she didn't want to say anything negative in front of Oliver.

But honestly, why did Daniel care? The judge had spoken true—he'd missed a third of his visits with Oliver over the past six months, which meant he'd only seen his own son for seven weeks this summer, and then eight times this year previous to that.

He didn't really want Oliver.

No, Ivory knew what he wanted. He wanted to hurt her.

"Let's celebrate," Tripp said. "I know this great place for ribs about a half an hour away." He took Oliver's hand and led him down the aisle to the exit. "You get to stay with us, bud. Are you happy?"

"Yeah," Oliver said, cheering. "And do I have to have ribs? I don't like the bones."

"'Course not," Tripp said as they left the courtroom. He paused and looked back at Ivory, who stood with Byron.

"Thank you," she said, her emotion overcoming her again.

"Of course, Ivory." He drew her into a hug, and Ivory imagined it to be the type of embrace and support she'd get from a father if she had one that cared about her. "We'll get everything filed, but I don't think you'll have a problem keeping your custody." He glanced toward where Tripp and Oliver stood. "Even Daniel can't compete with Tripp Walker."

Ivory wasn't sure what he meant, but she nodded anyway. She'd start paying him back that very day. Twenty dollars a week. Only giving him that much money would take a long time to pay him back, but she didn't care. She was going to pay him back every penny if it was the last thing she did.

———

IVORY AND TRIPP fell into an easy routine of eating breakfast together before she went to the dry cleaner. Oliver didn't wake that early, but when he did, Tripp fed him and took care of him.

They brought her lunch almost every day, and when she got home, Tripp had something to eat for dinner too.

He worked most afternoons, and sometimes Ivory would find him in front of all three screens, moving things around three-dimensionally, or coloring digitally while Oliver sat at the table where she normally made jewelry, doing something.

He read sometimes, and the first time she'd stood in the doorway and listened to her son read his book out loud to Tripp, Ivory had wept big, fat tears that didn't seem to stop. The sight was so beautiful and so close to heaven, that Ivory couldn't believe it was happening in her house.

"That word is dynasty," Tripp had said, and Oliver had repeated it correctly and kept reading.

The two of them were so...perfect together, and Ivory knew Tripp loved her son. And Oliver loved Tripp.

It was only Ivory that seemed incapable of feeling love

for a man. Yes, she loved her son. But her feelings for Tripp were still very knotted, and she wasn't sure how to get them to lay flat.

He'd been nothing but kind and patient with her, and she didn't deserve him. Sometimes she'd lie awake at night and listen to him breathe in the bed beside her. Even letting him into her bed had taken a couple of weeks, and Tripp had never once complained about sleeping on her lumpy couch.

A month passed, and they had to establish a new routine. "So I'll take you to school in the morning," Ivory said. "And Tripp will pick you up after school." She looked around the dinner table at everyone. Ivory hated that she wouldn't be there after school for her son, and Tripp must've been able to see the agony on her face.

"Baby," he said. "You don't have to keep working at the dry cleaner."

"Yes, I do," she said with conviction. She'd given him a twenty dollar bill every week for the past four weeks. He kept them in the top drawer of his desk, and one night when she couldn't sleep, she'd tiptoed over to it and peered inside to find the four of them there. So he wasn't spending them.

He didn't need her money, she knew that. She didn't care. They hadn't combined their bank accounts, and she bought groceries every other week, put gas in her own car, and paid as many bills as she could before her money ran out.

He bought groceries on the weeks she didn't and paid

the mortgage. A sense of helplessness filled her, because she was only falling farther behind with him.

*No*, she told herself as Tripp said something to Oliver. She only had to pay him back for the money he gave her before their marriage. Everything after that was combined and didn't count.

"Back-to-school night is Friday," Oliver said. "Can we go?"

"Of course," Ivory said. "Then we'll know what school supplies you need." She exchanged a glance with Tripp, who simply took another bite of the brisket he'd ordered for dinner.

He couldn't really cook much, and she let him buy lunch and dinner for her. She hated how consumed she was with what he paid for and what he didn't, but she hadn't been able to get those feelings to go away.

They finished dinner and Ivory sent Oliver down the hall to take a bath. "Gotta go to your first day of third grade tomorrow," she said with a smile. "Be sure to get all the way into your armpits."

"Mama," he said, rolling his eyes. He skipped down the hall, humming to himself.

"And take off that cowboy hat," she called after him.

"Yes, ma'am," Tripp said, removing his hat and pulling her toward him. She squealed and giggled, silencing when he kissed her. "Maybe you could take your lunch at pick-up time," he said.

"I can't leave the building, Tripp."

"Maybe Harmon could just come in for a half an hour." He swayed with her, always so willing to make things better for her.

"It's okay," she said. "You spend more time with him than I do anyway. I just want lots of texts about what he says, okay?" Oliver loved to talk about what had happened at school that day, and Ivory couldn't believe she was going to miss it.

"I'll text you everything," he said. "Tomorrow, we could do a live video, if you wanted."

Ivory didn't know what she wanted. Her blood had started to buzz with Tripp's touch, and yet she was still resisting his presence in her life.

"That would be great," she said, kissing him again. He deepened the kiss, pressing her into the kitchen counter behind her.

Later that night, after the kitchen was cleaned up, after they'd tucked in Oliver and had everything set out for his first day of school, after Tripp made love to her, Ivory lay beside him as he slept.

She reached over and touched his forearm, but he didn't stir. "You fit here," she whispered, and she knew she was right.

So why did she still want him to leave her alone to raise her son?

# 21

Tripp knew Ivory had something she wasn't telling him. They'd established an easy way of living, though mornings could be a bit chaotic sometimes. But she made it out the door with Oliver on time nine times out of ten, and she seemed happy at Verona's.

He took care of a lot of things at home, and he was extremely happy with his life with Ivory behind closed doors.

And yet...there was something between them, even when there was nothing physical between them.

"Fall Festival!" Oliver yelled one morning near the end of September. Tripp groaned and rolled over, knowing his step-son wasn't going to go back to bed and let him sleep. By the darkness still blanketing the room, he hadn't let them sleep in very long.

"Mama," he whined. "It's Fall Festival day."

"I know, baby," she murmured, scooting backward in bed until she bumped into Tripp to make room for Oliver on her side. He climbed into the bed, and Tripp gave up on going back to sleep. "But we aren't leaving for hours."

"I want to get a good pumpkin," Oliver said.

"The carving doesn't start until noon," Ivory said, barely flinching when Tripp rolled over and put his arm over her hip. "Why are you up so early?"

Oliver didn't answer, and that meant he'd had a nightmare. Not only that, but he'd be cranky by mid-afternoon, and Tripp really wished he'd go back to bed for a few hours right now. Then everyone would be happy now—and later.

"Baby, it's five-thirty," Ivory said. "Come on. It's too early to get up." She got out of bed and led him out of the room. Hope entered Tripp's heart as he breathed steadily in and out, waiting for Ivory to come back to bed.

When Tripp woke next, he was still in the bed, but the light streaming through the blinds indicated a lot of time had passed. He sat up with a groan, the weight lifting he'd been doing the past month or so still making his muscles ache. The scent of something sweet carried on the air, and he sat up and pushed the blankets off his legs.

In the kitchen, he found Ivory icing a pan of cinnamon rolls. "You didn't come back to bed," he said, wrapping his arms around her from behind. He touched his mouth to the back of her neck, immediately getting a cold vibe from her.

"I couldn't go back to sleep," she said. "Well, I dozed in Oliver's room for a while." She sighed, and Tripp let go of her so she could move over to the kitchen sink with the now-empty icing bowl.

"Ivory," he said, but she didn't look at him. Maybe it would be easier for both of them to have this conversation if there was no eye-contact. "I know you're not telling me something."

"Yeah." But she didn't volunteer what it was. Tripp, as skilled as he was with a computer mouse, couldn't read minds.

"Tripp," Oliver said, interrupting him.

"Yeah, bud?" He took his time swinging his gaze from Ivory's back to the little boy.

"Your computer keeps making noise." He twined his fingers together, and Tripp sensed something was wrong. Oliver never had that much anxiety on his face.

"Did you touch it, Ollie?" Ivory asked, stepping to Tripp's side.

"No."

"Don't lie to me, baby." Ivory moved over to her son. "What did you touch?"

"Just the mouse."

Ivory looked over her shoulder, and Tripp started toward the room where his computer was. "I'll fix it," he said, pure annoyance moving through him. A little bit at Oliver, who he'd told not to touch his computer, but mostly with Ivory. At least Oliver had said something when the machine had made a noise, alerting him of a problem.

Ivory had a problem and hadn't said anything. She still wouldn't.

His computer beeped in a way he'd never heard before, and he sat down to get it taken care of.

"We're eating," Ivory called a few minutes later, but his machine was in the middle of a reboot, and he didn't want to leave it. He'd had it custom-built at a shop that would do lifetime repairs and replacements, and if something was wrong with the machine, he'd have to make a trip to Austin.

He walked over to the doorway and called back, "Go on without me."

She moved to the mouth of the hallway, concern on her face. "Is it going to be okay?"

"We'll see," he said, flashing a brief smile.

"We can still go to the Fall Festival, right?" Oliver asked, standing half a step behind his mother's leg.

"Of course," she said, stroking his hair. "Tripp just needs to fix his computer. We've told you not to touch it."

"I know." The boy dropped his chin. "Sorry, Tripp."

"It's okay, bud," he said, and he went back to his station. All three screens stayed black for several more minutes, and a message finally came up, asking him to restore everything to the factory reset.

Sighing, he pulled out his phone. He was in the middle of a project, and he couldn't really afford to lose time. He dialed the shop in Austin, and said, "Hey, yeah, this is Tripp Walker, and I've got a problem with my computer...." He went through the details, and sure enough, they asked him to bring the machine in.

"I live in Three Rivers now," he said.

"Where?" the guy asked.

"Yeah," Tripp said, scrubbing his hand up the back of his head. "I'll see when I can get it there. How long will you have it?"

"It's impossible to know, man," the guy said. "Tony built your machine, and he'll be here every day next week. Uh... he's got a couple of other things on his table right now."

Tripp suppressed the sigh threatening to explode out of his mouth. "What time do you open on Monday?"

"Ten."

"Great, thanks." He hung up and looked at the message on the screen. Oliver probably hadn't been the one to cause this problem, but Tripp still didn't like that the boy had touched his computer. They'd been getting along so great, and he spent a lot of time in this room with Tripp. Sometimes he did his homework, or colored, or read to Tripp while he worked. Sometimes he sat in the chair Tripp had bought just for him and simply watched. No matter what, he knew better than to touch Tripp's computer.

"I'm jumping in the shower," Ivory said from the doorway, and Tripp swung his chair around.

"All right."

She entered the room instead. "That doesn't look good."

"I have to take it in." He stood up and looked at the table

where she made necklaces on the weekends. "Can I borrow your laptop to book a flight to Austin?"

"You have to take it to Austin?"

"Yeah, that's where I bought it."

"Maybe a shop here could look at it," she said.

Tripp shook his head. "I had it custom made, and they do lifetime work."

Alarm crossed her face, but he wasn't sure what had caused it. "How much does that cost?"

"Nothing," he said. "They have a lifetime guarantee." He didn't tell her he'd paid twenty grand to build the machine in the first place. Of course, the first thing Ivory worried about was money. He had a stack of twenties in his top desk drawer that told him that.

"I'll go eat, then I can shower when you're done." He gave her a smile though not much inside him felt like smiling, and she turned and went into her bedroom. The very fact that Tripp still thought of it as *hers* and not *theirs* said something about their relationship.

As he waited for his cinnamon roll to heat in her ancient microwave, he called Liam.

"Hey," his brother said, his voice somewhat chipper. "We were just talking about you."

Tripp thought of his brothers at the homestead out at Seven Sons, and he suddenly wanted to be there with them so badly. "Oh, yeah?"

"Yeah, Rhett and Evelyn just asked Jeremiah to cook for

Thanksgiving. Fosters and Walkers, right here at the ranch. Do you guys have plans with Ivory's family?"

"Nope," Tripp said. In fact, Ivory had said she didn't talk to her parents much, and that had been the end of that conversation. Tripp had gotten more out of Oliver, who said they never went to visit his grandparents in Tennessee, because "Grandpa's mean."

He also never saw his father's parents, who lived down in Corpus Christi. Tripp hadn't realized how utterly alone Ivory had been until then, and he wondered how she'd handle a huge dual-family party for Thanksgiving.

"Great," Liam said. "Jeremiah says you guys can bring soda, and he'll have punch to mix it with."

"I need to talk to Ivory," Tripp said. "Make sure she doesn't have any other plans." But since they'd been living together, he'd never seen her make more than oatmeal or scrambled eggs for breakfast. Dinner was usually something he ordered, or something simple like hot dogs, grilled cheese sandwiches, or spaghetti. He'd never seen her make mashed potatoes or anything in the oven at all.

"Oh, okay," Liam said. "How are...things?"

Tripp sighed, because Liam had picked up on something with him. His twin sense knew Liam had something going on too, and he said, "If I tell, you have to, too."

"I've got nothing."

"It's funny how you think you can still lie to me," Tripp said, smiling for the first time that morning.

"Fine," Liam said. "But mine is stupid, and I don't want to talk it to death."

"I'm not Rhett," Tripp said.

"You go first."

He glanced down the hall, but he couldn't see Ivory or Oliver. He pulled his cinnamon roll out of the microwave, which had finished a while ago, and said quietly, "Ivory's hiding something from me, and I don't know what it is. I'm a little frustrated with her."

"Ooh, trouble in paradise," Liam said, teasing. "Hey, at least you know she's not perfect."

"I know she's not perfect," Tripp said, rolling his eyes. The way she paid him twenty dollars every Friday told him that. As did the way she literally never made Oliver pick up after himself. She wasn't perfect, but Tripp could deal with shoes by the front door and dishes on the kitchen counter. Heck, he'd even tackled her yard for her and made sure they always had groceries.

"Your turn," he said.

"It's the same thing I've had trouble with for a while now," Liam said.

"Callie Foster," Tripp said without missing a beat. He also didn't make it a question.

"The Shining Star is going down fast, and she won't see reason," Liam said, obviously moving now. Probably away from the table where he'd been talking with the rest of their brothers who lived at the ranch. "Even with everything

Rhett did for them this year, their harvest wasn't enough to cover them through the winter."

"You didn't offer to buy the ranch again, did you?"

"I'm not suicidal," Liam growled.

"So you need a new solution," Tripp said. "That she might accept."

"Any ideas of what that might be?"

Tripp had one, sure. The same one he'd proposed to Ivory, though, technically, she'd proposed the idea to him. He'd just been the one to get the ring and ask her in a romantic way to marry him.

He coughed, because he wasn't sure his relationship was anything to be emulated. "I mean, maybe," he said.

"Don't hold back, brother," Liam said, but Tripp definitely wanted to keep his idea to himself. "Tripp?"

"Marry her," Tripp blurted, maybe a little too loudly. If Daniel had been lurking outside the window, he'd have heard Tripp. He left his breakfast on the counter and ducked into the garage as Liam laughed.

"I'm serious, bro," Tripp said. "It worked for me and Rhett."

"She didn't talk to me for a couple of weeks after I offered to buy her ranch and let her just keep it," Liam said. "She'll never speak to me again if I show up with a diamond."

Yeah, Tripp knew the feeling. "You might be surprised. I mean, you think you're perfect for each other, right?"

"Maybe," Liam said, because he was in some heavy denial.

"What happened to your plan to wait a bit and then ask her out again?"

"I'm still working on it."

"It's been months, man."

"I know that." Liam sighed. "I said I didn't want to talk this to death, and here we are, one breath away from me dying."

"Sorry," Tripp said.

"What are you going to do about Ivory?"

"I have no idea," Tripp said, sighing. "I asked her, but she just stood there."

"So talk to her about Thanksgiving," Liam said. "And work back to it."

"Yeah."

"I gotta go. I'll tell everyone you're a family of three for Thanksgiving." He hung up before Tripp could protest. In the next moment, the garage door opened, and Oliver stood there.

"He's out here, Mama," he called over his shoulder, and Tripp just wanted a moment to himself. Especially when the two people he couldn't get away from were the one who'd broken his computer and the one who wouldn't talk to him.

"Whatcha doin' out here?" Oliver asked.

"Just talking to my brother." Tripp held up his phone

and climbed up the steps to go back inside. "You ready for the Fall Festival?"

"Yep."

"What are you most excited about?" he asked. "Wait, I think I know. The donkey rides."

Oliver laughed in his childlike voice, and Tripp forgot his annoyance with the child. He ate his cinnamon roll while Oliver told him about the festival here in Three Rivers. He hadn't gone last year, because well, none of the brothers had left the ranch much last year at all, himself included.

Ivory came into the kitchen, her hair blown dry and straight. She wore more makeup than what she usually did to the dry cleaner, and her jeans had his thoughts racing toward getting them off later.

He cleared his throat and his mind. He wasn't going to let her distract him with kissing before she told him what was bothering her.

"Are you going to shower?" she asked, and Tripp stuffed the last bite of his breakfast in his mouth, nodding.

"Give me fifteen minutes," he said, leaving his plate behind for someone else to clean up this one time.

# 22

Ivory usually enjoyed autumn, but something about today felt too heavy. She kept her gaze out the window of Tripp's truck as he drove them to the downtown park, where the annual Fall Festival was held every year.

She'd taken Oliver to it before, and she'd felt like Mother of the Year afterward, because he loved it so much. She simply didn't want to go today. No, she wanted to hide.

From Tripp.

He'd let the conversation go for now, but Ivory knew he'd circle back to it—sooner than she'd like. Because she'd rather not tell him all of her darkest demons.

The fact was, she didn't believe he'd be in her life much longer. Watching Oliver grow more and more attached to Tripp had been hard for Ivory, and she'd fought the urge to take her son and run.

Because she knew love didn't last. Love left. Love broke hearts, and love was something to fear.

She clenched her arms across her middle, knowing Tripp could see the movement, had catalogued it, even as he said something to Oliver. What he'd said, she didn't know. She didn't know what love was, or how to show it, or how to accept it.

She couldn't believe she was still hemorrhaging from Daniel's decisions that had left her and Oliver to their own devices, but the truth was, she was. She wondered if she always would be.

"Mama?"

She looked over to find Oliver waiting for her, framed by Tripp's open doorway. "Coming," she said, pulling herself out of the darkness in her soul. She met Tripp and Oliver at the front of the truck, saying, "Wow, we had to park far away."

"I asked you if that was okay," Tripp said, glancing at her. He usually held her hand when they went out, but today, he didn't even try.

Ivory adjusted her purse over her shoulder. "Sorry," she said.

"What's bothering you?" he asked, his voice quite low.

But she didn't want to talk about this in front of Oliver, in front of anyone. Not at all would work for her too.

She shook her head and kept walking. Tripp's frustrated sigh came from beside her, but Ivory couldn't do anything about it right now. They arrived at the park, and Oliver ran ahead of them, chanting, "Pumpkins, pumpkins, pumpkins!"

That got Ivory to smile, and Tripp took her hand. "He'll be busy for a while," he said. "Let's wait in the shade."

Ivory did everything in the shade if she could, and she joined Tripp outside of the children's pumpkin-carving area while Oliver handed the cowboy his ticket and went with him to pick out his pumpkin. The joy on his face wasn't hard to find, and tears pressed behind Ivory's eyes.

"Tripp," she said. "I need to go see a counselor."

"You do?" He didn't sound shocked or incredulous, disgusted or worried. He'd simply asked.

"Yeah, I...." She swallowed, because she really liked Tripp, and she didn't want to lose him. And if he knew what she really thought....

"I don't believe in love," she said.

Several seconds went by. "What does that even mean?" he asked.

"It means that my belief system broke when Daniel chose his own selfish needs over me and Oliver. He left us with nothing, in a town we didn't know, to go hang out with his friends. To be this big-shot lawyer in Amarillo. I've been clawing my way back to normalcy for three years now, and the fact is, I couldn't do it on my own."

Her chest heaved now, and she struggled to breathe. Tripp put his hand flat on her back, and the contact was welcome and warm and wonderful.

"So that's why I give you a twenty dollar bill every week.

To prove to myself that I can do this, That I'm still here, and still fighting. But I have open wounds inside me, and I...I need them to heal before—" She cut herself off, because she couldn't tell him she didn't love him.

They were *married* for crying out loud. Doing married things that husbands and wives did. He was kind, and thoughtful, and caring. He'd provided everything for her these past few months, and she couldn't believe she'd just told him she was broken and needed to be healed before she could be with a man. Before she could ever love a man.

Because that meant she didn't love him—and now he knew it.

"Tripp," Oliver yelled. "Come see."

Tripp waved to her son, and then he faced her. So many things stormed across his face, and Ivory couldn't identify them all. She knew hurt when she saw it, though, because the emotion lived inside her constantly. Anger. Disbelief. Maybe some betrayal.

"I'm going to go see," he said, his voice deadly calm. Ivory nodded, because she'd already said way too much.

———

TRIPP DIDN'T SAY anything to her about her admission later that day. He still slept in bed with her, but he didn't reach over to touch her, didn't kiss her, didn't even say good-night. She knew better than most that people processed things in different ways, and all she could do was pray that the morning would bring new light to her mind, to their relationship, to their household.

She waited until Tripp's breathing evened, until she knew he was asleep, and then she slipped silently out of bed and dropped to her knees. No words came to her mind. She'd begged God to fix her before, and for a while there, she'd thought she might be ready to welcome a man back into her life.

In fact, that was the reason she'd contacted Evelyn all those months ago, Tripp's name the first one out of her mouth. She'd realized quickly, though, that she wasn't nearly as ready as she needed to be. More prayer. More soul-searching. Another try.

Then everything with Daniel and the custody had happened, and—"How did I get here?" she whispered. "I'm so sorry. I promised I wouldn't hurt him, but I can't love him? How can he possibly stay with me if he knows that?"

Her tears wet the blankets, and they didn't stop. She didn't know how to make them stop, and she cried harder with every passing second. Standing quickly, she ran from the bedroom, every cell in her body in the utmost pain.

"Ivory?" Tripp said behind her, but she hurried into the hall, sucking at the air, desperate for a release from this agony. She couldn't leave the house in her pajamas, but she did step out into the backyard, where she didn't have to muffle her cries quite so much.

Unfortunately, she was mid-sob when Tripp slid the door open and joined her. He said nothing. Simply took her into his arms and held her against his chest while she continued to storm through everything she'd felt in the past several years. She *hurt*, night and day, day and night.

She'd tried therapy before, and it wasn't enough. What would ever be enough? Or would she be truly broken for the rest of her life?

"What do you want me to do?" he whispered.

"I don't know," she said, gripping him with all of her strength.

"I'll stay," he said. "Or I'll go. Whatever will make things better for you. For that sweet boy in there."

Her heart felt so fragile, like one more beat would shatter it completely. And there Tripp stood, offering her his heart too, though it had to hurt too.

"I don't know," she repeated.

"How about we take it day by day?" he asked. "Right now, what do you want me to do?"

*Stay*, she thought, because she couldn't even fathom being out here in her backyard alone, in the middle of the night, sobbing.

"Stay," she whispered, and Tripp nodded.

"Then I'll stay."

———

THE NEXT MORNING, Ivory woke when Tripp leaned over and kissed her, saying, "We're going to church, baby. See you in a bit."

She opened her eyes, her heart skipping a beat. She didn't want to be alone. "It's time for church already?"

"Yes. I have Oliver ready." He gave her a timid smile. "We'll be back afterward, and if you feel up to it, we can head out to the ranch for lunch with my family."

They'd done that several times, and Ivory enjoyed Seven Sons Ranch and his brothers. The Foster sisters were usually there, along with their father and grandmother, and Ivory could usually just fade into the background.

Tripp lifted his hand in a wave and left. Panic reared up inside her, and she wanted to call him back. She breathed through it, and soon enough, she calmed. She didn't want Tripp to take Oliver out to his brothers' ranch without her, because then there would be questions.

So she got herself into the shower. Got her hair curled. Got herself dressed in a cute red-and-white striped blouse and a pair of jeans. She sat on the front steps when Tripp pulled up with Oliver, and her son leapt from the truck almost before it had stopped.

"Mama." He ran up to her and gave her a sloppy hug. "Tripp said I can change, and we'll go. I'm gonna wear my hat."

"Of course you are," she said with a smile. "Go on then, baby."

"Hang up that suit coat," Tripp said as he mounted the steps. He sank onto the top step beside her with a sigh.

"You know he's not going to hang up that jacket," Ivory

said, lacing her hand through his arm. She leaned against his bicep, a slip of happiness moving through her.

"I know." Tripp pressed his lips to the top of her head. "Staying here or coming with us?"

"I'm coming."

"Am I staying tonight or going?"

"I think staying," she said.

He nodded, his jaw jumping with a muscle that Ivory had seen before when they'd argued over money and her paying him back. "I'm trying to see how things are going to go," he said. "I just can't."

Ivory knew exactly what he was saying. "You don't want to stay."

"I do," he said, and she remembered when he'd said those two words to her before. "But—"

"You deserve better," she said, her voice cracking.

"Maybe with counseling," he said. "Maybe you just need more time. I can be patient."

Ivory didn't know what to say to him. A few minutes passed, and she finally asked, "How was church?"

"Confusing," he said, standing up. "I'm going to go change too, then we can go." He opened her front door and went inside the house, where she heard him chuckle before the door closed behind him.

A weight settled back on her shoulders, and foolishness descended on her, covering her, smothering her. She had no right to tell Tripp how to live his life day by day. And what? He was supposed to have a packed bag ready for whenever she told him to go? And he was supposed to kiss her and love her whenever she wanted him to stay?

"You're so stupid," she said to herself. Ruthless. Unkind. She hung her head, snapping it back up when the front door opened again.

"Mama, look at my hat." Oliver appeared beside her, and she did her best to smile at him. "Tripp says I can wear it to church next week, because I hung up my jacket." Pure light radiated from her son's face, and everything inside Ivory broke.

Because she'd not only hurt Tripp because of her inability to love. She'd hurt Oliver too. He'd be devastated when yet another man walked out of his life.

And that was Ivory's fault.

She stood up and smiled down at her son. "Mama's not feeling well, baby. I'm not going to come out to the ranch. Is that okay?"

"Yeah," Oliver said, some of the light in his eyes dimming. "Are you okay?"

"Yeah." She smiled, but she turned away from him because she was about to cry. Again. "You go have fun with Tripp."

She opened the door and stepped inside, locking the door behind her. She just needed a few minutes to talk to Tripp.

He came out of the bedroom at the same time she started down the hall. "Hey," she said, stilling.

"Hey."

"I'm not going to go with you guys," she said, wiping her eyes. "I'm so sorry."

"Let's not give up yet," he said. "You go to counseling, and we'll see how things go. One day at a time, right?"

Ivory knew in that moment that she would never deserve the love of this amazing cowboy. But she nodded. He did too, stepped aside, and she went into the bedroom they shared. The sound of his boots as he walked down the hall and out of the house sounded like him leaving her for good.

# 23

Tripp could drive from Ivory's house to Seven Sons Ranch on auto-pilot, which he did with only Oliver in the truck with him. He'd labored through church today, trying to find the right path for him and Ivory.

The problem was, he and Ivory seemed to be on completely different highways in completely different states.

She didn't believe in love.

She couldn't love him.

Familiar anger and frustration filled him, and he curled his fingers around the steering wheel until they ached. He released them, trying to get his negative emotions to go as easily. But how foolish he'd been, convincing himself that because she made love with him that she actually loved him.

That because she'd let him move into her house that he belonged with her. That because she allowed him to spend time with her son that she really wanted him.

None of it was true, and Tripp had never felt so stupid. He could barely look at himself in the mirror, and he definitely couldn't look at Ivory. He'd been working around her house, taking care of her son, completing his projects for his company while building their family, getting dinner, all of it.

And for what?

For Ivory to tell him he had no hope of ever being loved.

*She's right,* he thought. *You deserve better.*

Too bad he'd gone and fallen in love with her so completely.

He pulled up to the ranch, and Oliver whooped as he got out of the truck. He didn't even close his door before he ran off, yelling, "Penny! I'm here, Penny!"

Tripp dropped to the ground a little slower, hearing Penny barking from inside the house. He knew the moment someone opened the back door and let her out, and he rounded the truck to close Oliver's door.

Inside the homestead, chatter and laughter met his ears. Tripp paused near the front office, where he'd used to share a space with Liam. His brother's machines were still there, and Tripp realized how much he missed being here at the ranch.

He'd asked the Lord what he should do at church that day. He'd felt nothing. And now, standing in the homestead on this ranch that had brought him closer to his brothers and saved him from a darkness like that which lived in Ivory, he felt like he'd really like to be here.

Problem was, when he'd taken his vows, they were very real to him.

*But not to Ivory*, he thought, bitterness accompanying the thought.

"There you are," Callie said, appearing in the hallway. "Are you comin' in or what?"

"Yeah," Tripp said. "But is Liam around? I need to talk to him."

"I'll get him for you." Callie smiled at him, and a moment later Liam came out of the kitchen area.

"Hey, bro." He embraced Tripp. "Whoa, something's wrong." He peered at his brother, his dark eyes searching for the problem.

"Yeah," Tripp said. "Can I use your computer for a minute? I need to book a flight to Austin."

"Austin? Why?" Liam went into the office and sat in front of his screens. He tapped on the keyboard, and everything lit up.

"My computer died," he said. "It's got a weird factory reset on it. I need to take it back to Computer Solutions."

Liam got up and Tripp took his place, navigating quickly to an airline website. "So what else is going on?" Liam asked.

"Ivory and I...." Tripp didn't know how to finish. He booked a flight for tomorrow morning and turned back to his brother. "We're not getting along right now."

"Oh, I'm an expert at that," Liam said with a smile.

"You and Callie seem to be getting along fine," Tripp said.

"Yeah." Liam sighed. "I still haven't asked her out, and now we've got all these holiday plans with her family. It honestly feels like torture sometimes."

"What does?" Callie herself asked, coming into the office.

Tripp looked at Liam, who wasn't great in confrontational situations. It was why both of them were better behind screens.

"Being with you sometimes," Tripp said, stepping in front of his twin. He felt slightly crazy, and definitely out of control. "You have to know he *really* likes you."

Callie's mouth opened and she blinked at Tripp, silent.

"Come on, Liam," Tripp said. "Let's go see how close lunch is to being ready." He stepped past Callie, regret pulling through him. He didn't say things like that to others. He wasn't normally unkind. "Sorry," he said to Liam.

"Did you see her face?" Liam hissed. "Do you think she doesn't know?"

"If she doesn't, she's blind," Tripp said back. "But I shouldn't have said anything. Should I go apologize?" They entered the kitchen, and Tripp came to a halt when he saw Skyler. The two brothers seemed to spot one another at the same time, and Skyler's face lit up.

"Tripp's here," he said, and everyone looked toward the twins.

"When did you get here?" Tripp asked, striding forward now to embrace his younger brother. He hadn't seen Skyler since last Christmas in Grand Cayman, and that was entirely too long.

"Pulled in about an hour ago," he said, laughing. "Didn't you see my truck?"

"No." Tripp chuckled with his brother. "It's so good to see you. How long are you staying?"

"Forever," Jeremiah said. "He's going to be the ranch mechanic."

"Really?" Tripp really wanted to come back to Seven Sons Ranch now. He and Skyler had always gotten along great, and when the twins had gotten in trouble as teenagers, Skyler had always been right there, a couple of steps behind them, doing all of the same mischievous things.

So maybe Tripp had been a bad influence on his younger brother. Didn't matter now.

"Yeah, really," Skyler said, reseating his cowboy hat on his head properly. "I sold my shop and Jeremiah here convinced me I needed to get up here to Three Rivers to take care of his tractors." He grinned at the man pulling something out of the oven.

"They're not *my* tractors," Jeremiah said, rolling his eyes as he set the huge roasting pan on the stovetop.

"Yeah, I'm pretty sure I bought one," Rhett said.

"Yeah, the one that stops working in the middle of a job," Jeremiah said.

Tripp loved the energy in his family, and he was glad he'd come this afternoon even though he hadn't wanted to. "Anyone see where Oliver went?"

"Evelyn took him out to see the horses," Rhett said. "No Ivory today?"

And everything that had started to warm inside him iced over again. "She's not feeling well," he said.

"Oh, really?" Rhett's eyebrows went up. "Is she...?" He glanced at Jeremiah and then Liam. Skyler, and then Wyatt.

"Is she what?" Tripp asked, still not hearing the unspoken words.

"Pregnant," Jeremiah barked. All the chatter and laughter had been sucked out of the kitchen, and Tripp wanted the floor to open up and swallow him whole.

"No," he said with a scoff. As if sleeping with his wife was absolutely laughable.

"How's the turkey?" Callie asked, coming back into the kitchen. She obviously hadn't heard the previous conversation, and Jeremiah removed the lid from the roasting pan. "Wow, Miah. It's beautiful." She smiled at Jeremiah, and Tripp watched their friendly exchange.

"You made a turkey?" Skyler asked. "Oh, I'm definitely moving here."

The back door opened, and Oliver entered with Evelyn behind him. "Tripp, there's a new horse! You have to come see."

"After dinner, bud," Rhett said. "It's time to eat."

Tripp kept quiet for the rest of the afternoon, only talking to his brothers or one of the Foster sisters if they asked him a direct question. He basked in the spirit of the ranch, the people out here, all the while thinking of the home and the person he had to go home to.

And while he'd always wanted to go home to Ivory, tonight, he didn't want to.

Not even a little bit.

————

LANDED IN AUSTIN. He sent the text to Ivory, not that he expected her to text him back. He'd taken Oliver back to her house last night, and then he'd gone back to Seven Sons to sleep. He didn't want to talk to her, and he'd claimed it would be easier to get up early and make the hour-long drive to Amarillo for his five-thirty a.m. flight.

In truth, he simply needed some time to himself. Time to figure out what to do. He'd said he could be patient. He'd said they could take things day-to-day. But the more he thought about it, the more he didn't want to bend every part of himself to Ivory's will. He'd been the doormat in a relationship before, and that hadn't ended well for him.

He couldn't move across the state again, especially with almost all of his brothers now in Three Rivers.

He arrived at Computer Solutions right at ten o'clock, and he set his bag with the CPU on the counter. "Hey," he said to the guy behind the counter. "I called about this computer on Saturday. Is Tony around?"

"Yeah, let me grab him." He looked completely bored as

he walked away. A few minutes later, Tony came out from the back room to shake Tripp's hand.

"Hey, man. What's it doing?"

"Freezes on startup," Tripp said. "Says it needs a factory reset."

"Let's plug 'er in and see what's going on." Tony took the CPU and turned around to the counter behind him, littered with electronic parts, wires, and tools. The machine made that strange beeping noise, and Tony said, "Oh, I know what this is."

"You do?"

"Yeah, we just need to install the latest version of your operating system." He reached for a disk. "I've got it right here. This should be ready in about an hour."

"Really? An hour?" Tripp couldn't believe he'd flown for longer than that for such a simple solution.

"Yeah." Tony grinned at him. "They tried to push out an update, and things went haywire. We've had several people bringing in their higher-end machines with this smart operating system."

"Great," Tripp said. "I'll go get coffee." He left the shop and got behind the wheel of the rental car. He'd told Ivory he wasn't sure how long he'd be in Austin, because it could take days to fix his computer.

And now it would be ready in an hour.

He didn't want to go back to Three Rivers yet. And if Ivory didn't ask him specifically what was going on with his computer, he wasn't going to.

## Tripp

No, he needed to have a plan before he went knocking on her door again.

# 24

Liam purposefully waited until Tripp had left for the airport, waited until Jeremiah and Wyatt left to work the ranch, waited for the clock to click all the way to noon, before he left the safety of his office.

Tripp had blown everything wide open between him and Callie yesterday with just a few words. *You have to know he really likes you.*

And Liam had seen her face. She knew. Whether or not she'd known when he'd asked her out months ago, Liam wasn't sure. And he hadn't asked again.

He just wanted to be able to see her without any awkwardness. If all he got was a few conversations each week, and their texting sessions, and Sunday lunch with her, he wanted it.

And he knew that made him pathetic, but he wasn't sure what else to do. In the months since Tripp's wedding, he'd seen Callie retreat and come back to him more than once. Not physically, but emotionally. Mentally.

He'd seen behavior like this before in his ex-girlfriend. Portia had been yes-then-no and hot-then-cold with him for two years. And why?

She had a secret.

Callie did too. Liam didn't know what it was, but it was big. Part of him wanted to ask her, and the other part was afraid he'd lose her forever if he did.

So he said nothing. He smiled at her when she came over. He welcomed her to his office when she stopped by. He wandered the fence line in the early morning when she normally worked in the garden.

Today, though, with the sun directly overhead, heating the earth almost past bearable, Liam went out to the stables and saddled Pretzel.

"Come on, boy," he said. "Maybe if you stumble upon Callie, it won't be too awkward."

The horse didn't answer, of course. He did snuffle a little, and Liam pulled a butterscotch candy out of his pocket. "Would you do it for a treat?"

The horse would do anything for a hard candy wrapped in crinkly plastic, and Liam chuckled as he gave Pretzel the treat. "That's a good boy. And she likes you. She won't yell at me if you're there."

Callie didn't yell at all. No, her method of expressing her displeasure or hurt feelings was silence. And while she hadn't shut down in front of everyone at lunch yesterday,

Liam would be surprised if she approached him first after what Tripp had said.

Which meant he had to go to her. He swung into the saddle and aimed the horse west, moving him along the path that led out to the smokehouse that had become Orion's baby.

Jeremiah's beehives were out here too, and a stand of trees where Pretzel liked to snack. Liam let the horse graze while he pulled down a branch and started stripping the bark off of it.

He wasn't like Micah, and he couldn't create something beautiful out of the wood. It was simply something to keep his hands busy while his mind worked through how he could get over to Callie's and talk to her.

"Hey," she said, and surprise zinged through Liam.

"Hey." He looked back at the branch, the bright silver blade of his pocketknife glinting in the sun.

"Miah said I'd find you out here."

"Dunno how he'd know that," Liam said. "I didn't tell him I was coming out here." Mostly because he hadn't known.

"I guess he saw you saddle Pretzel and head west." She stopped on the outer cusp of the shade and stuck her hands in her back pockets.

She wore jeans and work boots, along with a purple shirt that had swipes of mud across it. Without makeup and with that dirty blonde hair piled up, she was basically an angel in human form, and Liam swallowed, trying to think of something to say.

"Water leaking?" he asked.

"Yeah...how'd you know?"

"Your shirt is covered in mud."

She looked down at it, and Liam dropped the branch. "I could come help you with it."

"I got it," she said, a dose of fear and worry in those pretty eyes.

Of course she did. Callie Foster didn't need help, and she wasn't shy about making sure everyone knew that.

"But thank you," she said. "I was wondering...never mind."

Liam watched her for a second, and she seemed to be like an ocean wave. Coming toward him, excited and roaring. Then pulling back, receding quietly, almost hoping he'd come chase her.

"You can say it," he said softly, almost like he didn't want to scare her away.

"I was wondering if what your brother said is really true." Callie looked right into his eyes, and Liam really appreciated that.

"Yeah," he said. "It's true." He wasn't sure if he should be hopeful or if his heart should be in the bottom of his cowboy boots.

She nodded, and helplessness moved through him. No matter how hard he tried, or how fast he could run, no one could catch and bottle the ocean tide.

"I didn't mean to talk to him about you," Liam said. "He's just...." He didn't want to betray Tripp's confidence either. "We sometimes just know when things aren't going great for each other."

"We're not great?" she asked.

Liam wanted to reassure her that yes, they were absolutely great. But it would be a lie. So he shook his head slowly.

"Are you angry with me?"

"No," he said. How could he explain that he simply wanted more than she had to give? And how unfair would that be? And it would hurt her, too, as Callie really did want everyone to be happy.

Which was exactly what he wanted for her.

"I can see you're not happy," he said slowly, trying to measure out the words the right way. "And I want to help. Sometimes I think you'll let me, but most of the time I can tell you won't. And...I feel like a bad friend." Or that he wasn't her best friend the way he wanted her to be.

Maybe she'd been confiding in Jeremiah all this time.

*Stop it*, he told himself. Both Callie and Jeremiah had assured him there was nothing between them. In fact, Jeremiah said Callie hardly told him anything anymore.

No matter what, he hated that he was over forty years old and still second-guessing everything when it came to matters of the heart.

"Liam," she said, and if she knew what happened to his pulse when she said his name, she wouldn't do it. "You're not a bad friend." She took a step closer, and then another. "You're my best friend."

"I thought that was Miah." The poisoned words left his mouth before he could suck them back in.

"Well, you're wrong," Callie said evenly. "And you're right. I'm not very happy."

Liam slid his pocketknife in his pocket and stepped toward her. His fingers slid down her arm and into hers. "What can I do about that?"

She looked up at him, and Liam thought now would be the perfect time to kiss her. Really let her know that he wasn't happy without her either. That everything Tripp had said was absolutely true, and Liam would do almost anything to have Callie in his life the way Tripp had Ivory, and Rhett had Evelyn.

"Nothing," she said, her eyes shuttering. "I mean, I...I just need to figure some things out first. And then I'll tell you."

"Tell me your secret?" he asked.

Fear crossed her face, and she stepped back, removing her hand from his. It was only twelve inches, but Liam felt like she'd just put a chasm between them.

"I know you have one," he said, undaunted. "I can see it in you, Cal. And I want to know it."

"I can't tell you," she whispered.

"Why not?"

"Because," she said. "I don't want you to think badly of me."

"I won't."

"You don't know that."

But Liam did. He also knew it was fruitless to argue with Callie. So he simply fell back a step too and pulled his knife back out. "When you're ready, then. You know where to find me."

Tears glistening in Callie's eyes, but Liam couldn't do anything about them. Absolutely nothing, and when she walked away from him, he felt his own heart cracking open a little bit more.

He finally released the breath in his lungs and tipped his head toward the heavens. "That could've gone better, you know. What was I supposed to do there?"

He wanted the sky to crack and bleed, the way everything inside him was. He wanted thunder and lightning. He wanted the Lord to *help him* help Callie.

Only the breeze blew, and Liam finally reached for Pretzel's reins. "All right, boy," he said. "You've had enough of this juicy grass. Let's go."

In the stable, he found Jeremiah refilling the hay bags. "Did Callie find you?"

"Yep," Liam said.

Jeremiah glanced at him. "She doesn't seem right."

"She's not." Liam unsaddled the horse and started putting everything away. He knew his brother liked that, and he wanted to be on Jeremiah's good side. The bad side wasn't pretty, that was for sure.

"She's retreated completely from me," he said, pausing

in his work. "When she does talk to me, it's about you." He studied Liam. "Are you guys seeing each other?"

Liam gave a barking laugh. "I wish."

"I know," Jeremiah said, hanging his head. "I was sort of hoping that was why she'd been acting so strange." He came over and they brushed down Pretzel together. "I've been thinkin'...."

But he let his words hang there, and Liam couldn't see inside his brother's head. "Thinking what?"

Jeremiah shook his head. "Nothing. Never mind."

Liam was getting that a lot lately, and he honestly didn't have room in his head to sit and worry about all the secrets everyone was keeping anymore. He had plenty of his own—starting with how far he'd go to help Callie.

# 25

"Okay, start the movie, baby," Ivory said as she pulled the popcorn off the stove. "This is almost ready."

"Is it like how Tripp makes it?" Oliver asked, and Ivory's last bit of patience withered.

"Yes," she said. "It's just like he makes it." Ivory honestly had no idea how Tripp made the colorful, candied popcorn. She'd tried to look up a recipe online, but all she'd been able to find was something for kettle corn. So she'd made that.

*Just another thing to thank Tripp for*, she thought as she poured the popped kernels into a big bowl. Her son's obsession with sugary popcorn. Ivory liked it buttered with salt, but Oliver had specifically requested "Tripp's popcorn."

He'd been gone all week, and Ivory both liked and disliked his absence in her life. Number one, she was incredibly lonely without him. Number two, she had to rely on someone else to pick up Oliver from school and watch him until she got off work. Number three, she had to make her own dinner.

When she listed things like that, she felt like a grade-A jerk. Like she'd just been using Tripp all this time.

"Which, of course, you have," she muttered as she handed the bowl of popcorn to her son.

"This isn't like Tripp's," he said in an annoyed tone. "It's not even colored."

"It tastes the same," she said, picking up a handful of the treat. She put several pieces in her mouth, and immediately spit them back out. "Okay, it doesn't taste the same." In fact, this popcorn tasted like burnt sugar and the bottom of her shoe.

"I wish Tripp was here," Oliver said, folding his arms as he pouted. Ivory could echo the sentiment, but she just got up and poured the ruined popcorn into the trashcan. A sigh pulled through her whole body as the cartoon Oliver had wanted to watch began.

A sense of helplessness so keen overwhelmed Ivory. She'd been in this position before. Not able to do anything right. No future to look forward to. Just her and her son, trying to make it through each day the best they could.

She hated that she was in this position again, and even worse, that she'd put herself there this time.

Last time, she'd at least been able to blame Daniel.

Someone knocked on the door, and she headed through

the living room to answer it. Tripp stood there, and Ivory's lungs seized.

"Hey," he said easily, like no time had gone by. Like he was there to pick her up for their seven o'clock Friday night date.

"Tripp!" Oliver yelled, flying into the man's arms. He caught Oliver laughing and crouched down in front of him.

"Have you been bein' good this week?"

"Yep," Oliver said.

"Got all your homework done?"

"Yep."

"Stayed away from that girl at recess?" Tripp grinned at Oliver, and Ivory's heart flopped around in her chest like a fish out of water.

"What girl?" she asked at the same time Oliver said, "Yep."

"Can you come in and make that popcorn?" he asked. "Mama tried, but it was nasty."

"Hey," Ivory said, though she couldn't really argue with her son.

Tripp straightened and met Ivory's eye. "I need to talk to your mama for a minute," he said. "Can I make it after that?"

"Sure." Oliver said, skipping back to the couch. "We're watching a movie."

"I can see that." Tripp nodded to the porch, and Ivory's stomach practically flung itself out of her body. She somehow managed to step onto the porch with him, and he closed the door behind her.

"You're back," she said.

"Well, I'm in Three Rivers," he said.

"You didn't need to knock," she said. "It's your house too."

"Is it?" Tripp stuffed his hands in his pockets. "Ivory, I've been thinking a lot, and I'm not going to stay here anymore."

Pure fear dove through her, rendering her speechless. She just looked at this handsome cowboy billionaire that had come into her life at the exact wrong time, but who did the exact right things.

"I'll help you with Oliver in the afternoons, and I can keep my office here. But I'm not going to *live* here. Or sleep here. Or any of that." He cleared his throat.

Ivory folded her arms, her mind racing. What was she supposed to say? She couldn't argue with him. Heck, if she were in his position, she'd probably be doing the same.

"What are we going to tell Ollie?" she asked, her voice much too high.

"You're his mother," Tripp said. "You tell him what you think will hurt him the least."

"Are you sure you have to do this?" she asked, very aware of what she was asking of him.

"Have you called a counselor?" he asked.

Ivory sucked in a breath and held it.

"I didn't think so," he said. "So yes, Ivory, I have to do this. I don't want to leave you and that boy in there, but I feel like it's the right thing to do."

She nodded, because again, she had no argument. "Will you stay for the movie?"

Tripp looked away, out toward his truck. "All right. I'll stay for the movie."

"And will you take Oliver trick-or-treating in a couple of weeks?"

"Yes."

Ivory just had one more question, but she felt like she was pressing her luck already. She reached down deep for her courage and took a breath before asking, "Can we still come out to the ranch for Thanksgiving?"

"I'm sure that will be fine," he said.

She nodded, put her hand on his arm, and waited until he looked at her. "I never wanted to hurt you. Ever."

"I know that, Ivory," he said. "But I just don't see how this can work with how we currently are."

"No, you're right." She hated that he was right, but he was. And she hadn't done anything this week while he'd been gone to change how she currently was.

He didn't say anything else, and Ivory had no idea how to break this silence. Tripp nodded, and shuffled back half a step. "Okay, I'm gonna—yeah." He reached for the door-knob. "Popcorn."

"Right," she said, following him inside, where Oliver sat on the couch like they could be a normal, happy family. Eat popcorn. Laugh at the silly cartoons he liked. "Popcorn."

———

THE NEXT DAY, Ivory woke to the sound of the television playing from down the hall. She had no idea what time it was, and her whole head ached from the way she'd been clenching her teeth while she slept.

A groan came out of her mouth as she sat up, her brain still trying to make sense of what day it was and what she had to do that day.

*Saturday*, she realized. And that meant she had necklaces to make. With her neglect over the past few months, she only got a few orders a week. She fiddled with them during the week, but she finished them on weekends, mailing them on Monday afternoon, just like her online shop said she would.

At the moment, she couldn't remember how many necklaces she needed to complete that day, and she looked over to the empty half of the bed where Tripp had been sleeping. She missed him, and that didn't make sense and it wasn't fair.

Before she went into her art studio—where she'd be faced with Tripp's triple computer screens—she padded down the hall to the kitchen. She started making coffee and then moved over to the kitchen table where her laptop sat.

An older model, the computer took a while to come to life and connect to the Internet. She tousled Oliver's hair and asked him if he wanted cereal.

"I ate popcorn," he said, and a slip of annoyance moved through Ivory though before Tripp had come back into her life, if there had been leftover popcorn from the night before, she wouldn't have cared if Oliver had eaten it.

She poured herself a cup of coffee and sat down at her computer. Verona's provided health insurance, but it didn't cover a huge network of providers. She pressed her eyes closed and drew in a deep breath, a prayer slipping through her mind.

*Please help me find someone who can help me.*

Then she logged into her insurance and started searching the database for a counselor. They wouldn't be open on the weekend, but Ivory made a promise to herself that she'd call first thing on Monday morning.

She hoped this promise was one she could keep.

———

On Monday evening, Ivory's heartbeat skipped and leapt when she pulled into her own driveway. Tripp's big, navy blue truck was parked there, and she eased to a stop beside it. He'd be inside. She'd have to see him. Maybe talk to him.

She sighed, her heart dropping to the bottom of her feet. She'd have to *see* him. *Talk* to him.

"Might as well get this over with," she said, wondering if all aspects of their evening routine would be the same. She got out of the car and went up to the front door, where the scent of food hung in the air. What kind, she wasn't sure, but it sure seemed like Tripp had gotten dinner, just like he had when they were married.

"You're still married," she muttered to herself, opening the door. Music filtered down the hall from her art studio, where Tripp's computer was. She knew she'd find him and Oliver there, and she couldn't get herself to go that way.

Containers of Chinese food sat on the counter from her favorite spot, and she had no idea what to make of it. Was he just being nice? Was China Isle his favorite spot too?

She went into the kitchen and leaned both palms against the counter. Her shoulders ached, and she was so far inside her mind that she didn't hear Tripp come down the hall until he said, "I'm going to take off."

"Okay," she said without turning around. Her pulse beat like a drum in her chest, echoing in her ears. "Wait. Tripp?" She spun around, everything clashing inside her.

"Yeah?" He turned back to her, settling his cowboy hat on his head. He was so sexy and so kind, and Ivory knew she didn't deserve him.

"I'm wondering if you can stay a little later tomorrow night." She wiped her palms down her thighs. "I, uh, have a therapy appointment at four-thirty." Looking at him like this. Talking to him about her counseling. Asking for his help. All of it was torture of the most exquisite kind.

"Yes," he said simply, and relief rushed through Ivory.

"Thank you."

He nodded and left. The house without him felt empty and desolate, and Ivory hated that her house wasn't the safe haven it had been before. Sighing, because she knew it was her fault, she rummaged through her purse until she found a twenty-dollar bill.

Then she went down the hall to get her son for dinner.

# 26

Jeremiah knew Tripp had moved back to the homestead. Kind of. His computer had stayed at Ivory's. He left every afternoon to get Oliver from school. He stayed in town for a while, and then he came home at night.

He didn't say much to anyone, and Jeremiah didn't know what to say to him either. In fact, he watched his brother disappear inside the shell of himself, the same way Callie had been doing for months now.

Neither one of them was very happy, and Jeremiah's heart constricted for them as he poured water into the coffee pot and got his morning dose of energy brewing.

He was actually glad his heart hurt. It meant he could feel something again. No, it wasn't anything soft for a woman, but it was something after a very, very long time of darkness.

"Mornin'," Wyatt said as he came into the kitchen. "I swear, I'm going to try to get up before you one day."

Jeremiah just smiled at him. He hadn't told anyone that he only slept four or five hours at night, because he still had nightmares from his would've-been-wedding day. Last night, he'd dreamed he'd gone to a deep, cool swimming hole. It had felt so great to dive in and cool off, as early October was still too hot for him.

While he was there, someone else had dove in, and the next thing he knew, he was being pulled down. Dragged under. No matter how hard he kicked or struggled, he couldn't get away.

The last thing he remembered was the perfectly polished red fingernails—exactly the way Laura Ann had painted her fingernails for their wedding.

He stayed in his room after the nightmares, and he had a secret drawer full of crossword puzzle books that calmed him and passed time until he could come brew coffee and fry bacon.

"Pancakes?" Wyatt asked, pulling open the fridge. "Sausage?"

"If you make it, they'll eat it," Jeremiah said. He was glad to have another brother in the house who liked cooking, though Wyatt only made breakfast a couple of times a week. Dinner was still Jeremiah's baby, and Wyatt said he didn't even want to make a meal that big.

But pancakes and sausage he could do, and he set the

cast iron skillet on the stove and put the sausage links in it while the first drops of coffee fell into the pot.

Perfect serenity filled the morning air at the homestead, and Jeremiah took a deep breath of it. His phone rang, shattering the silence and tranquility.

"If that's Whitney...." he said, knowing full-well that it was her. He'd told her no at least a dozen times. He'd taken to ignoring her calls, and then she'd cornered him at Wilde & Organic while he was just trying to get his groceries.

"It's her," he said, glaring at her name on his phone. Just the fact that he'd put her number in his phone angered him.

Every time he talked to her, it took longer to get her out of his head. And the one time he'd seen her, he'd dreamed of those perfectly kissable lips for a week straight.

Wyatt laughed and said, "Better answer it, or she'll show up at the door."

And Jeremiah didn't need that. He swiped on the call with, "No, Whitney. And calling me before seven a.m. isn't helping your cause."

"What will help my cause?" the woman asked, her voice diving right into the soft parts of his brain. He tried to shake it loose, because he could sometimes hear that pretty little lilt in the quiet moments out on the ranch.

"Not calling me for a year," he said.

"Very funny." She sighed, and Jeremiah thought she finally might be tired of their little game.

"You should just let her come on out," Wyatt said, and a keen sense of betrayal knifed through Jeremiah.

He'd practically yelled it, and Whitney said, "I don't know who that was, but I like him."

Jeremiah had tried reasoning with her. Telling her the ranch was a dangerous place, with wild animals and sharp tools. She'd laughed—which had taken him a month to get out of his ears—and said she knew the dangers of fences and windmills.

He'd tried saying she could come if she paid an exorbitant fee to shoot. She'd said she'd call back when she was ready to book. She hadn't, though, because no one would pay a thousand-dollar location fee.

He'd tried asking her what was so special about Seven Sons. She'd *gushed*—positively *gushed*—about the charm of the place, the amazing foliage—her word, not his—the "quaintness" of the pastures, the horses, the "cute" chickens. And on and on.

Now, every time Jeremiah walked past the Texas flag on the side of the barn, he heard Whitney's voice, talking about "how amazing" everything at the ranch was.

Jeremiah had to agree with her about that. He loved Seven Sons, and he'd worked his fingers to the bone to get it there and keep it that way.

"Are you even listening to me, Jeremiah?" Whitney's voice saying his name.... Jeremiah would be hearing that for ages. His four-syllable name sounded downright amazing in her sweet voice.

"I wasn't, actually," he said. "You can't come out to the ranch with your fancy brides."

"This isn't actually a bride."

*Curse her*, Jeremiah thought. "Look, I don't want everyone and their puppy out here. If I let you start shooting out here, then I'll be spendin' all my time fielding *annoying* phone calls like this instead of getting my work done."

"Jeremiah—"

"I'm hanging up now," he said, and he did just that. Wyatt chuckled, his back to Jeremiah as he flipped pancakes. "We're not talking about this."

Wyatt must not have heard the undertones of warning in Jeremiah's voice, because he said, "I don't get why you don't just ask her out and get it over with."

Jeremiah made a horrible squeaking noise. "I do not even *want* to ask her out."

"Yeah, okay," Wyatt said, heavy sarcasm in the words. "And I haven't been eyeing Hanna Nielson."

"Eyeing—what? Who?" Jeremiah couldn't believe what he was hearing. Of course, Wyatt hadn't taken the oath to avoid any and all women once he arrived in Three Rivers. Jeremiah couldn't be upset with him.

And yet, he was more irritated now than when he'd hung up with Whitney.

"Hanna Nielson," Wyatt said. "She doesn't know who I am, of course. She works at a restaurant in town." Wyatt turned to get the syrup out of the microwave. "And wow. I'm a little smitten."

"A little?" Jeremiah asked. He'd never admitted out loud

how much he liked a woman, but Wyatt had. He'd never been shy about who he liked, at least with the brothers.

Wyatt laughed, and the front door opened. He silenced almost instantly. "Not a word to Liam," he said.

"No?" Jeremiah took a few steps to his right and caught Liam ducking into his office. "Why not?"

"Oh, he's havin' a hard enough time with...you know. He doesn't need me yapping about my crush on Hanna."

Jeremiah didn't either, but he didn't say anything. He poured himself a cup of coffee and sat at the bar, letting Wyatt serve him a meal for once.

Liam did join them a few minutes later, looking exhausted and sweaty and a bit perturbed.

"You went to the gym?" Jeremiah asked.

"Yep." He reached for a pancake and slathered it with butter, completely counteracting the effects of his workout. "And Tripp was there again. He's in a bad way, guys. We need to pray for him and maybe start thinking about talking to him."

Jeremiah had always liked the brotherly intervention—when he wasn't on the receiving end of them. Thankfully, his brothers had accepted his decisions and mood for what they were. For the most part.

"Done." Wyatt flashed Jeremiah a wicked look, and Jeremiah glared at him.

"Don't you dare."

"Whitney keeps callin' Jeremiah."

## Tripp

"Yeah, great," Liam said, pouring way too much syrup on his pancake. Jeremiah watched him for a few seconds, and then looked at Wyatt.

Guess they'd start praying for both of the twins.

# 27

Tripp got very good at finishing up his work about five-fifteen, telling Ivory he was leaving, and driving back to the ranch. He enjoyed his afternoons with Oliver, and if the boy realized Tripp wasn't sleeping there anymore, he hadn't said anything.

He stayed late every Tuesday, ate dinner with Oliver, and put him in the tub about the time Ivory got home. She'd never said a single thing about her sessions, and Tripp's curiosity kept him awake at night.

But he refused to ask her. He'd caught himself once, about to ask, "How did it go?" but he managed to transform it into "How was your day?"

That had still gotten a narrowed-eyed look from Ivory, but she'd simply said, "Good. You?"

"Good," he'd said, and that had been the longest conversation they'd had in weeks.

Liam had told him that at some point, he was going to have to walk away from Ivory and Oliver completely. File for divorce. Move on.

Tripp had no idea how to do that. Well, Rhett knew how to file for divorce, and he'd told Tripp he could help with that. But Tripp didn't want to get divorced. He didn't want to walk away from Oliver and Ivory, the way her ex had done, and he didn't want to move on.

Every night, he prayed that maybe this could just be his life now, but he knew way down deep that it couldn't. He wasn't happy, and Ivory certainly wasn't. At least from what he could see.

As the weeks passed, the twenties in his drawer continued to mount, along with Tripp's frustration. But he'd promised Ivory he'd take Oliver trick-or-treating, and he'd told Liam that Ivory would be at Thanksgiving. No one else knew, but Jeremiah wouldn't care about two more. He'd make a ton of food, and there would be a lot of people at the ranch. Enough to keep plenty of distance between him and Ivory.

So he'd wait until after Thanksgiving. Then he'd do what he needed to do to get back on a path he could continue for the rest of his life. Jeremiah's complete swearing off of women sounded good, and his brother certainly seemed a lot happier than Tripp.

On Halloween, Tripp picked up a ninja from the elementary school. A skipping ninja. He laughed as Oliver got in the car, dragging an overly full backpack with him. "Wow," Tripp said. "What's in that thing?"

"We had a party," he said. "And I got the grand prize! Mrs. Letham said I could bring home the whole piñata." He started unzipping his pack and pulled out a pretty broken piñata.

"Holy cow," Tripp said. "Was that a jack-o-lantern?"

"Yeah, we made it," Oliver said.

"Oh, I remember that," Tripp said, easing out of the pickup line. "You told me about it."

"Yeah, and we got to have doughnuts, and these peanut butter cookies that had been decorated like ghosts. It was great."

"Sounds like a lot of sugar," Tripp said, wondering if he should be concerned. Probably. They hadn't even started trick-or-treating yet. At least it was Friday, and his teacher wouldn't have to deal with the hyped-up students tomorrow.

He wondered what Ivory would do tonight, prime date night. He hated that his thoughts went in that direction, because he still wanted to be the one she spent her Friday nights with. He wondered if he'd ever stop feeling that way.

He pulled up to Ivory's house, chuckling again as Oliver jumped out of the truck and ran for the front door. He'd always skipped or jumped as a way of locomotion, but the running was made of all sugar.

Tripp followed him into the house and then the kitchen, where Oliver stood in front of the fridge. "No sugar," Tripp said, glancing at Oliver, who already had a cup of chocolate pudding in his hand. "Nope. Not that."

"Why?"

"You've had enough for right now," Tripp said. "Have a piece of cheese or something. We'll have more candy tonight."

Oliver put the pudding back and pulled out a piece of string cheese. "What are you going to dress up as?"

"This," Tripp said, gesturing to his blue plaid shirt and jeans. "I'm a cowboy."

"You're always a cowboy." Oliver laughed as he shook his head. "You're supposed to be something else for Halloween."

"Are you?" Tripp grinned at him, this little boy he adored so much. "Well, I didn't know. Will you still go trick-or-treating with me?"

"Yeah, sure," Oliver said. "We're going at five, right?"

"Five," Tripp said. "I have some work to do this afternoon." He hooked his thumb over his shoulder, his chest suddenly collapsing. "You want to come help?"

"Yeah, sure," the boy said again, and Tripp smiled at him somehow.

"Okay." He went down the hall first, because he needed a moment to gather his thoughts. "Oliver? You know I don't live here anymore, right? Has your mom ever said anything about...that?"

"No," he said. "She cries a lot, and she looks sad."

"Yeah, we're both sad," Tripp said, sitting in his chair and turning to face the child. "I'm moving my computer station back to the ranch. We'll go out there in the afternoons until Thanksgiving, okay? And then your mom is going to find you another babysitter."

Oliver looked at him, his eyes widening. "But I don't want another babysitter." He stepped into Tripp's arms and hugged him tight. "You're the most fun, and I never bother you while you're working."

"I know that," Tripp whispered. "It's not about you, bud. You're awesome in the afternoons. I love spending time with you. It's just...me and your mom aren't going to see each other after Thanksgiving."

"Like my dad." Oliver stepped back, glaring at Tripp.

"Yeah," Tripp said, heavy guilt pressing against his shoulders. "A little bit like that, except I don't really want to go."

"Then why are you?"

Tripp looked out the window, so out of his league in trying to explain this situation to a seven-year-old. "I just have to, bud." He sighed and turned back to his computer. "So will you please help me get my station ready to load into the back of my truck? Then we'll get pizza like I promised, and then I'll take you up to that rich neighborhood where they hand out full-size candy bars."

———

295

Tripp's interactions with Ivory got easier and harder at the same time. He drove Oliver back to town from the ranch at five-thirty every evening, and he stayed in the truck while the boy skipped up the front sidewalk to the door, where his mother waited.

Ivory waved to him and went back inside. No words spoken. No smile.

She'd texted to ask him to drop Oliver at the pizza place with the kids gym on Tuesday evenings about seven, which he did. Again, he only saw a flash of her through the glass doors before Oliver went inside and Ivory disappeared like a ghost.

His unhappiness reached a new low, but he couldn't do much about it. He got through one day and actually crossed it off on a calendar. Three weeks until Thanksgiving. Then two. Then one.

Six days. Five, four, three.

He'd finished a project and hadn't picked up another one, because he'd lost his love for animation.

"Family meeting," Jeremiah said one night after dinner, and Tripp looked up from his plate. He honestly couldn't even remember what he'd just eaten, but his plate was clean and his stomach full.

A long silence followed, wherein Tripp realized everyone at the table was staring at him. "What?" he asked.

"Dude, what do you mean, what?" Skyler shook his head, and Tripp realized then that this was a family intervention, not a meeting. "You're like, pathetic, and I've never seen you like this." He wore concern in his light brown eyes, and he flicked them around to the other men at the table.

"Where's Evelyn?" Tripp asked, just now noticing that Rhett's wife wasn't there.

"Okay, I see what you mean," Rhett said, clearly not speaking to Tripp. "This is bad."

"We're worried about you," Liam said. "I see you sitting at your station, doing nothing."

"I don't have another job," Tripp said, every defense coming up. "It's not like I need the money."

"But you hate doing nothing," Jeremiah said. "Out of all of us, you twins have always been the busiest, because you like it."

Tripp looked at Liam, hoping for back-up. Instead, he got a very serious look from the person he was closest to. Something pinched in his chest, and he had no idea how to make it stop. His eyes actually filled with tears, and he blinked furiously to hold them back.

"Tripp." Rhett reached over and put his hand on Tripp's. "Just tell us everything." He leaned down and looked under the brim of Tripp's cowboy hat. "Remember when everything fell apart with Evelyn?"

He nodded, because he was in immense pain, not suffering from amnesia.

"Remember what *you* said when you found out we'd broken up? That our marriage wasn't real?"

Tripp shook his head.

"You said, 'Come home, Rhett. We're here for you.'" His

brother's voice choked, and Tripp finally looked away from the tabletop. Rhett ducked his own head and did his own blinking. "So I know I'm not here as much as I used to be. But we're still all family, and we're all here for you." He looked around at everyone seated at the table, and Tripp missed Micah so much in that moment. "For everyone, no matter what. Right, guys?"

"Right," Wyatt said loudly while everyone else murmured some form of assent.

"Is this how you felt?" Tripp asked in the resulting silence. "Like someone was stealing half of every breath while you desperately try to inhale? Over and over and over." His voice broke, and foolishness made anger shoot to his head. "I hate feeling like this."

"You're in love with her," Liam said.

"I've never denied that," Tripp said. "She's...incapable of loving me back." He wanted to get up and throw his plate at the nearest wall. Toss it in the sink and go down the hall to his room, pack a bag, and just drive until his truck ran out of gas. Oliver didn't have school this week, and no one needed him.

Absolutely no one.

"I know exactly how she feels," Jeremiah said quietly. "And it's no picnic either."

"Jeremiah," Wyatt said. "You're not broken."

Jeremiah gazed evenly at all of the brothers, and Tripp wished he had half of his brother's confidence and power over his emotions. "I feel *nothing*," he said. "Absolutely nothing. I'm *exactly* like her—incapable of feeling anything for a woman."

Tripp knew his brother's heart had been shredded when his fiancée hadn't shown up to the altar. But he had never heard Jeremiah talk like this.

"I'm not making excuses for her," Jeremiah said, meeting Tripp's eye. "I'm really not. But you should know she's in complete turmoil too."

Tripp nodded, because he did appreciate the insight. He'd seen Ivory, and no, she didn't look happy either. She wasn't raging the way she had in the parking lot that day he'd almost hit her. But he knew she'd only taken the storm and hidden it behind a carefully placed mask.

"Our marriage wasn't really real," he said quietly, studying the table again. "I married her so her ex-husband wouldn't get full custody of Oliver." With that weight off his shoulders and out of his mind, he felt so much better. His brothers had always helped him carry his burdens, and shame moved through him that he'd stopped talking to them. Really talking.

"Maybe I could—" he started, but Jeremiah shook his head.

"No, Tripp. I would never want a woman to stay with me when I'm completely incapable of loving her back. Trust me, Ivory doesn't want that either."

Utter helplessness filled him. "So what do I do?" If someone, anyone, would just tell him what to do to stop feeling so miserable, he'd do it.

"You get up every day," Rhett said. "And you do good things in the world."

"Ethan needs volunteers out at Three Rivers," Wyatt said. "He and Brynn have a ton of horses right now, and they can't keep up."

"I need help packing and moving here," Skyler said. "You could come back to Austin for a bit with me, if you wanted."

"You could take another job," Liam said.

"You could keep Whitney Wilde off my back about shooting at the ranch," Jeremiah said with a smile. "And that's a full-time job. The woman is relentless."

That got everyone to laugh, including Tripp, and some of the cracks he felt splintering through his whole body fused back together. He reached out, searching for a human connection, glad when all of his brothers reached over and put their hands together.

"All right." He drew in a deep breath. "I'll go home with Skyler for a bit, and then I'll go volunteer at Three Rivers." Maybe that would get him through Christmas and the New Year.

Then he'd figure out how to become a new man again.

"Perfect," Jeremiah said. "Phew. That was hard. Who wants ice cream?"

Tripp added his voice to the rest of the brothers, glad he'd survived this difficult family meeting. Before Rhett got up, he added, "And Tripp, go file for divorce. That'll give you some closure, too."

He nodded, but he didn't want closure. He didn't want the door between him and Ivory to be completely shut. If he thought he was unhappy now....

He added it to his list of things to do once he was ready to be the new Tripp Walker.

In January.

# 28

I vory stalled in the doorway of her art studio, because that was all it was now. An art studio. Not the place where she'd be able to catch a whiff of Tripp's cologne or see evidence that he was still in her life.

Because he wasn't.

She folded the twenty-dollar bill in her hand, shocked she'd forgotten he'd taken his computer station back to the ranch. When he'd moved out, she'd expected to get something in the mail notifying her about a divorce filing. Nothing had come. Why he was dragging things out, she wasn't sure.

*Yes, you are*, she thought. He hadn't filed for divorce because he loved her and didn't want to end their marriage.

At least that was what Doctor Feldman had said.

Ivory had actually enjoyed her sessions with the psychologist, and she felt like she'd made some great progress. Last week, they'd talked about Daniel and his decisions that had left Ivory with the belief that love wasn't worth having.

And today, she was going to ask Doctor Feldman if it was fair of her to take her son out to Tripp's for Thanksgiving. After all, she didn't need to keep reopening the gash in her heart. Or his.

She retraced her steps and clipped the money to the fridge, along with the other twenties she'd put there after Tripp had taken his desk out of her art studio. After grabbing a bottle of water from the fridge, she headed back out to her car to get to her appointment.

Along the way, her phone beeped, indicating a text. She waited until she'd pulled into the parking lot at the office complex before checking her device. Kate had texted with, *You need me to start picking up Oliver next week, right?*

*Yes,* Ivory sent back. *Is that still okay?*

*Of course. I just found out I'm pregnant again, so I might have Jennika pick up the kids if I'm not feeling well.*

*That's fine,* Ivory said. *I can come get Ollie anywhere. Thank you SO much for doing this.*

*We still need to get together,* Kate said, and Ivory looked up from her phone. She hadn't been walking with her friends as fall arrived and then winter. Not because she didn't need the exercise, but because she didn't want to leave her son home alone in the early mornings.

Kate had noticed, of course, and she'd asked Ivory why she'd stopped coming. Ivory was done with lying about things, so she'd said her and Tripp were separated and he'd moved back to the ranch.

*Congratulations on your pregnancy!* Ivory said, because she should be glad for her friend. As she sat in the car, thinking, she realized she did feel...something. Happiness for Kate. Joy for the thought of a new baby.

A smile pulled at her mouth, and pure relief filled Ivory. Her phone beeped, but she ignored it as she grabbed her purse and practically leapt from the car. "I can feel something," she said to the other cars in the parking lot, as if they cared about this breakthrough.

"I can *feel* something."

She burst into the building to an empty lobby, but her excitement didn't fade. Up the elevator and through the check-in process, she still bubbled. When she finally sat down across from Doctor Feldman, she said, "I can feel something."

"Oh," the woman said. "Tell me what happened."

Ivory quickly related how she'd felt at the news of Kate's pregnancy. "And I'm not faking. I'm not pretending. I can actually *feel* that I'm happy." She laughed for maybe the first time in two months.

Doctor Feldman made a note on her pad, smiling—and that was something as the woman was as stone-faced as they came. "This is great, Ivory. What else are you feeling?"

"Hopeful," Ivory said, still riding the high. "And like maybe I can find myself again."

"I have in my notes that we're talking about the holidays this week."

"Yes." Ivory straightened, folding her hands in her lap. "Tripp invited us out to the ranch for Thanksgiving, and I told him a long time ago that we'd come."

"I believe you asked him if you could still come," Doctor Feldman said, looking up from her notebook.

That was right, she had. "Yes," she said. "I was worried about going. Like, maybe it's not the right thing."

"Think about what you just said," Doctor Feldman said, cocking her head.

Ivory went over the statement again, but she didn't know what the woman wanted her to hear.

"Was," Doctor Feldman said. "You said *was*. Are you still worried about going, or you *were*, but now you're not?"

In that moment, Ivory realized she needed to go to Thanksgiving dinner at the ranch. "I'm still worried about it," she said slowly. "Because I don't want to hurt Tripp. But I need to go and...see him. Maybe I'll be able to feel something again."

"Ivory," Doctor Feldman said. "You don't have to do everything in the same day. Remember?" She actually did smile then, a quick movement of her lips.

"I know," Ivory said. She'd gotten a lot better about managing her expectations for herself, for Tripp, for Oliver. Even for Daniel. Doctor Feldman had helped her with an easy list of things to make sure she did each day.

Spirit, self, space, significant others.

She needed to take care of her spiritual side each day, and she'd been doing that by putting a Bible on her nightstand and reading before she fell asleep. Sometimes she woke up in the middle of the night, the lights blazing and that heavy book on her chest. But she did it.

She had to do something for herself every day. Doctor Feldman had told her that sometimes, for her, that meant taking a ten-minute lunch when she was already behind on her appointments.

Ivory had been taking more bubble baths than ever before, because she loved the hot water and scented air.

She had to do something to keep up her space each day. Could be something easy like washing the dishes or folding laundry, and included mowing the lawn and mopping the floor. Anything to take care of the spaces God had given her.

And lastly, she had to do something for her significant others. Right now, that was Oliver, and she counted making his lunch or being on the front porch when Tripp brought him home as her way of taking care of her significant others.

Doctor Feldman said they could expand on those things once Ivory felt like she had control over the ones she'd already been given. She loved the feeling of accomplishment she got when she could look back at her waking hours and check off each item. Her self-confidence had grown, and she did feel like there was hope for her.

Finally.

Now, whether there was hope for her and Tripp, she didn't know.

"Tell me what you're worried about," Doctor Feldman said, and Ivory brought herself back to the conversation at hand. She'd learned how to be more present over the last two months of weekly sessions with Doctor Feldman, too.

"Well, for starters," she said. "His parents will be there, and I've never met them...."

―――――

IVORY CHANGED her mind four times on Thanksgiving morning. She was going to go. She wasn't. She was. She wasn't.

In the end, the envelope she'd gotten yesterday had convinced her to go. Tripp deserved to know Daniel really hadn't given up on his quest to prove their marriage had begun under false pretenses.

Never mind that he hadn't seen Oliver since July. Not even once. She'd gotten another notice for a custody hearing, this time in a family court in Amarillo. Daniel had moved the venue, citing that the judge in Three Rivers was prejudicial.

Ivory knew everything that had gone on behind this new motion. Daniel hadn't given up on trying to find a crack between her and Tripp. And right now, there was an entire ocean between them.

"Come on, baby," she called down the hall to Oliver. "Time to go." She swiped the envelope off the counter and folded it in half before stuffing it in her back pocket.

# Tripp

Oliver came zooming down the hall, making race car noises with his mouth. Ivory hated them, but she said nothing as he flew past her and into the garage. The drive out to the ranch seemed to pass in a blink, and she pulled up in front of the homestead to find several extra cars there, mostly rentals.

Her heartbeat shook through her body. Tripp's whole family was going to be here. All of his brothers. His parents. The Fosters had also been invited, and Ivory felt like a complete outsider. All of her worries about this event came pouring back through her, though Doctor Feldman had had her say them all in their session on Tuesday.

"Now you won't have to worry about them," she said, looking up from where she'd written them down. "I've got them here, and I'll worry about them."

Ivory shook her head, in disbelief that she'd thought her psychologist could actually do that for her. Oliver had reached the front door far ahead of her, of course, and she froze as the sound of Tripp's laughter rode on the air.

Oh, that laugh.

She really missed that laugh.

Their eyes met, and Ivory knew she missed a lot more than his laugh. She missed those dark eyes looking at her, tracking her movement, trying to figure out what would make her happy. She missed that smile. She missed the very presence of this man in her life. She missed the ability to text him whenever she wanted.

Her blood rushed through her ears, the dull roar of a

river all she could hear. So many emotions moved through her body that she gasped.

All of this feeling...maybe she wasn't up for it.

Then Tripp turned and took Oliver into the house, leaving the door open for Ivory. She got her feet moving again, got herself up the steps and through the front door.

"There she is," a woman said, and Ivory barely had time to breathe or blink before an older woman had her locked in a tight embrace. "Tripp's Ivory. We've heard so much about you." His mother released her and stepped back, positively beaming with joy.

"I'm Penelope. My husband, Gideon, is around here somewhere." Plenty of chatter came from the back of the house, where Ivory knew the kitchen was, and she couldn't imagine the crowd there.

"So nice to meet you," she said, wondering what in the world Tripp had told his parents about her. About their marriage. But she put her plastic smile on and let Penelope take the cake pan from her.

Jeremiah had not asked her to bring anything, but she couldn't just show up and eat the Walker's food. Could she?

No, she couldn't. So she'd made a cake and brought it. They could throw it away later, if they wanted to.

Ivory paused on the cusp of the huge back room that housed the kitchen, dining room, breakfast nook, and living room. It seemed like fifty people had congregated, though there were probably only a dozen or so.

She counted in her head quickly—sixteen. It felt like sixty.

Penelope moved over to the countertop and set down Ivory's cake, her attention diverted by one of her sons before she could come back to Ivory. She stood all alone, wondering what in the world she was doing there. The envelope in her back pocket felt like it had turned to lead, and she couldn't bolt and couldn't stay either.

"Heya, Ivory," a man said, tipping his hat at her. It wasn't Rhett or Jeremiah or Liam or Wyatt—she knew and had met them. So one of Tripp's other two brothers. She couldn't even remember their names right now.

Simone Foster came toward her, a smile developing on her face with every step. "Hey." She gave Ivory a quick hug that did nothing to soothe Ivory's nerves. "Come get a drink. Oliver went outside with Tripp and Liam to see the horses."

"Oh, great," Ivory said. She did go with Simone, who she'd sat by at the fall fair a time or two. The woman scavenged through flea markets and garage sales to find unique pieces. Then she restored them and sold them as must-have pieces for the farmhouses that dominated in Three Rivers.

Ivory wouldn't categorize Simone as a friend, but she was definitely an acquaintance. A friendly face. Someone Ivory knew and could talk to. She accepted a glass of sparkling cider and glanced around the ranch.

"Oh, their Christmas decorations are already out," she said.

"A few," Simone said. "Apparently, they have a family

tradition of putting the tree up on Thanksgiving morning. And then Rhett said they had to put the stockings up too."

Evelyn joined them, a glass of cider in her hand too. "Don't let him fool you," she said. "We barely got our place decorated before Christmas last year."

"Well, that was because you guys weren't really together until almost Christmas," Simone said.

"Yeah, and he's trying to make up for it this year," Evelyn said dryly. "They all are. I guess Skyler's moving in soon, and they're trying to get Micah to come too."

*Skyler and Micah*, Ivory recited, letting the two sisters talk about Tripp's family while she sipped and nodded like she knew all the things they did. But she didn't.

And the fact that she didn't really bothered her.

The back door opened, and Oliver came skipping inside. "Jeremiah," he said, his higher voice ringing out above the other lower ones. "Tripp said you'd show me how to ride that big lawn mower."

Jeremiah laughed, the sound full of so much...joy that Ivory couldn't even comprehend it. "Is that what he said? You're too little for that still, bud."

Liam entered the house, and then Tripp did, and time stilled completely. Ivory couldn't look away from him. It was as if he'd swallowed the most powerful magnet in the world and her whole body was made of steel.

His soul simply called to hers, and she knew in that moment that she had to figure out how to get him back into her life.

Permanently.

She'd once wondered if he could be a permanent part of her life. At the time, she hadn't wanted him to be. Heck, even last week, she'd have told Doctor Feldman that she didn't know how to love. Didn't know how to open herself up to that level of risk again.

But now, faced with the man, she thought she'd do anything if she could wake up in the same bed as him.

Her breath caught when she realized what cowboy hat he was wearing.

His wedding hat.

Tears pressed behind her eyes, and she absolutely could not contain them. "Simone," Evelyn said, a heavy dose of warning in her voice. She stepped in between Tripp and Ivory, hissing, "Get her a tissue."

"Oh, sweetie," Simone said, hurrying to tear off a paper towel from the roll sitting on the nearby table. "Let's go outside. We can sneak out of the garage."

Ivory didn't want to sneak out anywhere. She wanted to march right across the room and tell Tripp she could feel something.

And it wasn't much, but it was the start of something amazing. Something amazing *with him*.

But she let Evelyn and Simone shuttle her out into the garage, where she pressed the paper towel to her eyes. "I'm so sorry," she whispered. "I don't know what happened."

Evelyn kept one palm on her back while Simone looked

for something else Ivory could use to wipe her tears. Everything on her face seemed to be leaking.

"It's okay," Evelyn said. "He didn't see you."

Simone returned, this time with a blue mechanic rag that looked mostly clean. "This is all I could find."

"It's fine," Ivory said, taking it. "I don't know what's wrong with me."

But she did, and it scared her more than anything.

"I love him," she whispered. "And I can feel it." She looked up, realizing too late that she'd spoken out loud.

"Of course you love him," Evelyn said. "And that's okay."

Ivory nodded, sure the two women helping her had no idea what kind of light had just entered her entire being. Loving Tripp *was* okay, and she just hadn't realized it until that very moment.

Love could be beautiful too. Love could heal wrongs and make bad things good again. Love could make a beautiful baby, and a family. Love didn't have to walk away.

Love was imperfect, like she was, but she knew in that moment that love could overcome the lingering darkness in her soul.

She just had to let it.

# 29

Tripp had seen Ivory duck into the garage with Evelyn and Simone, and everything inside him wanted to follow them. Ivory was his *wife*, for crying out loud. If there was something wrong, *he* should be the one to hustle her outside and make sure everything was okay.

"Oliver," he said, keeping both eyes on that garage door. "Stay here with Liam, okay?" He looked at his twin, whose eyebrows went up. Tripp just shook his head and started for the garage.

He wasn't sure what he'd find out there, but it was time to do something about his wife.

*His wife.*

The door opened easily, and Tripp hesitated, his eyes falling on the three women at the bottom of the steps. Evelyn, Simone, and Ivory looked up at him, and Ivory immediately wiped her eyes and cleared her throat.

"Evelyn," Tripp said, his heart pounding now. "Simone. Can I talk to Ivory for a second?"

The Foster sisters looked at Ivory, and Tripp immediately started pleading to God that she would give her permission.

"It's okay," she said quietly, and Evelyn and Simone came toward Tripp.

Evelyn gave him a small smile and patted his forearm. "She loves you. Be kind," she whispered as she walked by, no hesitation at all in her step. Simone said nothing, but she looked apprehensive as she went inside and left Tripp alone with Ivory.

"Hey," he said as kindly as he could. "Are you okay?"

She sniffed and pulled something out of her back pocket. "Daniel's trying to get custody again."

Tripp went down the few cement steps to the floor of the garage and took the envelope. Ivory tucked her hands in her back pockets and fell back several steps. "What?" He opened the already open envelope and pulled out the single sheet of paper. Reading quickly, his anger grew. "In Amarillo?"

He shook his head, his frustration with Ivory's ex at an all-time high. "He won't win this."

"I've already emailed a copy to Byron," she said.

"I can get someone to look at the case too," he said. "If you want."

She shook her head, but her eyes held so many unsaid things. Tripp didn't know what to say or do. She wasn't volunteering any information about her therapy sessions, and she rarely told him how she felt about anything. He didn't want to push her away by pushing her, but he wanted to know what to expect.

"You haven't filed for divorce," she said, her voice timid.

"I know," he said, lowering the sheet of paper. He focused on tucking it back into the envelope. "I don't want to get divorced, Ivory. I still love you."

Tears filled her eyes, and a sort of explosive sound came out of her mouth. Her tears fell, and she nodded. "You know what's so great?"

He had no idea, so he just watched her.

She smiled, and she was so beautiful. "I actually believe you love me. I feel like I can be loved for the first time in years."

Tripp's heart started thumping with hope between every beat. He tried to stop his spirits from rising, but they did anyway. Up and up and up they went, and he simply looked at her.

She reached up and cradled his face in one palm, and Tripp couldn't help himself as he leaned into the touch he craved more than any other. They breathed in together, and then she stepped back, her hand sliding away from his face.

"I'll take care of this," he said, lifting the envelope. Before she could answer, the garage door opened, and Rhett stood there. He took a few precious seconds to take in the scene while Tripp and Ivory looked up at him.

"Time to eat, guys," he said. "Jeremiah's about to lose his mind, and I don't think any of us want that."

"We'll be right there," Tripp said. Rhett nodded, the door closed, and Tripp looked back at Ivory. "We really don't want to see Jeremiah lose his mind."

Ivory smiled and gestured for him to go up the steps first. He did, but he opened the door and held it for her, making her press in close to him to get back into the house. Their eyes met, and for the first time since he'd asked Ivory to marry him, Tripp felt like their marriage wouldn't be so trivial for much longer.

*Don't get carried away*, he told himself as he joined the fray of people in the kitchen. Jeremiah looked at him and said, "All right, now that we're all here, let's go over what we've got." He proceeded to detail the mashed potatoes, the yams with brown sugar, the sweet potato mash, the green beans, the stuffed mushrooms, the turkey, the gravy, the cranberry sauce. The list of items went on and on, and Callie leaned over to Liam and said something that made Tripp's brother light up like a Christmas tree.

He laughed silently, and Tripp could only hope that his brother could find a way to get his happily-ever-after with Callie. And while he was at it, he added a prayer for himself too.

"Let's say grace," Jeremiah said. "Rhett?"

"Wyatt, will you say it?"

Tripp removed his cowboy hat like the rest of his brothers, and Wyatt's deep, calm voice thanked the Lord for the food, for the family, for the friends, the good state of Texas, and the ability to eat.

"Amen," he said, and Tripp couldn't help the chuckle that burst from his mouth. Thankfully, he wasn't the only one, and Wyatt asked, "What?"

That only made everyone laugh harder, and Skyler stepped over to Wyatt and clapped him on the shoulder. "The good state of Texas, bro? You know there are forty-nine other states, right?"

"Texas is great," Wyatt said. "I'm not the one who painted a huge state flag on the side of the barn. Or put *seven* Texas stars on the front gate.

"Seven Sons," Rhett said, still laughing. Tripp picked up a plate and joined the buffet-style line to get his Thanksgiving feast. With so many people here, there were several conversations happening at the same time. Tripp made no effort to join any of them, and Evelyn situated herself right next to Ivory and engaged her in something going on in town for the holidays.

"Oh, sure," she said. "We've been going to the Christmas parade since we moved here." She smiled at Evelyn, who asked if she and Rhett could sit by Ivory and Oliver this year.

Tripp appreciated his sister-in-law, and Rhett, and everyone else in the room. An overwhelming sense of gratitude filled him, and he took a seat next to his father.

"Hey, Dad."

"Tripp." His father leaned closer so he could whisper. "Why aren't you sitting by your wife?"

"Dear," his mom said. "I told you about this. They're having some problems right now. He'll work them out." She patted Tripp's hand and smiled at him like he had the ability to solve any problem.

If only that were true.

But hey, he'd spoken to Ivory, and it had been really positive. He'd take anything he could get from her at this point, and he held onto the hope that there would be more conversations in the future. Good conversations.

———

TRIPP COULDN'T WAIT to get out of the moving truck. He and Skyler had been driving for what felt like days, and Tripp's legs were starting to go to sleep. He'd enjoyed the week in Austin, if only for the fact that it got him out of Three Rivers immediately following Thanksgiving.

The guilt he carried for turning Oliver back over completely to Ivory's care was ridiculous, but only if he thought about it too hard. He loved the boy, and he was married to his mother, and Tripp somehow felt like he was abandoning the child the same way Daniel had done.

Ah, Daniel.

Another reason Tripp wanted to get away for a bit. He'd called Byron and asked him to please make this situation go away. That he'd pay for whatever it took—another lawyer. More hours. Whatever. Just make sure Daniel would leave them alone for a while.

"Oh, holy tinsel," Skyler said, leaning forward to peer up and out of the windshield. Tripp did the same, though he knew what to expect. "They decorated the oak tree."

"Yeah," Tripp said. "Liam and I did it last year. Looks like it's a tradition now."

"You decorated the oak tree last year? Why?"

"No pines here," Tripp said. "We might have been bored. But then on Christmas Eve—well, it wasn't really Christmas Eve, because we went to Grand Cayman last year. But before we went to Cayman, we each brought our gifts outside and opened them here. It was a little cold, but it was fun."

"Will we do that again this year?"

"I hope so," Tripp said. "It was actually fun. Jeremiah made hot chocolate and lots of coffee, and he bought all these syrups to flavor everything. I enjoyed it."

"What does the inside look like if this is what the outside looks like?" Skyler asked, keying in the code to open the gate. Ornaments had been hung on the gate rungs, and long strings of pine garland had been laced through the fences that led up to the homestead.

"There's a big tree," Tripp said. "And the stockings. Liam burns this candle on his desk that smells like pine trees. Sometimes he'll light a cinnamon one, but I hate that

323

one. So I usually sneak it outside to the trash when he's out doing chores or something."

Skyler chuckled. "Sounds about like you two. Always bickering over little things."

"Yeah, well, the cinnamon one stinks."

Skyler pulled to a stop and exhaled. He looked at the house, which had lights strung along the pillars and the roof. "Look, don't tell anyone this, okay?"

"Okay," Tripp said, sensing something big was about to happen.

"I'm happy to be here," Skyler said. "I am. I just…I'm not a good mechanic, and I'm worried Jeremiah will think badly of me once he finds out." He skated his eyes over to Tripp and then moved them back out the window.

"Not a good mechanic? Skyler, you had your own shop in Austin."

He shook his head. "I had to file bankruptcy. Or rather, I just kept pouring my own money into it." He drew in a deep breath and blew it out. "I just…I want to be here. I *need* to be here. But I need to figure out what to do with my life."

Tripp didn't know what to say. His brother had been tinkering with machines for as long as Tripp could remember.

He suddenly remembered something he'd said to Rhett too. "Well, it's a good thing you're here," he said. "We're family, and we'll be here for you, no matter what happens."

With that, he got out of the truck, glad when Skyler did

too. "All right, let's go see how many of Santa's elves threw up in the house."

"Oh, boy," Skyler said. "Tell me now if my eyes will be offended with red and green."

"And gold," Tripp said, laughing as he went up the front steps. Sure enough, they opened the front door to the scent of that nasty cinnamon candle, Christmas tunes playing on the speaker system in the homestead, and a legit paper chain running down the hallway.

"What is going on here?" Skyler asked, fingering the paper chain. "Do we actually rip these off?"

"Hey," Liam boomed, coming out of the office. "There you are. How was the drive?"

"Forever," Tripp said. "How long did it take you guys to decorate the house?"

"Forever," Liam said back. "But now that Wyatt's here, Jeremiah has a partner in crime, and I couldn't hold back the tide." He glanced down the hallway. "And Tripp, you should know that they made that paper chain for Oliver."

"Oliver?"

"He's still out here every afternoon," Liam said.

"What? I told Ivory—"

"Her babysitter canceled on her," Liam said. "And I said I'd take him." He shrugged. "I didn't want to bother you or Skyler in Austin."

Tripp had no idea what to say. His twin could've sent a text. And then the boy was running down the hall, yelling, "Tripp! Tripp! Tripp!" and Tripp didn't care that Liam had gone behind his back and said he'd take Oliver in the afternoons.

He scooped the little boy up, both of them laughing, and hugged him hard. "Oh, bud, I missed you."

And bonus, he'd get to see Ivory tonight too.

# 30

I vory wished she had a job she could leave early on a
Friday afternoon when she had somewhere else she'd
like to be. But Verona's was open until five, and there wasn't
anyone else to cover for her so she could drive out to Seven
Sons and pick up Oliver.

And if she was being honest with herself—and she really
wanted to be—she wanted to see Tripp, not just pick up her
son. Liam had told her Tripp would be back today, hope-
fully by afternoon, and her heart had been beating irregu-
larly all day.

Her phone chimed, and she looked at it, too hopeful that
it would be Tripp, asking her when she'd be out at the ranch.
But of course, he'd already know that.

The text was from Kate. *Bleeding. Had to go to the hospital. Can you somehow get my kids after school?*

Her heart fell all the way to the soles of her feet. Kate

had never badgered her to tell more than Ivory wanted to tell. She'd stuck by her when Tripp had moved out, and she'd been willing to help with Oliver.

Ivory had gone over to Kate's on Sunday night, and her friend hadn't looked good at all. That was when she'd called Liam, desperate for help. And of course, the part-time cowboy had agreed to pick up Oliver and take him out to the ranch, the same way Tripp had done.

Ivory had gone to see Kate every evening after work, and she'd been starting to feel better last night. "Oh, no," she whispered to her device. She started tapping out a message. *I'll take care of them.*

Then she turned, almost like she'd be able to talk to Harmon or Verona right now and get the afternoon off. Of course, they weren't there. She'd been working the dry cleaner for almost six months, and they trusted her explicitly. She did all of the books. She took care of the deposits. She had their systems working like well-oiled machines, from the filing to the computer system to how they categorized clothing.

She'd weeded out all their old clothes, and she called people who didn't come pick up within two weeks. She liked her job, and she loved Verona and Harmon. She dialed Harmon, hoping she wasn't disturbing his lunch.

"Harmon," she said when he answered. "My friend is in trouble, and I need to leave at three to help her. Could you or Verona cover the last two hours today?"

"Of course," he said easily. "I'll be there at three."

Relief filled Ivory. "Thank you so much."

"No problem, Ivory. You never take time off. We understand emergencies."

"Thank you," she said anyway, her anxiety for her friend returning the moment she hung up. She called Kate, but her friend didn't answer.

"I'll be there," she said out loud as she typed it out. *I'll call the school.*

She made that phone call next, saying, "Hey, Fawn, it's Ivory Osburn."

"Heya, Ivory," she said, her Texan accent heavier than most. "What can I do for you?"

"I need to get Kate Pearson's kids from school today. Can you let them know for me?"

"Of course, honey."

"Great, thanks."

The chime on the door sounded, and Ivory turned to help whoever had just walked in. Jennika stood there, and she looked terrified. "Have you heard from Kate? I went to her house to take her lunch, and she wasn't there, and there's blood everywhere." She held up her phone as a tear rolled down her face. "She's not answering her phone."

Ivory stepped over to the other woman and hugged her. "Yes, she just texted me a few minutes ago. She started bleeding and went to the hospital."

"Oh, no," Jennika said, her shoulders shaking as she cried. Ivory's own tears welled up, and she smiled, because she could *feel* how sad this was.

"I'm leaving here at three to get her kids," she said. "I hope Don is there already."

"I'll find out." Jennika stepped back and kept her eyes on her phone. Her fingers flew over the screen, and she let out a shaky breath. "Should we go to the hospital?"

"No," Ivory said firmly. "Kate won't like that. No, I'll get the kids, and I'll keep them until I hear from her or Don." That would be what she'd want. She nodded like that was that.

"How are you so calm?" Jennika asked, her tears flowing freely again. "This is just so sad."

Ivory just looked at the other woman. Yes, losing a baby was sad, especially because she knew Kate and Don had wanted another child for a while now. But Ivory had been through much harder things, at least in her opinion.

"My husband left me and my four-year-old son to join a bowling club in Amarillo," she said. "Of women. And then he'd stay out all night, drinking with his buddies. Before I knew it, he'd moved there, with the words, 'I need to live my own life, Ivory.'"

Jennika's eyes widened, and Ivory saw the horror in her eyes.

"And that's what he's been doing ever since—whatever makes *him* happy. The rest of us—my son and I—are casualties of his decisions. I mean, I don't work nine hours a day at the dry cleaner to keep busy."

She didn't mean to sound so acidic, but Jennika had to know that they hadn't been dealt the same hands in life.

Ivory used to be bitter about that, used to wish God had given her a different path to tread.

But now, she knew her experiences had made her the person she was. At least that was what Doctor Feldman had said on Tuesday. She'd been very happy with Ivory's conversations with Tripp at Thanksgiving, and she said Ivory was making such good progress, they could probably take their sessions down to twice a month instead of every week.

Since then, Ivory had been trying to find a way to get Tripp—her husband—back into her life. All the way back. She had no money, so expensive gifts were out. But Christmas was approaching, and she really wanted to spend the holidays with him.

Jennika grabbed onto her again, holding her tight. "I'm so sorry, Ivory."

"I'm surprised Kate didn't tell you."

"Kate is a good friend," she said, stepping back. "Okay, I'm going to...go, I guess. I'll leave the food at their place, and you'll call me if you or they need anything?"

"Yes," Ivory said, her emotions all over the place.

Jennika nodded and started for the door, and Ivory looked helplessly at her phone. She wanted to call Tripp, but she didn't quite dare. *Soon*, she told herself. She'd call him soon.

"Jennika?" she said, and the woman turned back. "If you were trying to get...if you wanted your husband to know you cared about him, had been thinking about him...what would you do?"

Jennika looked like she'd been hit by a brick. "I'd make his favorite food."

Ivory nodded at the same time her heart fell to her toes. "Thanks." She wasn't great in the kitchen, though she could put together simple meals. Tripp's favorite meal...Tripp's favorite meal....

He loved that colored, sugared popcorn—and the last time she'd tried to make it, it had come out "nasty."

"Gotta start somewhere," she muttered to herself.

———

HOURS LATER, she walked with Jenny's hand in one of hers and Dexter's in the other. "I think it's just down here," she said, craning her neck to see around the corner. Don had asked her to bring the kids to the hospital, and she did need to go pick up Oliver. She had texted Liam about the situation, and he'd replied with, *No problem, Ivory. Ollie's fine.*

*Oh, and Tripp's back.*

That was it.

Before she'd been able to figure out how she felt and what she should do, Don had called. She reached the door and knocked lightly before entering. Kate laid in the bed, but Don blocked Ivory's view as he stood up from the chair beside the doorway.

"Daddy," Jenny said, and he scooped her right into his arms.

"Hey, baby," he said, closing his eyes as he held his daughter tight. "Dex."

"How's Momma?" Dexter asked, peering around his father's back.

"She just needs to rest," Don said. "She wants to talk to you, Ivory. Kids, let's go get a drink."

Don took the kids and left the room, and Ivory wiped her palms down her jeans. "Kate," she said, her voice breaking.

"Oh, don't cry," Kate said, a shaky smile on her face. She lifted her arms, and Ivory flew over to her and held her tight.

"I'm so sorry," she said.

"I'm okay," Kate said. "Thank you for getting the kids."

"Of course."

"I feel like such a bad friend," she said. "You need my help with Oliver, and I couldn't do that. And now—"

"Stop it," Ivory said as she straightened. "There's no score to keep here. We help each other when we need it, if we can. I have a whole ranch full of cowboys to help with Oliver."

Kate's smile was stronger now. "Yeah, I wonder what that would be like."

Ivory shook her head. "I—I need to get Tripp back."

"Yes, you do," Kate said.

"What should I do?"

"Take him a burger and tell him you love him."

"Just like that?"

"Just like that, Ivory." Kate looked so tired, and Ivory loved her so much.

"What can I do for you?"

"Oh, it's the weekend," she said with a sigh. "I'll be fine. They're just keeping me overnight, and then Don will take me home and bring *me* the burgers and tell me he loves me." She closed her eyes and leaned further into the pillows.

"I know Jennika has dinner at your place."

"I'll tell her thank you."

Ivory nodded and took a step back. "Call me the moment you need anything."

"I will."

She left the hospital, waving to Don and the kids as she went. She had some time before she absolutely had to be out at Seven Sons to get Oliver. In fact, her son could sleep over out on the ranch, and he'd think it was the greatest thing that ever happened to him.

Behind the wheel of her car, she thought quickly so she wouldn't chicken out and tapped on the phone icon to call Tripp. The phone rang, and rang, and rang, and finally his voice said, "Heya, Ivory."

Oh, so he wasn't planning to play fair, using that deep, Texas drawl and saying her name like that? So sweet and so playful and yet so serious too.

"Hey, Tripp," she said, her tongue almost tripping over his name. "Look, I have a huge favor to ask you. You can say no."

"I won't say no," he said, and Ivory knew he wouldn't.

She drew in a deep breath. "Can Oliver sleep over at the ranch?"

"Of course. Is everything okay?"

"My friend is in the hospital, and I need some time... here."

"But you're okay?"

"I'm hungry," she said. "But other than that, I'm good."

"I can bring you food."

"Tripp," she said, ducking her head as if she could flirt with him over the phone. "I don't need you to do that. I need you to tell Oliver I'll be there in the morning."

"It's Saturday," Tripp said. "And Jeremiah makes waffles on Saturday mornings."

"From scratch," Ivory said. "Or so I've heard."

"Come see for yourself," Tripp said.

"I will," Ivory said.

"Great, see you then." The call ended, and Ivory looked out her windshield. It was five-thirty. She had the rest of the night to figure out how to make that popcorn—and what to say to Tripp to let him know how she felt, what she wanted, and if any of it was even possible.

# 31

Tripp woke when a little seven-year-old boy came barreling into his room and jumped on the bed beside him. "Tripp," Oliver said, laying his head down on the same pillow Tripp was using.

"What, bud?" he asked, reaching over to smooth the boy's hair down.

"Jeremiah says if you don't get up and come help, there won't be any bacon."

"Oh, that would be terrible, wouldn't it?" Tripp smiled at his step-son. "Your mama's coming this morning, and she likes bacon, doesn't she?"

"I can help with the bacon," Oliver said. "So will you get up?"

Tripp groaned and sat up, chuckling as Oliver ran out of the room, already shouting to Jeremiah that Tripp was up and to get the bacon out of the fridge.

Tripp pulled a T-shirt over his head and yawned as he walked down the hall to the kitchen. Jeremiah grinned at him and nodded to the bacon on the countertop. "Morning."

"Mornin'," Tripp said. "Any sign of Ivory yet?"

"Nope." He reached for the remote that would start the Christmas music and pressed a button. Festive bells rang out, and Oliver started singing along in a clear, high voice.

"Hey, the kid can sing," Jeremiah said. "Nice, Ollie." He danced with the boy, and Tripp thought Oliver had impacted a lot more than just him. He grinned at the two of them and got busy laying bacon strips in a frying pan. Jeremiah would kick him out of the kitchen in a minute anyway, and he could go wait for Ivory on the front steps.

Sure enough, Jeremiah shooed him out of the kitchen before he could even flip the bacon, and Tripp padded down the hall to the front door. The air was crisp this morning, but he settled on the top step and looked down the driveway.

Maybe their holiday decorations were over the top, but Tripp loved Christmas. Absolutely loved the spirit of it, the magic of Santa Claus, the joy of buying the perfect gift for someone and watching their face light up when they opened it.

He hadn't bought anything for Ivory yet, but he'd been thinking through a few things. He wasn't sure where they'd be in their relationship, or how she would take a gift from him. She already felt indebted to him, and Tripp didn't need to add to that.

His heart pulsed out a couple of extra beats when he

saw her car turn the corner and continue toward the ranch. He got up and opened the front door to get the gate sliding open for her, and then he went down the steps. He was waiting on the sidewalk when her car came to a stop, and she took several long moments to get out of the car.

She carried a tin covered in snowflakes in her hands, and she glanced around at the ranch. "You guys really know how to do Christmas, don't you?"

"A little bit," he said. "Haven't you been out here all week?"

"Yeah," she said. "I just haven't...talked to you about it." She kept taking steps closer and closer to him, and Tripp felt like he was having an out-of-body experience. "Liam said it was a twin brainchild to decorate the oak."

"Yeah."

She paused a few feet from him. Close enough for Tripp to see the pure fear in her eyes. He hated that, and he wanted to turn and walk away from her. He couldn't inspire fear in her for the rest of his life, could he?

"I made you an early Christmas gift," she said, thrusting the tin toward him. "And I just want you to know that it might not be exactly right, but I spent a lot of time on it last night."

Tripp took the tin, and it was surprisingly light. Instinctively, he knew it contained popcorn, and he opened the lid. "Wait, last night?" He looked at her even as the smell of sugar wafted up from the tin. "I thought your friend was in the hospital."

"She was," Ivory said with a smile. "I visited her and then worked on this." She nodded to the tin, and he looked down at the rainbow-colored corn in the tin.

Pure love flowed through him, and he hadn't even tasted the popcorn yet. He didn't even care what it tasted like.

He looked up at Ivory, unsure of what to say.

"I'm in love with you," she said, her voice trembling slightly. "I've been working really hard to figure out how I feel—*if* I could feel love again—and my therapist says I've been making really good progress."

Tripp had to agree. He could count on one hand how many times Ivory had admitted vocally how she felt about him.

Ivory took a deep breath. "I don't want to get divorced either. I want to come out to this ranch for everything we possibly can, and I want to buy a house with you in town, and I want us to live there together as a family. And I want to wake up next to you and I want to go to sleep with you breathing beside me, and I want to have more kids with you."

Her chest heaved, and she worked for a moment to calm herself.

Tripp didn't want to be calm. Everything inside him buzzed and vibrated, and he covered the few feet between them, took her face in his hands, and kissed her.

She kissed him back, and Tripp could hardly believe what was happening. "I love you," she whispered against his lips, but he just kissed her again.

"Tripp," she said, breaking their connection again. She looked him straight in the eye. "I don't want our relationship to be trivial. It's—*you're*—one of the most important people in my life."

"I love you so much," he said.

"Can you forgive me?"

"Always," he said, wondering if that made him stupid or weak. He decided he didn't care. He'd loved and wanted Ivory Osburn for a very long time. "So we don't need to get divorced?"

"I don't see why," Ivory said. "We just need to talk, work out what we want, and then do it."

"Rhett and Evelyn got divorced and then remarried."

"Maybe we could just renew our vows or something."

Tripp gazed down at her, this woman who meant so much to him. "Yeah, I like that idea."

"Okay." She bent and picked up the tin of spilled popcorn. "You didn't even try this."

Tripp took a handful and popped it into his mouth. It was sticky and sweet but she'd used way too much coloring, and the popcorn had a terrible, synthetic taste.

"It's great," he said, regretting the big handful he'd taken.

Ivory laughed and pushed against his chest. "You're not a good liar."

"Thank goodness for that," Tripp said, swallowing with difficulty and then laughing. "Okay, so what's the first thing we need to talk about?"

Ivory drew in a deep breath. "A place to live. A new place. For us."

*For us.* He liked the sound of that. "I *would* like a place with a dedicated office space," he said.

"You definitely need that," she agreed. "And I can have a jewelry studio too."

"And if you want more kids, we need more bedrooms." He laced his hand through hers and led her slowly toward the homestead.

"So we'll start by looking for a house," she said. "And I'll list mine for sale." Ivory looked up at him, those blue eyes filled with so much hope. "Sound good?"

Tripp pressed his lips to her temple. "It sounds amazing."

———

Tripp pulled up to the house he'd just finished buying, the new keys sitting in the cupholder beside him. He'd loved this house when he'd first looked at it, and he'd maybe been a little aggressive to get the deal closed before Christmas.

But once he'd said he'd pay in cash, wouldn't require an inspection, and would pay all the closing costs, the owners had agreed to be out by the twentieth.

He'd closed this morning, and now the house was his.

His and Ivory's, even if he hadn't told her about it yet. Buying the place where they were going to build their future, their family, without her input was probably a stupid thing to do, but she'd suggested they wait until her house sold before they started looking.

Tripp didn't want to wait. He wanted to start his life with her as soon as possible, and they weren't going to get divorced. They weren't renewing their vows until July. And yet, they weren't living together again.

She wanted a fresh start. He had money.

"Your fresh start is right there," he said, still looking at the house. He slid out of the truck and approached the front door. The key worked, and he stepped inside. A large office sat to his left, with a wide open living room to the right. A Christmas tree right there in front of the window would be the perfect welcome for the holidays.

He stepped through a doorway that could close, separating the rest of the house from this front part. He really liked that, because he could work up front, or Ivory could have guests over in the formal living room, and the chaos of the rest of the house would be contained behind the closed door.

Through that doorway, the rest of the house opened up to a huge kitchen, family room, dining room, and laundry room. There were two bedrooms and two bathrooms behind the garage, including the master suite.

Upstairs, the house had a giant playroom, as well as four more bedrooms and two more bathrooms. Plenty of room for a family, a jewelry studio, anything else they wanted to do.

Tripp returned to the truck and retrieved the giant red ribbon he'd ordered online. He opened the garage and got the ribbon in place, because Ivory and Oliver would be arriving soon.

His nerves bubbled, but he kept himself moving. Orange soda for Oliver, in the old-style bottles he liked, went on the top step of the porch. He retrieved the sparkling apple cider for Ivory and himself.

The sound of a car approaching had him spinning back to the truck. This house sat on a curvy road with several others, though he couldn't see any of them from anywhere in the house or yard. He'd checked. The east side of Three Rivers had rolling hills with farms and estates, and Tripp would be surprised if Ivory didn't know why he'd given her this address and asked her to meet him there.

He stood next to his truck as she pulled into the driveway, and he smiled at her as she got out. She took several seconds to look at the house, especially the bow on the garage, before she faced him.

"Merry Christmas," he said.

"You bought this house, didn't you?" she asked, and he couldn't tell if she was upset or not.

"Yes," he said.

"Whoa," Oliver said. "You bought this house?" He skipped over to Tripp, who scooped him into his arms.

"I did, bud. We're going to live here, as a family." He switched his gaze to Ivory on the last few words. "I want to live with you guys again, Ivory. You don't want the memories in the other house. So I thought a house for Christmas would be a good *family* present."

She circled her car and stepped to his side. "You're going to be impossible like this our whole lives, aren't you?"

"Probably," he said with a chuckle.

"Show me the house, cowboy," she said, taking his hand in hers.

Tripp set Oliver down, saying, "Wow, you've gotten big, bud."

"Mama says my jeans are too short. We measured last night, and I've grown a whole inch."

"Amazing," Tripp said, following Oliver up the steps. "I got drinks for everyone, for the tour." He removed the lid from Oliver's bottle of soda and handed it to him. "Don't spill, bud."

He poured two glasses of cider and handed one to Ivory. "To us. To our future, and family, and happiness." He clicked his glass against Ivory's, and all of her icy exterior melted. He took a drink, and so did she. So maybe everything would be okay.

Tripp opened the front door, pure happiness filling him. "I have a Christmas tree in the back of my truck. I thought we could set it up right there." He indicated the perfect spot in front of the window. "My office there."

He led Ivory through the rest of the house, as well as out to the backyard, which had a large, covered deck, with plenty of trees for privacy.

"All right, Tripp," she said, leaning against the railing on the deck, surveying the land. "You're right. This is an amazing house." She looked up at him, a glint in her eyes. "Exactly what I would want if I could afford it."

"Well, you can afford it now," he said, slipping one arm around her waist. "I want to spend Christmas with you, in *our* house. I want to wake up next to you in the morning. I can't do that right now, and I'm dying." He whispered the last couple of words and ran his nose down the side of her face. She turned into him and kissed him, removing his cowboy hat and holding it against his back.

"I know it's sudden," he said, breaking their connection. "But will you guys move in tonight?"

"There's no bed here," she said.

"I have my brothers on stand-by," Tripp said. "I'm packed, and I have the furniture store delivering tomorrow." He'd tried to think of everything they needed. A dining room set. New couches for the bigger space. Silverware and pots and pans and cups and plates. Towels.

"What do I need to pack?" she asked.

"Clothes," he said. "I've taken care of everything else."

"Tripp."

He looked into her eyes. "Merry Christmas," he said, hoping she'd just accept his gifts for her.

"I love you," she said. "Merry Christmas." She kissed him, and Tripp sure liked that. He could feel the way she loved him, and feel her acceptance of his gifts, and Tripp couldn't wait to live with her again.

# 32

Callie's stomach dropped to her toes when she saw the envelope with the logo from the Bank of Three Rivers.

"No," she moaned. "No, no, no."

She glanced toward the front of the house, but Simone wasn't even out of bed yet. The sun had barely come up, for crying out loud.

And Callie was about to be crying out loud.

She turned her back to the front door, just in case Simone did get up and come outside to see what was taking Callie so long at the mailbox. Then she opened the letter, her heartbeat bobbing in the back of her throat.

The letter outlined what she already knew. She'd read the other letters before burying them in the garbage can outside, never taking the terrible notices into the homestead.

But she couldn't ignore this anymore. The ranch was

fifteen days away from foreclosure. The huge block letters at the top of the letter imprinted themselves on her retinas, and she looked up.

"Please," she begged, but God had not been listening to her. Every day, she was a little further behind. A week would pass, and she'd buy groceries with a credit card.

*It's time to stop*, she thought. Or maybe the Lord had finally spoken to her. No matter what, Callie couldn't ignore this letter.

Tears streamed down her face, because burying her reality hadn't made it go away. Pure desperation moved through her, and she looked east, where the posh, thriving Seven Sons Ranch sat serenely in the rising golden light.

She shoved the rest of the mail into the box, slammed it shut, and started down the dirt lane. It was a half-mile, but she hadn't lost her adrenaline by the time she arrived at the homestead.

It was very early, but she climbed the stairs steadily, ready to wake them all if she had to. She needed to talk to Liam, now. Even she was a bit surprised that she wanted to divulge this secret to him, and not Jeremiah.

She rang the doorbell and started knocking on the door before the chime had quieted. She wanted to call for him, but she paced away from the door so she wouldn't.

"Callie?"

She turned to Miah, her panic rising. "Where's Liam?"

"He's at the gym." Miah came out onto the porch. "What's wrong? Maybe I can help."

He probably could, as every Walker brother had billions and billions of dollars. But she didn't want Miah to help her. He wasn't the man who'd been over at her house for the past year—or maybe longer. He wasn't the cowboy who'd offered to buy her ranch. He hadn't asked her out. He wasn't Liam.

"No, it's okay, Miah." She was glad she'd folded up the letter and shoved it in her pocket as she walked over.

"You sure?" He didn't move to embrace her or comfort her, though Callie's face felt dry and crinkly from the tears she'd cried.

Liam would've hugged her the moment he'd opened the door. He'd have stroked her hair and whispered that she'd be okay. Whatever it was, he'd fix it.

"I'll just wait for him," she said, sitting down on the front step. Miah sat beside her, sighing in such a way that alerted Callie to his own distress.

"What's going on with you?" she asked, the letter in her pocket weighing as much as a ton of bricks.

"I'm...good," he said.

"Come on, Miah," she said, nudging him with her shoulder. "I know you, and you're not good."

Several seconds went by, and Callie just let Miah have his time. She knew him well enough to know he needed a moment to organize his words. He never said a whole lot anyway, but when he got fired up, he could talk and talk and talk.

"Okay, I'm going to say something you can't tell anyone

else." He cut her a look, and she couldn't believe he was already wearing that cowboy hat. "Not even Liam."

"Fine," Callie said. "Because you'll just end up telling him yourself."

"I'm serious, Cal."

And he was. "Okay," she said.

"I can't get this woman out of my head."

Callie sat up a little straighter. "What woman?" She tried to make her voice nonchalant, but she totally failed.

Miah laughed and shook his head. "I shouldn't have said anything."

Funny, Callie thought he should've been saying a lot more. "Well," she said. "Whoever she is, she'd be thrilled to know you're thinking about her."

"I just don't...see myself ever going very far with a woman," he whispered. "And how is that fair to her?" He looked openly at Callie now, and she found utter turmoil in his eyes.

"I see," she said. "Well, Miah, maybe you need to stop thinking about your life being over. Maybe it's just the second act."

A truck turned into the driveway, and Callie stood up, putting a bunch of distance between her and Miah. "I have to go," she said, flying down the steps toward Liam's truck. He'd barely gotten out when she said, "I need to talk to you. Can you walk with me?"

"Sure." He glanced toward the porch. "How long have you been here?"

"Just a few minutes."

"Why didn't you just go inside?"

Callie glanced toward the porch, but Miah was long gone.

"It's cold out here," he said, looking down at her. "You're not wearing a jacket or anything." Liam put his arm around her. "What's going on?"

Callie's nerves quivered, and she took several seconds to try to find the right way to tell him. She couldn't. So she reached into her pocket and pulled out the envelope.

She gripped it tightly in her fingers, crushing the paper. Liam stood there and looked at her, and then it, and then back to her.

"What's that?"

"This is the secret," she whispered. "And I'm so scared, and you're going to think so, *so* badly of me." Her chin trembled, but she forced herself to thrust the envelope toward him. "Try to understand."

Liam took the envelope, worry in his dark eyes. He took the letter out, and Callie turned away from him. She couldn't stand to watch him read about her complete ruin. Couldn't stomach seeing the disgust and disappointment in his eyes.

"Callie," he whispered.

She didn't turn back to him, but he gently turned her around. She kept her head down, and Liam gathered her into his arms. "I'm so sorry."

"I can't lose the ranch." A whimper came out of her

mouth despite his strong arms, the warmth from his body, or his complete non-judgement of her.

Liam stroked her hair, the way she'd imagined he would. He took a deep breath and stepped back. "Callie, at the risk of making your day worse, I'm—you know what the solution here is."

"Do I?" She shook her head. "I'm not taking your money. I just can't."

"It's either take my money or lose your ranch." He looked down at her, something sharp in his eyes. "And I can't believe you've been dealing with this on your own. You should've told me a long time ago."

"I couldn't," she said, wishing he could understand.

"We still have fifteen days," he said, embracing her again. Callie stepped into the comfort of his arms, because she'd been shouldering everything by herself for so long, and she was so tired. She also really liked how he'd said *we*, and she clung to him as if they really were a *we*.

# 33

The next morning, Liam pulled up to Callie's house, dread mixing with excitement in his gut. Maybe some hope too. Tons of fear. After Callie had shown him the letter of foreclosure on her ranch, Liam's only idea was to ask her to marry him.

"You're an idiot," he said to himself, watching the front door of her house. Callie got up early; he knew that. He also knew it was winter, and she wouldn't go out to the ranch as early as she normally did.

He looked over to the passenger seat, where the little black box sat. He'd gone to town yesterday and bought a ring, so nervous he couldn't work for the rest of the day.

Today would be a bust too, and he'd actually planned to propose to Callie and then saddle Pretzel and disappear for a while. There was a cabin on the northern edge of the property, and he was planning to stay there for a couple of days. Then he wouldn't have to be around Callie after she told him no.

"Just do it," he muttered to himself. Before he could chicken out and go home, he grabbed the ring box and got out of the truck. He strode to the steps and took them two at a time to the porch.

He rang the doorbell. He reminded himself to breathe. He waited.

Callie came to the door, surprise in her expression. "Liam?"

He dropped to both knees and held out the black box. "Callie Foster," he said, everything inside him aligning. This was right. This could be good. "I know you won't just take my money. You wouldn't go out with me either. But maybe you'll marry me, and allow your husband to help you carry some of the load you've been burdened with for so long."

His fingers fumbled as he tried to open the ring box, but he finally got it.

Callie sucked in a breath and looked at the ring, then back to Liam. "Liam." She shook her head, her ponytail swinging. "I—"

"Don't say yes or no," he said. "I think you should think about it. Really think." He got up and closed the ring box. He put it in her hands and covered everything with both of his. "Please, Callie. Pray about it. Think about it. Consider everything."

## Tripp

Their eyes met, and Liam couldn't help the hope streaming from him. Surely she'd say yes. But maybe her stubbornness would cost her the ranch.

She nodded, her eyes bright. "I'll think about it."

# 34

I vory groaned when she heard Oliver yelling at her from
the living room. Everything in this new house echoed so
much, and Tripp had promised they could get curtains and
rugs to help with the noise.

"He's up." She groaned as she rolled over and cuddled
into Tripp's chest. It wasn't even light outside yet, and she
should've put blackout material over Oliver's windows.

"Mm," Tripp said, clearly still half asleep.

"He's going to come in here in a minute," she said.

"You shouldn't have bought him so many gifts," Tripp
said, chuckling.

She pushed against his chest, a smile on her face. He'd
bought all of the gifts. Ivory had just been trying to keep up
with everything that needed to be done. She'd been going
through everything at her house, deciding what to keep,
what to sell, and what to throw away.

They'd been living in the house for four days, and she had to admit she loved the house, loved the land, loved the decorations, loved the man in bed with her.

"Mama," Oliver said, bursting into the room. "Come see! Tripp, get up. Santa came!"

"Did he?" Tripp asked, groaning as he rolled over. "All right, bud. I'll be there in a sec."

"Mama." Oliver climbed onto the bed and put his face inches from hers. "There's a bike out there, Mama."

"I hope it's for me," she said, and Oliver burst out laughing.

"It's too small for you, Mama."

"Dang." Ivory kissed Oliver's cheek. "Give us a few minutes, okay?" she said. "I have to go to the bathroom and find my slippers."

Oliver slid off the bed. "Hurry, okay?"

Ivory didn't hurry, but she and Tripp eventually made it out to the family room, where they'd put up a second Christmas tree and started putting out their presents for each other. There were significantly more now, including that bicycle Oliver had mentioned.

"Wow," Ivory said, gazing at the wealth before her. Pure gratitude overcame her, and she started crying before she'd even realized it.

"Sweetheart," Tripp said, and she turned into his arms.

"I'm sorry," she said. "I'm fine, really."

Tripp held her and told Oliver to go ahead and start opening the presents. She quieted and sat on the couch as she watched her son's joy. As Tripp made coffee and then waffles in the shape of Christmas trees.

Ivory knew happiness and joy could be had without money. She knew Tripp would do whatever he had to do to take care of her and Oliver. And she loved him more and more every day because of that.

"Don't eat too much," Tripp said when Oliver reached for his third waffle. "Jeremiah is making lunch today, remember?"

"All right," Oliver said, but he still ate the third waffle. "Can we have these waffles every year?"

"Sure thing," Tripp said.

"And will we do that Christmas Eve tree every year at the ranch?" Oliver asked. Ivory wasn't sure why Oliver was asking these questions.

Tripp seemed a little confused too. "If you want." He looked at Oliver. "What's that about?"

"I don't know," Oliver said. "I just...are you guys going to stay together? Or will you go back to the ranch?"

All at once, Ivory realized that Oliver was searching for some stability. Her heart thundered in her chest, because she didn't know how to reassure him. She felt like a complete failure that he even had these questions.

"Baby," she said. "We're going to stay together. This is our house now. Mine and Tripp's and yours." She smoothed his hair off his face.

"Yeah," Tripp said. "I'm not going back to the ranch.

This is my home now. Our home. Me, and you, and your mom."

Oliver looked back and forth between them. "Okay," he said simply.

"Okay," Tripp said, getting up and pouring himself more coffee. "Do you want to go ride your new bike?"

"Yeah." Oliver cheered and slid off the barstool.

"Okay, go get dressed," Tripp said. "Real shoes," he called after him as Oliver ran for the steps to head up to his bedroom.

Ivory just looked at Tripp. "Sounds like he's a little unsure about some things."

"We'll make sure he feels safe and secure," Tripp said. "We'll establish our own family traditions, but we can participate at the ranch any time we want."

"I like the Christmas Eve tree at the ranch," she said. "It was really fun."

Tripp opened a drawer and pulled something out of it. "I have one more gift for you." He put a plain white envelope on the counter in front of her.

Ivory just looked at it. "Tripp. What is that?"

"Open it."

With buzzing nerves, she picked up the envelope. It wasn't sealed, and she pulled out a few sheets of paper. They looked like legal documents. Her eyes caught on the word *custody*....

"Tripp," she said, looking up. "What is this?"

"The custody case was dismissed in Amarillo," he said.

"The judge there even agreed not to revisit custody unless you bring it to the court for twelve full months. Said Daniel was abusing the system and causing unnecessary trouble."

Ivory looked back at the paper, a little dumbfounded.

"And if he ever does bring up custody again," Tripp said. "We'll handle it together. He can't touch us, Ivory."

"Because this marriage isn't trivial," she said.

"Not at all," he agreed.

———

"Merry Christmas," Liam said when Tripp and Ivory walked into the homestead at Seven Sons later that day. Choruses of the same greeting rang throughout the house, and Ivory stepped over to Evelyn and hugged her hello.

Jeremiah worked in the kitchen, as always, and Callie and Simone came toward Ivory to say hello. Oliver disappeared among the other cowboys, and Ivory sank onto the couch, a happy sigh coming out of her mouth.

"How's the house?" Callie asked.

"So great," Ivory said with a smile.

Callie leaned forward. "How do you do it?"

"Do what?" She accepted a bottle of water from her husband, who immediately left the women alone again.

Callie exchanged a glance with Simone and then Evelyn. "I told you we should do it," Simone said.

"There's no *we* about it," Callie hissed.

Ivory ignored the bottle of water and looked around at

the Foster sisters. "Maybe you should start at the beginning."

"I don't want to hurt your feelings," Callie said, and something was clearly troubling the woman. "But...how do you accept Tripp's...charity?"

"It's not charity," Ivory said, truly believing her words. "He loves me. I love him. We're on the same page."

"See?" Evelyn asked. "I told you."

"What's going on?" Ivory asked.

"Liam offered—" Simone started.

"Shh," Callie said, casting a long look over her shoulder to the huge kitchen table where most of the Walkers sat. When she turned back to Ivory, she looked absolutely miserable. "I don't want to use him."

"I told her to use him," Evelyn said.

Ivory thought she knew what was happening here. She wanted to say the right thing without betraying any confidences she had with Tripp. "I know exactly how you feel," she said. "Tripp has done a whole lot for me. Stuff he didn't have to do, and it was really hard for me to accept the help."

Another rush of gratitude filled her. "But after a few months of therapy, and lots of time on my knees, I've realized something. The only thing preventing me from being able to love Tripp fully and find happiness was my own pride."

"Where have we heard that before?" Simone muttered, earning her a dirty look from Callie.

"God finally let me get out of my own way, and when I

learned to accept help from who God put into my life, everything got better."

"So, you're saying...accept that God put Liam in my life, and let him...." Callie shook her head. "I just don't know."

"Dinner's ready," Jeremiah yelled, and the noise quieted. "Let's gather over here."

The women got up and joined the Walker brothers in the kitchen. "We're so glad to be here," he said. "Merry Christmas, everyone. Wyatt, Skyler, Liam, and I put together a gift for all of our guests." He nodded to his brothers, and they started passing out what looked like tickets.

"These are for the New Year's light celebration downtown," Jeremiah said. "We'd love to go together as a family."

"Wow," Ivory said, taking her ticket from Liam. These weren't cheap, and the fireworks on New Year's Eve were a sight to behold. The city brought in a band and had a huge buffet, and Ivory had always wanted to go.

"Thank you," she said to no one in particular.

"And now, announcements," Skyler said. "I'll go first." He adjusted his cowboy hat, and while Ivory didn't know this Walker brother super well yet, he had a good air about him. "I'm not going to be the mechanic here on the ranch. I'm going back to school in business and accounting, so I can run the ranch's affairs." He looked so happy, and everyone cheered for him. He had the personality to perform, and he obviously loved being in the spotlight.

"All right, all right," he finally said, raising both hands in the air to get everyone to be quiet. "Anyone else with any announcements?"

Ivory might have missed it had she just not spoken to Callie, but it felt like Skyler looked at Liam *and* Callie for a little bit too long.

"We have one," Rhett said, stepping to the front of the crowd from behind Liam. "Evelyn is expecting a baby this summer."

A shriek went up from Evelyn's sisters, and even Ivory's excitement grew. Choruses of congratulations went around the kitchen, and everyone hugged Rhett and Evelyn.

"Anyone else?" Skyler asked, obviously the official announcement-person.

No one said anything, and Jeremiah said, "All right. Let's pray and eat. This ham isn't getting any more candied."

# 35

Tripp tied his tie, the air conditioning working hard against the disgusting July Texas heat. But he and Ivory had first tied the knot in July, and this vow renewal needed to happen on the same date.

The date their family had started, whether they were both on the same page then or not. No one was in the room with him, and only his brothers would be in attendance today. The ceremony would take place on their own back deck, with a small family dinner afterward.

A small hand knocked on the bedroom door where Tripp had been getting dressed. Oliver. "Yep," he said, and the boy came inside. "You ready?" He could see that Oliver was indeed, ready. He wore a similar suit to Tripp's, and their hats were identical. Liam had helped get him ready, and all three Foster sisters were currently in Tripp and Ivory's bedroom, getting her ready for the simple ceremony.

"I'm ready," Oliver said. "You?"

"Almost." Tripp finished with the tie and reached for his cowboy hat. He settled it on his head and looked in the mirror. "Ready."

He crouched down in front of Oliver. "You know I love you, right? I know you're not my biological son, but I love you like you are."

Oliver hugged Tripp, and he closed his eyes and held onto this little human who, besides Ivory, was his best friend. "I love you too, Tripp."

"To the moon and back?" Tripp asked.

"To Saturn," Oliver said.

"Jupiter." Tripp laughed, this game between them making his heart melt.

Someone else knocked, and Rhett stuck his head into the room. "We're ready for you guys."

"All right." Tripp straightened, and he took Oliver's hand and led him out of the room. Down the hall and through the family room to the sliding glass doors that went onto the deck.

All of his brothers, including Micah, sat in chairs, and Callie and Simone came onto the deck behind Tripp. "She's coming," Callie said, and she quickly took her seat in the front row next to Liam.

He patted his pocket for the vows he'd written, and he stepped to the side when Ivory came out on the deck too. She wasn't wearing a white wedding gown, but a beautiful pearly pink dress that fell to her ankles. Her blonde hair was down, curling in waves over her shoulders, and she carried a simple bouquet of red roses.

Tripp leaned down and kissed her sweetly.

There was no pastor. No escort down the aisle. They linked arms and walked toward the railing, facing their families and then one another.

"Tripp Walker," Ivory said, no paper in sight. "The past year with you has had some ups and downs. I appreciate your patience with me, your undying affection, and your bottomless love. I am whole because of you. You taught me that love is kind, and love is good, and love endures. I adore how much you love Oliver, and I can't wait for us to welcome another son to this house." She smiled, her way of covering up her emotions.

Tripp's muscles tensed and released, so much joy flowing through him.

"I love you with my whole heart," she finished, her voice high-pitched and wobbly. She nodded once, and that was Tripp's cue to start speaking.

He took an extra moment to draw in a deep breath, and he left his penned vows in his pocket. He knew how he felt about this woman.

"Ivory," he said. "I'm so glad you took a chance on me, a cowboy who tried to run you over in a parking lot."

She half-cried and half-laughed, and Tripp was glad for the lighter mood. "I know it's hard for you to accept help, and I appreciate how much you've allowed me to give you. I enjoy taking care of you and Oliver, and I hope I'll have many more years to do so. I love being a father, and a husband, and my love for you has no bounds."

His were shorter, but it wasn't a contest. She tipped up onto her toes and kissed him, and Tripp's love for her swelled and grew, though he'd previously thought it was as large as it could get.

His brothers and the Foster sisters cheered, and Tripp broke the kiss to hug everyone. There were some days—like right now—that Tripp couldn't believe this was his life.

"All right, all right," he said. "Let's go inside. It's too hot out here, and we have food and cake inside."

"You had me at cake," Jeremiah said, heading for the house. He escaped quickly, and Tripp had a moment of regret that his brother had to be involved in ceremonies like this. He sent up a quick prayer that Jeremiah's heart would be healed, and then he picked up Oliver and took Ivory's hand before going inside with his family.

———

Keep reading to find out if another Walker brother can get his happily-ever-after in Three Rivers! What will Callie say to Liam's proposal? Chapters one and two of **LIAM** are next!

# Sneak Peek! Liam - Chapter One

Callie Foster sat on the edge of her bed, the magic of Christmas hardly touching her heart. She normally loved the holidays, especially since the Walker brothers had moved in next door and started sprucing this lane up. They put up garlands and hung Christmas balls on their fences. And the giant oak tree Callie had always coveted in front of their house was filled with lights, tinsel, balls, and even a popcorn string.

That had been added quite last minute for Oliver Osburn, Ivory's son. Ivory was married to Tripp Walker, and Callie couldn't think about the Walker brothers or the ranch next door without thinking about Liam Walker.

"Oh, Liam." She sighed as she ran her hands through her dirty blonde hair. She hadn't showered in a couple of days, but she had plenty of time before the big Christmas dinner at Seven Sons Ranch.

Callie normally loved going next door and eating a meal she hadn't had to think about or cook. Or clean up after. Not only that, but Jeremiah Walker was a fantastic cook, and Callie's mouth was already watering for some of the ham candy he'd serve for lunch.

But it wasn't Miah that made Callie's pulse skip around, and it wasn't Miah she dreamed about at night, and it wasn't Miah who'd asked her out or offered to buy her ranch or actually proposed a crazy idea to help her and Simone keep the Shining Star.

"Actually *proposed*," she said aloud to herself, the sight of Liam down on both knees, holding that giant diamond out to her, so much hope on his face.

Callie hadn't answered him yet, but she couldn't say yes. She was not going to take Liam Walker's money, even if her ranch was only a week away from getting foreclosed on. She was not going to marry him for his money either, though she'd been all for the idea when it was Evelyn walking down the aisle.

"That was different," she told herself as she padded down the hall to the kitchen. Everything around the ranch was just on the wrong side of shabby-chic, with more shabby than anyone would like.

She set the coffee to brew, no sign of Simone yet. Her sister loved to sleep late, and they had no reason to get up early even if it was Christmas morning. If Callie wanted to get Simone out of bed, she'd make a bacon quiche, the saltiness of the bacon a scent her sister couldn't resist.

Callie had no room to talk, as her brands of kryptonite included ice cream and potato chips. She'd had to go up a size the last time she bought jeans, and the stress of keeping the ranch afloat hadn't helped her ease up on her comfort foods.

So she didn't tempt her sister with bacon, and she went back down the hall to shower while the coffee brewed. She took a long time in the hot spray, first spritzing her eucalyptus mist and inhaling the clear, clean scent to clear her mind, and then reaching for her purple shampoo.

Her hair was naturally blonde, but her stylist had told her to use the brassy-reducing shampoo a few times a month, and Callie was a little bit protective of her hair. At this time, this was all she had in her life.

She hadn't been out with anyone in several years, as she spent all of her time, energy, talent, and money on the ranch. In quiet moments while she stood in the shower, Callie wondered what her life would be like without the Shining Star.

*What should I do?* she prayed, tilting her head back as if that would allow the prayer easier access to God's ears. He hadn't answered any of her previous prayers about the ranch, and though she felt a bit abandoned by Him, she still went to church every week. But she hadn't felt anything there either. She wondered if she was completely past feeling and should just give up.

On everything.

She and Simone could sell the ranch and get a house in

town. Simone could still do her antique restoration, and her craft fairs, and Callie would...be completely unhappy.

Completely.

She loved the ranch with everything inside her, and she couldn't imagine her life without it.

*You've gotta do something then*, she thought and she reached for the lemongrass soap, the scent another of her favorites.

By the time she'd dried, dressed, curled, combed, painted, and plaited her hair, she could smell the evidence that Simone had beaten her to making breakfast. Thankfully.

"Merry Christmas," her sister said from her spot in front of the stove. She grinned like she was thirty years younger and Santa had brought them dozens of toys.

"Merry Christmas," Callie said, getting down a mug for her coffee. "What are you making?"

"French toast," Simone said. "And Mom's hash brown hash."

"Mm." Callie smiled at her sister and opened the fridge to get out some cream for her coffee. She couldn't find it, and she straightened, remembering that she hadn't bought more cream when she'd gone grocery shopping last time.

Because they couldn't afford it.

She turned back to the island and set her coffee down, sighing.

"Why don't you just tell Liam you'll marry him?" Simone asked.

"Because," Callie said.

"Because why?"

"Because I'm not taking charity from any of those Walker men."

"Because you're prideful," Simone said. "If one of them was proposing to me, I'd not only say yes, I'd say *heck yes*." She smiled and flipped the French toast. "I mean, what's not to like? Liam is super good-looking, he—"

"You said hot last night," Callie said, cocking her eyebrows and adding too much sugar to her coffee. But she had to do something to make it palatable without cream.

"Fine, he is hot," Simone said. "They all are, and if you can't admit it, you're blind."

"I can admit it," Callie said.

"Good." Simone flipped the three pieces of French toast onto a plate from the pan and set it on the counter next to Callie. "And he's rich, and he wants to help, and he's liked you for a very, very long time."

Callie thought of something Tripp had said to her months ago. *You have to know he really likes you.*

Callie knew, and she felt really bad for keeping Liam at arm's length. Especially because her own feelings for the "super good-looking" cowboy next door were too high and too advanced for her to ignore. If she went out with Liam, she just knew she'd end up kissing him, and then she wouldn't have any choice but to walk down the aisle with him.

And that scared her more than almost anything.

*More than losing the ranch?*

That was the million-dollar question, and if Callie could just answer it....

"Morning," Evelyn trilled as she came through the front door, her own cowboy billionaire husband right behind her. Rhett had helped a ton on the ranch over the past year, and Callie was extremely grateful for him. But one cowboy's work wasn't enough to save the Shining Star, and Callie had hidden everything from her sister and her brother-in-law. Because Rhett had plenty of money too, and Evelyn knew how to login to the mortgage company and pay the bills.

"Merry Christmas," Simone said gleefully. "Did you bring the syrup?"

"Right here," Rhett said, setting it down on the countertop before kissing Simone's cheek and then Callie's. "Whoa, what's wrong here?"

"Nothing," she said, putting a smile on her made-up face.

"You look nice." Evelyn sat at the bar, her eyes sharp and all-seeing. "What's going on? You gonna try to win over Liam?"

Rhett chuckled. "She already has, like a year ago." He slung his arm around Evelyn and grinned at Callie. "All you have to do is say the right word."

Callie's misery knew no bounds, and she nodded. "I'll be right back."

"Cal," Evelyn called after her, but she couldn't stay in the kitchen for another second. She was going to cry, and nobody needed to see her mascara mask. Frustration and anger combined with her misery, and she barely made it behind a closed door before the first sob pulled through her throat.

————

SHE ENTERED the homestead at Seven Sons Ranch last, automatically looking around for Liam. He wasn't in the room yet, and Callie relaxed a little bit.

"Hey, Cal," Miah said as he came in behind her. "Wow, you look nice. Merry Christmas." He smiled at her and squeezed her hand as he moved past her. "Liam's right behind me, and he's pretending to be happy."

*Join the club*, Callie thought, but she just turned around and saw Liam coming toward her. The butterflies that lived perpetually in her stomach intensified, and she tucked her hair behind her ear.

She went to step back outside, her thoughts tangled. But maybe she could tell him she'd been thinking about the proposal. Maybe she could say yes.

Her foot caught on the edge of the sliding glass door, and Callie stumbled. A cry came from her mouth, and everything started to move so, so fast.

"Whoa," she heard Liam say as if she was a horse. Humiliation filled her as her knees hit the deck just outside the door. Her hands landed next, and then Liam was there, one of his warm hands on her back, the other on her arm.

"Hey, it's okay," he said as if he knew she was only a breath away from crying for the second time that day.

She looked up at him through her lashes, feeling stupid for so many things. This latest fall was just one of them. Liam was downright gorgeous, no "super good-looking" or "hot" about it. He'd always made her heart flutter as if it had grown wings, and she couldn't believe he liked her.

She wondered if he liked her for her, or because he felt some sense of duty to help her. She'd never asked him that. Never mentioned it to anyone. And she wasn't ever going to.

Liam certainly looked at her like he liked her, but Callie wasn't sure why. She carried too much weight, and her greatest asset was kindness. Well, that, and her perfectly non-brassy hair.

"Are you okay?" he asked. "You wanna try getting up?"

"Yes, please," she said, accepting his help for this. Why couldn't she accept it when it came to taking thousands and thousands of dollars from the man?

She got to her feet, the steadiness of Liam's hand in hers so comforting. It was starting to get colder in Texas, and she felt a shiver run down her spine. "Merry Christmas, Liam," she said.

"Yeah," he said. "It could be." He grinned at her and reached out and tucked her hair. "Have you—?" He cut off the sentence and held up his hands, backing up. "Never mind. Of course you have."

Callie didn't know what to say. She needed more time to think. To talk to Evelyn and Simone again.

Tripp

A general wave of hellos went up, and Liam nodded toward the house behind her. "Tripp and Ivory are here."

And Callie wanted to talk to Ivory. Thankfully, Oliver came skipping out to the deck. "Tripp, can we go see Pretzel real quick?"

"Sure thing, bud," he said, glancing at Callie. "But we have to be quick, okay? Jeremiah will have dinner on soon, and he doesn't like it when things start late."

"We'll be so fast." Oliver zoomed away from them, making race car noises with his mouth. Liam chuckled, nodded at Callie, that edge of hope in his eyes, and turned to follow the boy.

Callie let him go without even saying thank you for helping her stand up. Pure humiliation filled her, and she turned back to the homestead. It was almost time for lunch, and she wanted to talk to Ivory. She knew Tripp had married her to help her catch up with her bills and help her keep full custody of her son.

And Callie needed to know how Ivory did that, because then maybe she would be able to do the same thing with Liam.

# Sneak Peek! Liam - Chapter Two

L iam Walker grinned at Oliver Osburn, the boy's enthusiasm exactly what Liam needed to get through this day.

And of course, the very first person he'd seen upon coming off the ranch was Callie Foster. The very scent of her perfume had met his nose before he'd come out of the barn, and he hated that his pulse still pumped out too many beats at the thought of seeing her. But it did. He liked her a whole lot, despite the last few rocky months.

Very rocky months.

And "few" wasn't the right number. Ever since Rhett and Evelyn's wedding, which was six months old now, had Liam and Callie been fighting over whether or not he could help her keep the Shining Star Ranch in the Foster family.

Every month, he watched the desperation in her eyes grow. Every month, he watched her dig her heels in harder.

He'd suggested everything he could think of, and Callie had done some of them. But the Historical Society of Texas had denied her application for historical status at the ranch. That would've at least prevented the land sharks from circling.

Liam had seen another fancy town car drive down the lane just last week. He hadn't left his office and gone next-door to comfort Callie. She knew where to find him, and she hadn't come to his office.

In fact, Callie very rarely came to Liam, not that he was keeping track.

"Liam, hurry *up*," Ollie called, and Liam pulled himself out of his thoughts. He joined the little boy at the fence that kept the horses in their pasture, laughing at the squirrely child. "You got any peppermints?"

"It's *have*," Liam said. "Do you *have* any peppermints?"

Oliver bent down and ripped out a handful of grass without saying anything. He held his palm out flat for Pretzel to take the fresh grass, which the horse did.

Liam put his hand in his pocket, the faint crinkling of the wrapper enough to bring over another couple of horses.

"Liam," Oliver whined. "You got 'im all riled up."

He chuckled and took the candy out of his pocket. "It's fine," he said. "I have plenty." He handed the treat to Oliver, who struggled to open it, almost tossing it on the ground once the wrapper gave against his grip.

Pretzel pulled back his lips and gave a disgruntled noise, which made Oliver laugh. "He wants the candy."

"He sure does, bud. You better hurry up and feed them. Jeremiah—"

"I know, I know," Oliver said. "He doesn't like it when we're late." He held out the red-and-white striped candy, and Pretzel sucked right into his rubbery lips. Oliver giggled and giggled, and Liam kept giving him peppermints for each horse.

"All right," he said, once they'd each had one. "That was their Christmas gift. Now, let's get inside so we're not the last ones there."

"All right." Oliver skipped away, and Liam followed him, taking in a deep breath of the Texas Christmas air.

"Is today a good day, Lord?" he asked. Maybe today would be a good day for him to talk to Callie, though he sort of already had.

When he entered the homestead, he swept the large room for Callie, his stomach plummeting when he saw her sitting on the couch in the family room, her sisters and Ivory gathered around. Their heads were all bent together, and he could only imagine what they were talking about.

Nothing good, he knew that. Probably him and his insane marriage proposal. His face burned, and he wanted to leave. Surely there was a restaurant or church group serving Christmas dinner today. The only thing that kept him there was Jeremiah. Oh, and his mother and father, who'd come all the way from Grand Cayman.

Everyone seemed to be talking, and with the number of people who'd come to celebrate the holiday, the noise level was off the charts. Liam stood by the back door and watched for a moment, usually not one to sit on the sidelines. He'd just stepped over to Tripp and Rhett when Jeremiah yelled, "Dinner's ready. Let's gather over here."

He stood between the island and the stove, various dishes on the counter in front of him, with more pots and pans on the burners behind him. He wore a black apron, and while Liam had some skills in the kitchen, he never minded when Jeremiah put food in front of him.

Jeremiah surveyed the group, and Liam remembered what he'd said at one of their family meetings. It was more of an intervention for Tripp, a few weeks ago when he'd been so miserable about Ivory breaking up with him.

*I feel nothing. Absolutely nothing.*

Liam was starting to understand how his brother felt, and he wished he'd honored the no-women rule the brothers had established for themselves when they'd first arrived in Three Rivers.

"We're so glad to be here," Jeremiah said. "Merry Christmas, everyone. Wyatt, Skyler, Liam, and I put together a gift for all of our guests."

Liam jumped into motion as Jeremiah nodded at him. He took a handful of tickets from Wyatt and started passing them out while Jeremiah continued.

"These are for the New Year's light celebration downtown. We'd love to go together as a family."

Liam handed his last ticket to Ivory, glad someone else had to pass one to Callie and her sisters. Yes, he thought of the Foster women as family, but not in the sisterly way. Well, Simone and Evelyn. But Callie had always accelerated his heartbeat, from the very moment he'd met her.

He retreated back to Tripp's side, because his twin was a safe zone for him. "I love the fireworks on New Year's Eve," Tripp said, grinning at his ticket.

"Yeah," Liam said. "And this year, Jeremiah donated a bunch of money to the celebration, and we have a reserved spot."

"Wow," Tripp said. "Jeremiah's a smart one. Fighting the crowd is half of the problem."

"You just don't like crowds," Liam teased.

"And you do?" Tripp nudged him and laughed, and Liam was glad his brother was here. He sure was going to miss him in the office with him, though he'd had a few months alone and done okay. But Tripp and Ivory had just bought a new home out in the eastern estates of Three Rivers, and Liam knew his brother wouldn't be coming back to Seven Sons permanently.

"And now, announcements," Skyler said. "I'll go first." He adjusted his cowboy hat, and Liam could feel his nerves from several feet away.

"What's goin' on with him?"

"He'll say," Tripp said.

"I'm not going to be the mechanic here on the ranch," Skyler said. "I'm going back to school in business and accounting, so I can run the ranch's affairs." He looked so happy, and while surprise moved through Liam, he clapped along with everyone else.

"Wow, college," he said. "I'd rather die than go back to that life."

"Right?" Tripp laughed again. "But it'll be good for him. He never really went."

"All right, all right," Skyler finally said, raising both hands in the air to get everyone to be quiet. "Anyone else with any announcements?"

Liam hated with the fire of a thousand suns that Skyler's gaze landed on him. He pressed his lips together in a tight line and practically willed his brother to look somewhere else.

How humiliating. Of course, everyone at the homestead knew he'd asked Callie to marry him. Jeremiah hadn't even been upset. Well, he'd been a little bit upset, but he'd stayed in the room, so Liam thought he was making real progress.

"We have one," Rhett said, stepping out from behind Liam. "Evelyn is expecting a baby this summer."

A shriek went up from Evelyn's sisters, and Liam sure did like watching the joy as it crossed Callie's face. Liam loved kids, and he grabbed Rhett and hugged him, saying, "Wow, congrats, brother."

He wanted to congratulate Evelyn too, but she stood too close to Callie, and Liam actually stepped out of the way so everyone could hug Rhett. The din died down, though Momma was actually weeping, and Skyler retook his role as announcement-giver.

"Anyone else?" he asked.

No one said anything, and Jeremiah said, "All right. Let's pray and eat. This ham isn't getting any more candied." That caused more noise as everyone moved over to the table, where Daddy stood at the head of it and grinned around at everyone.

"I know I don't live here," he said. "But we have a tradition in the Walker family to go around the table and say one thing we're looking forward to in the New Year. Sort of a reflection time. Anyone who wants to participate, can. Anyone who doesn't, can simply say they don't want to." He looked at Momma. "Are you in, Penny?"

"Yes, of course," she said, and Grand Cayman hadn't beat the Southern accent out of her, that was for sure. "I'm looking forward to a new grandbaby."

Liam almost rolled his eyes. When it was just the nine Walkers, this tradition was great. But with the additions to the guest list, Liam felt his attention wandering. He perked up when it was Callie's turn, but he refused to lean forward to see her. He'd deliberately sat on the same side of the table as her, so he wouldn't have to look at her or talk to her.

He was interested in what she'd like this upcoming year to be for her, but she just waved her hand and said, "Merry Christmas, everyone."

Liam's heart filled his throat as Simone said she was looking forward to new opportunities, and Micah said, "I'm looking forward to coming to the ranch...permanently."

That only made everyone roar with questions, Liam included. "What?" he demanded. "When? You're coming?"

Micah smiled around at everyone and said, "Jeremiah said he needs me, and I've...met a wall in Temple."

*Met a wall.*

Liam had run into a few of those himself, right here in Three Rivers.

"I'll be moving here as soon as I can get things tied up in Temple," Micah said, turning to look at Liam. His eyes begged Liam to move the conversation to something else.

He'd never passed in this tradition before, but today, Liam didn't want to speak.

"Liam?" Daddy asked.

"I'm looking forward to seeing my CGI in theaters this year," he said. His family cheered for him too, and Liam ducked his head. He hadn't meant to brag, but he had worked hard to get the four-year contract, and he worked almost full-time at the computer now, despite his constant wearing of his cowboy hat.

The tradition finally finished, and Jeremiah got up to get the ham out of the oven. "Let's eat."

Relief filled Liam, because maybe he could just stuff himself and go take a nap. Even as he thought that, he knew he wouldn't. They'd done their Christmas Eve gift-exchange last night, but that was one gift per person. Liam had opened a pocketknife from Rhett, and he expected other gifts from his brothers.

*From Callie?*

He banished the idea from his mind, though she'd given every Walker brother a gift last Christmas. And the one before that. But Liam knew she had no money, and honestly, if she gave him anything of any worth, he'd give it right back.

He talked to Micah on his left and Wyatt on his right, and Liam managed to make it through dinner without wanting to take too big of a bite of ham just to choke himself. He honestly wasn't sure how much longer he could continue in the manner he'd been these past few months.

As he sat there at the dinner table, the holiday merriment around him, he made a decision. If Callie turned him down and gave back the diamond he'd bought her, he'd pack up his bedroom and his huge computer station, and he'd leave town.

He could work from anywhere, and it might actually be easier to be in LA as he worked on the Marvel project. He'd be lost without his cowboy hat, but he could wear it in the privacy of his apartment.

"Let's do presents in a little bit," Rhett said, blowing out his breath. "I'm stuffed and need a few minutes to recover."

"You didn't have to have seconds of literally everything," Evelyn teased him, and Liam thought they were a perfect match for each other. Of course, he thought that about him and Callie too, and she just couldn't see it.

He got up and picked up his plate, along with Wyatt, who said, "Thanks, Liam." He took them over to the kitchen sink, where he leaned into his palms and wondered if he could make a hasty escape down the hall and out the front door. The air was so scented and so noisy, that Liam was having a hard time breathing in here.

"Hey." Callie appeared at his side. She looked up at him, and Liam lost himself in the depth of her brown eyes. "I was, um, wondering if you'd like to go for a walk with me." She put her dishes in the sink too and brought her gaze back to his.

"Right now?" he asked.

"Yes," she said. "Right now."

———

**Liam** is available now in paperback. Get it here by scanning this QR code with the camera on your phone.

## Seven Sons Ranch in Three Rivers Romance™ Series

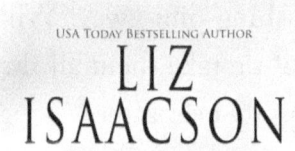

**Rhett (Book 1):** To save her business, she'll have to risk her heart. She needs a husband to be credible as a matchmaker. He wants to help a neighbor. **Will their fake marriage take them out of the friend zone?**

**Tripp (Book 2):** She needs a husband to keep her son. He's wanted to take their relationship to the next level, but she's always pushing him away. Will their trivial tie take them all the way to happily-ever-after?

**Liam (Book 3):** She's desperate to save her ranch. He wants to help her any way he can. Will their invented I-Do open doors that have previously been closed and lead to a happily-ever-after for both of them?

USA TODAY BESTSELLING AUTHOR
LIZ ISAACSON

Jeremiah

**Jeremiah (Book 4):** He wants to prove to his brothers that he's not broken. She just wants him. Will a fake marriage heal him or push her further away?

**Wyatt (Book 5):** To get her inheritance, she needs a husband. He's wanted to fly with her for ages. Can their pretend pledge turn into something real?

**Skyler (Book 6):** She needs a new last name to stay in school. He's willing to help a fellow student. Can this wanna-be wife show the playboy that some things should be taken seriously?

**Micah (Book 7):** They were just actors auditioning for a play. The marriage was just for the audition – until a clerical error results in a legal marriage. Can these two ex-lovers negotiate this new ground between them and achieve new roles in each other's lives?

**Gideon (Book 8):** It's 1971, and Gideon Walker is on the cutting edge of all the technology coming out of Texas. He has big dreams and wants to make something of himself. Then he meets Penny Aarons, and everything changes. He only has eyes for her, but she's got plans and dreams of her own...

Read this origin romance for Momma and Daddy from the Seven Sons series today!

# Coral Canyon Cowboys Romance Series

Visit stunning Wyoming for another family of cowboys...
The Youngs! The series includes second chance romance,
friends to lovers, family saga, Christian values, clean and
sweet romance, single dads, equine therapy themes, police
dog training, brotherly relationships, return to hometown,
fish out of water, and country music stars!

**Tex (Book 1):** He's back in town after a successful country music career. She owns a bordering farm to the family land he wants to buy...and she outbids him at the auction. **Can Tex and Abigail rekindle their old flame, or will the issue of land ownership come between them?**

# Three Rivers Ranch Romance Series

Escape to Three Rivers, Texas for small-town charm, sweet and sexy cowboys, and faith and family centered romance. You'll get second chance romance, friends to lovers. older brother's best friend, military romance, secret babies, and more! The Three Rivers cowboys and the women who rope their hearts are waiting for you, so start reading today!

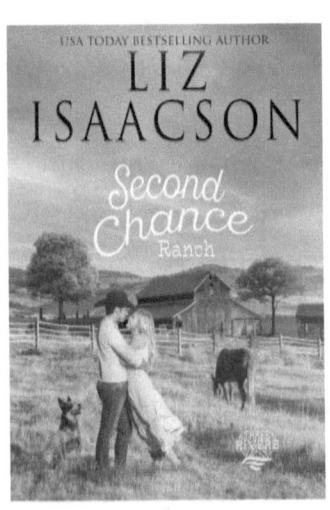

**Second Chance Ranch (Book 1):** After his deployment, injured and discharged Major Squire Ackerman returns to Three Rivers Ranch, wanting to forgive Kelly for ignoring him a decade ago. He'd like to provide the stable life she needs, but with old wounds opening and a ranch on the brink of financial collapse, it will take patience and faith to make their second chance possible.

## Steeple Ridge Romance Series

Get cowboy brothers working together at a horse farm in beautiful Vermont in the Steeple Ridge Farm romance series! With sweet, clean, and faith-filled western romance in a complete series, you'll get a cowboy billionaire, friends to lovers romance, holiday romance, and second chance romance with fun and unique plots (aquaponics, anyone?).

**Her Billionaire Cowboy (Book 1):** Tucker Jenkins has had enough of tall buildings, traffic, and has traded in his technology firm in New York City for Steeple Ridge Horse Farm in rural Vermont. Missy Marino has worked at the farm since she was a teen, and she's always dreamed of owning it. But her ex-husband left her with a truckload of debt, making her fantasies of owning the farm unfulfilled. Tucker didn't come to the country to find a new wife, but he supposes a woman could help him start over in Steeple Ridge. Will Tucker and Missy be able to navigate the shaky ground between them to find a new beginning?

# About Liz

Liz Isaacson writes inspirational romance, usually set in Texas, or Wyoming, or anywhere else horses and cowboys exist. She lives in Utah, where she writes full-time, takes her two dogs to the park everyday, and eats a lot of veggies while writing. Find her on her website, along with all of her pen names, at authorelanajohnson.com

www.ingramcontent.com/pod-product-compliance
Lightning Source LLC
Chambersburg PA
CBHW020523110726
47899CB00004B/1219